Sauce for the Goose

'You asked for this and you're going to get it,' he shouted, chasing her to her dressing room.

She was crying, 'I dare you, I dare you. I bet you wouldn't dare,' and laughing wildly.

They disappeared into her dressing room and he locked the door, amid shrieks of hilarity and protest. Once inside she turned to face him and her eyes were bright and wild. He stripped off his tights. There would be no denying him now. Fully aroused he stood before her, his massive erection thrust in a pulsing curve up against his ribs.

Her eyes nearly fell out of her head. 'Oh my God,' she gasped, and for the first time in his life he saw awe tinged not with terror, but greed. He felt a surge of joy. He knew he was going to be able to do exactly as he pleased with this one.

Sauce for the Goose

MARY ROSE MAXWELL

BLACK
lace

Black Lace stories contain sexual fantasies.
In real life, make sure you practise safe sex.

First published in 2000 by
Black Lace
Thames Wharf Studios,
Rainville Road, London W6 9HA

Typeset by SetSystems Ltd, Saffron Walden, Essex
Printed and bound by Mackays of Chatham PLC

ISBN 0 352 33492 4

Contents

Acknowledgements

My thanks must go to three wanton women: Mandie, Nadia and Renate, without whose enthusiasm and encouragement I would never have discovered that writing saucy stories is the most terrific fun.

M.R.M.

Secrets

*S*itting on her favourite bench in the park in the pale wintry sunlight, munching her peanut butter and cucumber sandwich, Annette was painfully aware that she was unremarkable and invisible. She would have described herself as dumpy and plain. Dressed for warmth and comfort in shapeless, heavy, tweedy layers, with her medium-mouse, frizzy hair brutally cut just above her earlobes and still uncontrollable, Annette felt as if she had been middle-aged all her life, although she was only thirty-one.

She was not a virgin. That had been taken care of in the fumbling, bumbling attempts of the spotty, bespectacled boy next door many years ago. They had tried several times and her only memory of it was the snorting sound of his blocked adenoids as he breathed noisily into her ear. Each time they tried he had spilled himself – with no noticeable pleasure for either of them – the moment he entered her, after only a brief tweak on a nipple and with all their clothes still on. Eventually she had given up and never bothered again.

But Annette had a secret – a personal, private secret that she had never shared with anyone, nor ever would.

1

Annette's secret afforded her quite a lot of pleasure and in her mind she thought of her secret as a 'fetish', because it made her seem more interesting; and certainly there had been times when those around her would have been deeply shocked had they but suspected. Every day of her life Annette experimented with kinky underwear. Take today, for example. Today it was very tight green PVC which caused her to sweat profusely and itch with both the heat and the hots. If she was very lucky and it got hotter, she knew if she walked around the park for long enough with her pelvis tight and her pudgy thighs sticking together in the damply pinching PVC, she could make herself come, right there in public, without anyone guessing – because no one ever looked at her. She flushed with expectancy and a tweaking thrill clutched at her cunt. After her sandwich, she would go for a walk. As she sat unnoticed, she could feel the clingy PVC causing rivulets between her dimpled thighs. Just one circuit of the lake would do it, and her crotch began to throb at the thought of the warm, coursing glow that would ripple through her and flush her bright pink in the broad daylight.

Once, she had worn a disposable nappy, and that had been a particularly rewarding experience because the train home had got stuck in a tunnel for ages. She had been bursting for a pee and, after hanging on in unbearable agony for what felt like hours, she had quite suddenly realised that she didn't have to and, blissfully letting go, had pissed herself inside the nappy. The forbidden, self-indulgent release of the warm stream had been so exciting that she had felt a sudden surge of arousal almost cramping her and had crossed her legs quickly. But instead of dampening her ardour, the hard pressure of the deliciously, wickedly wet nappy on her overexcited nub had triggered the unexpected thrill of a spontaneous orgasm, which made her heart pound and her breathing jagged. That had been a bit tricky to conceal but she had pretended to be faint with the heat of the Underground and people had been sympathetic. On 'normal' days she just wore men's underwear: jockeys, Y-fronts or boxers. Sometimes she didn't bother and wore nothing, no bra or pants at all. Corsets were not her favourite as she wasn't keen on feeling girly, but she did like the way her large matronly breasts overflowed around them and jutted bouncingly over the top, and the way her privates were so nakedly exposed below.

Her hunger was stirring undeniably now so she finished her sandwich and set off on her walk around the lake, with her thighs clenched and drenched, trusting that no one else could hear the tiny, rhythmic squeaking sounds.

Clive had spotted the frumpy woman on the bench but his only thought had been, Bother, that's my favourite bench; so as soon as she got up he sauntered over and sat down – or, rather, he would have liked to think he sauntered but, with his short legs and bulging tummy, what he actually did was waddle. He plopped himself down with a grunt and took out a sticky bun and his thermos of sweet, black coffee. Clive was in his mid-thirties and bald already. Unprepossessing, he walked, or, rather, waddled, with his paddle-feet at ten to two, and his love of sticky buns and gooey burgers ensured that he would never be any slimmer than portly. Faded and colourless, he didn't expect any more from life than what he already had, which was a daily unremitting routine from home to work and home again. He lived alone, watched a lot of TV and built ships out of matchsticks.

But Clive had a secret which he was ashamed of and would never confess to. In his mind he called it his 'fantasy', because that made it seem less real and therefore less shameful. Clive came to work in ladies' underwear, upon which he lavished a great deal of what he

3

earned. He spent a lot of time in underwear shops and had designed for himself a scarlet corset with lots of black lace above and below and real tie-up laces down the back. He hooked himself into it down the front and loved the sight of his erection blatantly upright and straining in a most unfeminine manner beneath it. He watched in a mirror as he pleasured himself and the gushing spurts of his creamy-white semen against the bulging mountain of shiny red and lacy black was the most erotic sight he could imagine.

Today he was wearing crotchless pink nylon knickers that he had bought in Ann Summers and he knew that, before the day was out, he would have to take a break in the gents and five-finger himself through the fragile gap, his cock hard and virile and aggressive against the pretty, delicate pink. The idea brought a blush to his cheeks.

The following day she was there again, on his favourite seat. Bother the woman. He looked about but there were people on every seat and he had no choice, so he plonked himself down at the other end of the bench and they sat silently munching and avoiding contact.

Under their respectively mild ordinariness, Clive was wearing softly brushed, velveteen leopard-skin and Annette had on an athlete's jock-strap stuffed with a dildo for realism. During the course of the day she would make use of the dildo more than once. And he had discovered that, with judicious positioning against the shredder as it vibrated, hidden behind the filing cabinet, if he stuffed paper into it for as long as necessary, the softly sensuous luxury of the velveteen was so stimulating that he could reach ejaculation very quickly and furtively with no one noticing.

As the season became sunnier and hotter, it was inevitable that they shared the bench on a number of silent occasions, initially barely noticing each other except to be vaguely annoyed at the intrusion of their privacy but eventually becoming used to the other's presence.

Finally, one day, to his utter astonishment, Annette said, 'I'm sick of peanut butter and cucumber sandwiches. You don't fancy a swap, do you?'

Forward hussy. But no one ever spoke to him and he was, in some strange way, grateful. After a long, confused silence he finally replied, 'I'm sorry, I don't like peanut butter, but you can have one of my doughnuts. I've got more.'

And she did. She sat there eating his doughnut exactly as if they had known each other for years.

However, it took him several more days to get out the next sentence: 'Would you like some hot coffee? There's plenty here but I've only got one cup.'

She turned and looked at him, her small, grey eyes puzzled and slightly alarmed but she, too, was grateful. They shared the coffee cup and the sticky, black treacle tasted like nectar.

It was another week before he stammered almost apologetically, 'We could go to a coffee bar if you like and have some cream cakes. That is, if you want a real change from peanut butter and cucumber?'

Annette blushed crimson. She only had her boxers on today, so she felt relatively normal. He had carefully dressed in a pair of floral white panties so he, too, was quiescent and didn't feel selfconscious. Unbelievably, she said yes, she'd like that, and they went on the first date either of them had ever had. And continued to do so once a week throughout the summer. They discussed their work and their hobbies – what there were of them – and quite often sat in companionable silence but they never, ever confessed their libidinous and unmentionable secrets. Both continued to indulge them but now they were finding thoughts of each other creeping into their private moments of pleasure and eroticism. For fear of exposure and shame, both were unwilling for the friendship to develop any further, and so it continued until the autumn when it became too chilly to sit in the park. Instead, they occasionally went to a movie and, one day, surreptitiously and hesitantly, Clive took Annette's hand in the dark and held it silently throughout the movie. Neither of them mentioned it. Both were in a turmoil. If it came down to a choice, neither of them was willing to give up their privately and sensually fulfilling secret compulsion but also, neither was willing to confess and face the ridicule and rejection. And so it went on for several more months.

It was Clive who accidentally changed things. Unable to resist his achingly lonely hunger a moment longer, comfortably familiar with this dowdy little woman who had become his trusted companion and friend, he put his hand up her unattractive woollen skirt and encountered . . . leather. Leather?

He withdrew instantly with an audible gasp, unable to comprehend the enormity of his discovery and Annette sat in frozen silence, dully sure she had lost him for good. But as he sat next to her, his cock was potently alert, thrilled into instant tumescence and hugely interested.

He began to sweat. He had no idea how to proceed, so he did nothing, but his aroused prick was lurching and twitching with an urgency such as he had never experienced. The desire to explode left him speechless. He knew without any doubt whatsoever now that Annette was all he would ever want: the perfect woman, the partner of his dreams – if he had ever dared to have any.

They parted silently as he saw her on to the bus as usual and, noticing that she was almost in tears, he squeezed her hand especially warmly and pecked her on the cheek. He needed to think.

She could barely believe and hardly dared to breathe

but that reassuring pressure on her hand gave her a glimmer of hope, so she waited.

After a few days he phoned her. 'Let's go out to dinner tonight, somewhere special.' Then, after a very long pause and a deep breath, he said, 'Wear whatever you want,' and put the phone down.

Annette felt faint and had to sit down suddenly. Of outer garments she had no alternative: tweedy skirt, jumper over her lumps and bumps, flyaway hair and brogues, as usual. But underneath she had decided on her Victorian grandpa-drawers, which covered her from her shoulders to her knees like a bathing costume. The woollen drawers were genuine, with a slash-slit in the front and a capacious buttoned crap-flap behind.

She was being conservative. She didn't want to go too far too soon. This was the most terrifying moment of her life. She had never dared to imagine that she could ever share her secret, her 'fetish', with anyone, but she had become utterly dependent on the easy company of this fat, pale, stodgy little man, who hadn't run away and didn't seem to despise her for her sordid weakness. Her heart was pounding.

They went somewhere very special and expensive and Clive's pale eyes were bright and feverish. The conversation was stilted and embarrassing until suddenly, without warning, Clive blurted out, 'Annette, will you marry me?'

She trembled all over like a leaf in a storm.

'Oh, Clive, will you have me – knowing – what you know?'

In a flurry of uncontrollable desire he begged her, 'Let's go home. Please. Now. Please. Will you come with me?'

And so they went back to his flat, where they could barely speak to each other in their mutual terror. He approached her gently, placing his hands up under her

7

skirt to the chastely thick wool and, discovering the gap in the front, with a long shuddering moan, ferreted his way inside and placed his plump, warm palm under her quivering bush, electrifying her loins.

Never one to rush, he held it there for a few moments, stirring lightly with his fingers, and she felt a surging heat blaze through her nether regions, pounding furiously against his gently cradling hand. He withdrew his hand and slowly, clumsily, began to remove his own clothes.

Annette's eyes grew wider and wider as she gradually realised what was being revealed to her enraptured gaze. He stood, sheepishly, plumply, shyly erotic in his scarlet corset with suspenders and black stockings, his penis fully erect in its palely curling fuzz, the veins swollen and pulsing beneath the black lace. She stared breathlessly, her blood thumping in her ears and her groin awash with waves of searing desire. His cock leaped towards her under his lovely, fat, corseted tummy and without further hesitation she fumbled hastily for her own buttons and zips, impatient to remove all womanly accoutrements and stand bountifully overflowing before him in her man's Victorian drawers, with easy access.

Now they couldn't move quickly enough. He slipped her shoulder straps down to her waist, freeing her abundant, deeply cleavaged, bouncing bosom. Grasping it in both hands, he plunged his face into its buxom depths, turning to kiss and suck at the full moons of her large, pink, stiff nipples. She clasped him to her, feeling the satined bones beneath her hands and running them joyously up and down the tightly laced sheen constraining the rolls of his fleshy back. Unable to wait any longer, he took his pleading cock in one hand and, ripping her crap-flap in his haste with the other, guided it into the open gap.

She was dripping wet from years of spinsterhood, her

labia swollen and throbbing. She placed one short, stumpy leg around his thigh, sliding her foot up and down the silky black stocking, and then they were on the floor, carpet beneath them as he placed his savagely engorged knob inside her cunt-lips and rubbed it around gently to encourage relaxation and flow, but Annette was in no mood for niceties. She ground her powerful hips against him and, thrusting her bare, mountainous buttocks upwards, she forced him to enter her tight, wet warmth deeply and fully, sucking and pushing in a timeless, ageless rhythm that needed no practice.

He groaned painfully and she cried out sharply as her clutching, slippery tunnel fully enclosed him, and then their lust took them over and they bounced and bucked and heaved about on the floor, pounding and pumping, lips and tongues fastened together, him still encased in his tightly laced scarlet and stockings and her with her ripely full hips and thighs still swathed in woollen drawers. The molten rush of their mutual climax was swift and simultaneous, cresting and crashing in great gushing spasms of unbound joy as, with one final juddering thump hard into her, he released his pent-up semen in torrents.

She shuddered several times and then sighed a long, grateful, welcoming sigh. He collapsed beside her, spent and satisfied.

After some tenderly silent moments, she turned and nibbled his ear-lobe. 'To think all this time – both of us – and we never knew. Did you – you know – every time we met?'

'Yes. And you?'

'Yes, every time.' She grimaced. 'What a waste of time. Well, we won't waste any more, will we?' And, as she turned and cuddled into him, kissing his dear mouth, she scratched lightly and teasingly at the pale chest hair peeping cheekily over the black lace of his corset.

On the day of their wedding they walked hand-in-hand to the registry office, a colourlessly plain, uninterestingly fat and dull couple that no one noticed, and no one would ever have suspected that the bridegroom wore a beautiful one-piece in white lace with a frothy-petalled, lacy rose delicately and strategically placed over his crotch so that he would arise from its centre like Venus from the foaming briny, or that the bride wore an elegantly simple two-piece in plain white leather, which featured three flaps, two long metal chains and a padlock with a tiny key which she would furtively give him as they exchanged wedding rings. Combustion upon the contact of lace on leather was guaranteed, but that was their secret.

The Fruit Pickers

The fruit pickers were all young: mostly college students from the city, taking advantage of the harvesting season coinciding with their annual summer break, but some were locals on their school holidays or temporarily unemployed.

Belinda was in her third year at university and this was her third season fruit picking. She preferred to be independent of her parents and it helped with those extra expenses not covered by her grant. Besides, she liked the added advantages of spending all summer in the sun and keeping fit. She knew most of the others and found them easy and stimulating company.

Garth was the exception. He was a local lad who found seasonal work on the farms throughout the year: shearing, milking, hedge trimming and haymaking, as required. He was field-hardened, sun-ripened, ruddy and rather liberally freckled. His manner was bluff, direct and rather hearty but, by his irrepressible cheerfulness and good humour, he had charmed his way into their company. He was refreshingly frank and his vigour and lack of sophistication gave him entertainment value.

Belinda found him somewhat irritating but harmless.

They didn't see much of the other locals, who were younger and went home at the end of each day, but no one seemed to know where Garth lived; he did not appear to have a home to go to and remained behind drinking with the students in the village pub each evening after work.

It was hard work. There were acres of strawberry beds as well as rows of fruit trees, mostly apples, and it took a week or two to get into the rhythm and adapt to the physical requirements.

Like all the other girls, she wore small, tight, blue-denim shorts, frayed at the edges, and a floral cotton top tied in a knot under her breasts. Her naked midriff was taut and golden-smooth. She did not wear a bra as her breasts, while perfectly rounded and as firm as oranges, were not large and did not require support. They nestled comfortably in the fold provided by the tight cotton knot.

Her legs were as fine and strong as a racehorse's, with the same narrow ankles and long, firm shanks. She was a thoroughbred, her skin never darkening to more than lightly gilded and her blonde hair very short, with a feathered fringe. Her accent was neutrally correct and regionless. Her subject was archaeology and she hoped eventually to combine it with travel. She liked company and relaxed confidently in the evenings over a pint with the others, sharing experiences and philosophies.

Garth was always there and, although naive and untutored, proved to be not unintelligent. He had theories to share and surprised them all with his unconventional and original slant on current politics and policies. He was revealed as being thoughtful and articulate behind the brash blokiness. His presence expanded them and they learned not to judge him by his rough manner and simple forthrightness. He was also generous, offering assistance without arrogance whenever his physical prowess was advantageous – carrying ladders, or hefting

12

heavy boxes – and he never seemed to begrudge an extra few minutes to show someone a trick of the trade or a short cut.

Although she still found him irritating, she respected his presence among them. The group formed a social closeness, as sometimes happens in such intense environments.

One afternoon, exhausted from the heat and effort, Belinda took a moment's break and leaned against the trunk of an apple tree, with her eyes closed. Without warning, she suddenly felt two large, powerful hands slip inside her top and place themselves warmly over her breasts, covering them comprehensively and kneading them, tweaking the nipples teasingly. She jumped, insulted and offended, and opened her eyes sharply to look straight into Garth's grinning freckled cheerfulness.

He removed his hands quickly, holding them palms outwards in front of his chest and, before she could speak, he said, in his broad rural accent, 'Sorry. Just couldn't resist. Too tempting, stood there all pert and perky.' And, still grinning, he strolled off nonchalantly to the other side of the orchard.

Dumbstruck, she remained rooted to the spot, the firm, warm pressure of his hands still imprinted on her naked skin. Bloody cheek. Still, no harm done, and it hadn't been an entirely unpleasant experience. She decided to ignore it. Apparently, so did Garth, for he treated her just as distantly as usual in the bar later and she forgot him. She did not mention it to the others but, that night in bed, she could still feel her skin prickling and tingling at the remembered touch and her nipples became tightly aroused. Damn the man. She didn't need this.

Several days later, just as she had put it out of her mind, she was standing stretched upwards at the top of a ladder in an apple tree, picking down the elusive fruit just barely within her reach, when the unthinkable happened. After a slight wobble of the ladder, she felt a strong finger slide straight up inside the leg of her shorts, right past the side of her knickers to insert itself deep into the personal, private sanctum of her cunt. She gasped and clenched her thighs together in self-defence. The abruptness of the unsought intrusion left her feeling vulnerable and unprotected. The assertive finger probed and wiggled.

She yelled and nearly overbalanced the ladder. 'Get the fuck out of there unless you want to become a soprano!' she screamed at him, helplessly clinging to the ladder and trying to kick his face at the same time.

With a hoot of laughter, he withdrew and leaped off the ladder. He stood below her, looking up, sniffing at the offending finger then licking it, and she felt naked and exposed above him.

'You can't blame me, now, can you? You're very tasty and it was right there in full view, ripe and juicy.'

Cheeky bloody pervert! This was unpardonable. She was speechless with rage. Her pussy, though, was open and awake, and she could feel the warm thrill of arousal rushing around her pelvis. Her legs trembled and she climbed shakily down the ladder and sat on the ground to put out the flames. She felt dampness between her thighs and was furious. He was obscene.

But his presence became a magnet and she was newly aware of his power and potency, his hard body, his rude virility and now, as well, his availability. In the bar that evening, she did her best to ignore him, turning her back towards him, but his magnetism called to her as if they were the only two in the room and she could sense without looking that he was grinning. She hated him. Pervert.

For the next week she did her best to avoid him and generally succeeded, though erotic images which included freckles and a wide grin were pervading her dreams. She threw herself into the work. In order not to have to see him in the orchard daily, she went to work in the strawberry beds – where she did not have to climb trees and she felt a little safer. Kneeling and bending all day was back-breaking but she was fit and didn't mind. She was alone between two rows and had just about reached the end when she leaned back to rest her aching muscles – and there right in front of her eyes, just a foot away at the end of the row, he was standing with his naked dick erect in front of him, poking fat and hugely upright above the waist of his shorts. He put his hand around the base of it and jiggled it at her.

Her fanny jerked awake and an electric shock wave shot through her. She bit down hard to deny it and gritted between clenched teeth, 'You're obscene. Put that disgusting thing away before I tell someone.'

'You won't tell.' His cheeky, dappled face grinned at her. 'You want it. I can tell. I bet you're all juicy. I've never seen anyone so fruity and fragrant. You're ready to be enjoyed, all lush and full blown. No one else makes me hard like this. I can think of nothing more delicious than plucking you.'

How dare he? This was obscene.

'Piss off!' she hissed at him. 'You disgust me!'

He chuckled throatily. 'Yes, and I think you like being disgusted,' he mocked her.

Then he was gone and where he had stood there was an empty space. She stared at it for a moment, hearing his cheery whistling as he disappeared among the rows of strawberries. She was beside herself with fury but her body was quivering and dissolving with a yearning desire that she was not glad of.

He obsessed her. She couldn't stop thinking about him and every evening in the bar his cheeky, knowing grin taunted her. He was waiting, she knew, as if she were a mare about to come on heat. He was sensing out her readiness and his instincts would be true. He would know exactly when to pounce. He knew her better than she knew herself and she was determined to make him wrong. What an animal! What a crude, uncivilised peasant! She was far too good for him!

But she had to masturbate every day now to control her lust, in the hot showers or furtively under the bedclothes in the dormitory when the others were asleep. Even during the day an aching hunger would overpower her and she would have to excuse herself and go behind a hedge for a quick relieving wank. It did not satisfy. Every time she thought of him, her cunt pulsed and became moist, and her knees would give way.

She was alert now, never knowing where or when he might spring upon her next, both terrified and expectant, not knowing which was worse. The sight of that stiff, hungry rod jumping about in front of her would not leave her alone, and she ran her imagination over his solid, sinewy thighs and his hard-etched, swelling biceps. His laughing freckled face with the loose, wild curls hanging around it floated into her near vision; his mocking lips fluttered over her breasts and played about in her valleys and crevices with a touch like electrical currents.

She supposed he would have hair all over his chest and stomach. Ugh! How bestial!

She was in torment. She had become naked, base lust and her hunger was rampant, but she was determined to stay in control. After all, she was educated and refined, not a farmyard animal in rut. She made sure they did not meet and attached herself firmly to the sophisticated young men that she was familiar with, whose careful manners, even if suggestive, could be easily managed and deflected.

She engaged earnestly in philosophical conversation and debate which did not, however, occupy her attention. Such men held no interest for her. She was at all times acutely aware of where Garth was and that he was watching her, observing her minutely from the other side of the room. The tentacles of a ravenous desire had begun to wind their way around them both, bonding them in its heat and suffocating them with breathless longing. She was surprised that no one else had noticed.

One of the other girls from the city, a wanton hussy who had gone through all the boys in their group and was now bored with them all, had begun to flirt with Garth. Her behaviour was a little bold, as they had all had rather much to drink, and she was standing intimately close and pouting provocatively up at him. She lifted a leg and wrapped it seductively around his thigh. He stooped and took her open mouth full in his, pressing hard upon her lips and crushing her to him in a vice-like semblance of passion.

Belinda felt a hot flush like a fever rush through her with a violence she was unprepared for. Totally overwhelmed by this floodtide of engulfing desire and rage, she banged her glass down on the bar and rushed out into the night.

She didn't know where to go to vent herself and eventually ran into the open door of a barn where hay was being stored. She screamed her agony into the empty barn.

'Bastard! Bastard! Fucking bastard!' She grabbed a wooden handled pitchfork that was leaning on a hay bale and drove it again and again into the hay as if it were him, grunting loudly.

Suddenly, he was there with her, battling with her for the pitchfork, hay flying in all directions. 'It's you! It's you! It's you I want, not her!' he was yelling.

She was sobbing and screaming and beating her fists upon his chest, 'Bastard! bastard!'

And then they were on the floor among the bales, tearing and pulling and yelling at each other. Her shorts came off, her cotton shirt and her panties; his shorts and shirt and shoes went flying, and without preamble he

17

was shoving his angry, swollen cock deep into her like a weapon, thrusting and grunting, and she was opening to him and thrusting back with fury, thumping her hips savagely against him, biting him hard on the neck, the chest and the arms, drawing blood. He pushed her so hard against the hay bale that the sharp stalks dug holes in her flesh, scratching welts like fingernails as they pounded and plunged, bucked and reared like wild animals locked together, grunting and yelling their rage and lust in passionate fury.

Their mutual climax was swift and violent, breaking over them like a red-hot torrent bursting from a dam and wracking them with shuddering tremors of black oblivion. He lunged powerfully one last time, crashing against the neck of her womb with a juddering thump, wanting to punish by uniting, unleashing torrents of hot, thick semen deeply inside to claim her, and she clung to him, quivering with satiation. They collapsed upon the hay, still clinging to each other and rocking together in a hard, close embrace. Belinda was sobbing.

He stroked her hair with his rough, calloused hand. 'Ssssh. You're mine now, mine: just as I always knew you should be. I don't want anybody else.'

She clung and sobbed, still trying to fight him with her willpower, but surrendered within. She knew there was no going back now and his animal power frightened her. She felt abandoned, helpless and out of control.

It was not entirely unpleasant.

Over the next few weeks, they could not keep their hands off each other. He would appear at the end of a strawberry bed, grinning cheekily, his ever-ready cock sticking out of his shorts, and she would take him in her mouth and relish the brutal force of him as he pumped himself in and out of her luscious and lascivious lips until he shot his hot, creamy semen down her throat. At such times they had to be quick, in case someone else appeared and caught them at it. She no longer com-

18

plained when he stuck his long, strong fingers up her shorts and into her wet, sucking cunt as she was picking apples, but squirmed and wriggled against his probing and prodding until the crest of her orgasm broke and washed over her, turning her legs to jelly.

Somehow they still managed to get the job done and to meet their quotas, even sometimes volunteering for overtime so that they could be alone in the orchard. Then he would take her roughly and forcefully, standing up against a tree trunk, which flayed her back and left her bruised and sore. He spurted quickly and voraciously with loud cries of pleasure.

She could not get enough. At lunch-break they would disappear behind a hedge and fuck hard and fast, fumbling with clothing, her shorts and pants pulled aside and ripping, and his cock protruding fatly from beneath the leg of his shorts. It was animal sex, wild and abandoned, lusty and brutal. She particularly enjoyed the times he took her from behind unexpectedly, placing his hands around her waist to unzip and lower her shorts and then cradling her breasts as they swung loose beneath her while he pounded vigorously against her buttocks, his dangling balls slapping softly, all the while watching for the others in case they got caught.

In fact, no one knew. It was, anyway, a totally unlikely match. In the bar each evening they pretended to ignore each other, only communicating in a social way, as if they were no more to each other than working acquaintances. Belinda did not want anyone to know, for she was still not quite comfortable with this raunchy, bestial side of her sexuality. She felt coarsened but at the same time exhilarated and expanded. Freeing the beast within her had confused her and made her uncertain of herself.

Garth was just as confused but in a different way. He was attracted by her earthy passion but only because it was contained in the packaging of sophistication and class. He aspired to her polished refinement and her brittle self-assurance. He did not feel that she was superior to him; it was more as if she brought out qualities in him that his country upbringing could not. He believed they were equals in every way and sought for his passport into her deeper favours. He tried to find a way to reveal himself more fully to her. He could not take her back to his home, for he lived in a caravan, but he searched for a place where he could show her a different side of his character that she did not suspect. He knew that she did not imagine that he loved her, but he did, and longed to prove his worthiness.

Eventually, he got his chance, when a friend left for a trip overseas and asked him to house-sit. It was a lovely country cottage with all the traditional features: dark wooden ceiling beams, hand-painted china, deep pile sheepskin rugs, and an open fireplace. He invited her back for an evening meal, which astonished her. He placed flowers in vases, lit the log fire – even though it was midsummer – and cooked a simple but delicious meal of grilled salmon with fennel, minted new potatoes and home-grown salad. She was agog at this new image. He had chosen a very good white wine; they had got through two bottles of it and, once they were in front of the fire on the soft rug, he had wooed and seduced her lingeringly and patiently.

Taking his time and making her wait, he had touched her gently and caressingly, tracing every curve, slope and valley, searching out her points of pleasure and sensitivity. He had delicately taken her firm, round breasts in his mouth and sucked gently, raising her nipples with his lips and tongue and savouring her slow, wide-eyed arousal. Using his tongue to discover her, he had lapped at her vulva with long, slow strokes, teasing the clitoris to a stiffened bud and licking up her juices from within. He missed nothing, gliding smoothly from her pursed anal rose up the honeyed rift, pushing deeply to explore her slippery depths and sucking on the bush-clad mount, drawing from within ripples of pleasure and desire.

Then he kissed her long and tenderly on the mouth, seeking her tongue and drinking her moisture. She was fascinated by this new lover who found her every response and touched her every nerve with his carefulness, stirring up new hungers that came from deep within and creating a slow-burning, empty ache in her core that was unlike the fiery greed she had had for him until now. This was deeper, softer, more intimate, and when he finally penetrated her, gently, hesitantly, lovingly, she felt herself open and expand like a flower to receive him.

They rocked and swayed slowly and lingeringly, in perfect unison, locked in close embrace and, as the rhythm quickened, it was mutually fusing and simultaneous, mounting with a trance-like dreaminess. The crest that finally broke over them was long and slow and breathtakingly complete, fulfilling and uniting them in a new togetherness of gentleness and awe.

When they finally emerged from out of their drugged and semi-conscious state, she prised herself apart and gazed at him with wonder. This was not the man she had fucked to a pulp in the fields. This was a new man, a complete man: many men. This was a lover, one who had the capacity to keep surprising her. Could this, she dared to ask herself, be the only man? Time would tell and she, with her sharp, analytical intellect, was prepared to take the time to find out.

He, with his finely-tuned, earthy instincts, had never been in any doubt.

21

Sad Malcolm

Malcolm was a dirty little pervert but he couldn't help himself. The pleasure he gained from his filthy habit was greater than his sense of shame and was the only point to his life, really. In his local neighbourhood there were several telephone boxes and they were always littered with the colourful cards left there by prostitutes, offering sex. Some of them had pictures of a woman with enormous boobs, half-clad, in obscenely inviting postures, and the type of sex on offer was very varied.

Late at night, usually after midnight, Malcolm would slink out into the street to any one of the phone boxes and, glancing about furtively, he would shut himself in and wank himself off while he read all the cards, fantasising about the kind of sex they described. With his long, disguising grey coat unbuttoned, he would unzip his trousers, take out his erect cock and slowly rub himself to rock-hard fullness while he talked dirty to the telephone, as if one of the girls was at the other end. As his mounting ejaculation became more urgent, he would point himself at the phone, rapidly pump himself to orgasm and then splash his viscous streams of creamy semen triumphantly all over it, at the same time calling it a filthy slut and other such names.

One night, plucking up his courage, his hands sweating, his mouth dry and his heart pounding, he had called one of the telephone numbers and tried to talk dirty sex to the girl at the other end: but it had been an answering machine and his efforts had been for nothing, though his prick had been achingly hard and hot. So far, he hadn't had the courage to try again. The idea of quick, hard, dirty sex with a tart excited him unbearably but, besides having no money and no self-confidence, Malcolm knew he was not particularly prepossessing. He was all skin and bone and sharp angles and he stooped badly; his chest caved in and his head was held low like a turtle. He tried to be as invisible as possible and spoke hesitantly, if at all, with a slight stutter. He wore glasses and his sandy hair was wiry and tufty and unmanageable. His clothes all looked the same: colourless, shapeless and unfashionable.

The only thing Malcolm liked about himself at all was his prick. Slightly darker than the rest of him, it was long and dangly and smooth and when it was hard, it curved up and out in a bow shape with the head fully exposed. He was now in his early twenties, but he had never had sex with a woman; he masturbated obsessively, talking dirty, using all the filthy names and obscene language he had read in the magazines he used to turn himself on. It was the one single pleasure he had in life, besides smoking. There hung about him the lingering odour of stale cigarettes, sweat and semen, and his bedsit reeked of old socks and unwashed armpits and underpants. He worked in a warehouse, stacking boxes on shelves.

Malcolm's nocturnal habit was frequent, so he alternated the phone boxes, careful to choose the most deserted. He was building himself up to make another phone call. He wanted to shoot his come and his verbal filth at a real voice but he was terrified of being found out and getting caught by the police if the call was traced. He hated attracting attention to himself. Shuffling along to a phone box in his usual style one night, he stopped outside it and checked the empty street.

'Pssst!'

He looked about him for the origin of the sound but could see nothing.

'Pssst. Over here!'

He spun around and peered into the dark. He could just make out a bulky shape lurking in the narrow alleyway between two buildings.

'Come here, you!' the voice hissed.

He sidled over suspiciously, squinting into the shadows and she came a little way out towards him, where he could see her. She was young and sullen-looking, and very cheaply tarty. She wore a short nylon coat with leopard spots and fake-fur trim, and high white PVC boots. Her full, pouting, sulky mouth was crimson but the dark lip-liner wasn't quite straight and her black eyes looked smudged. Her wispy, short, straight hair straggled about her face in several shades of red. She looked like a scrubber.

He was immediately interested and felt arousal stirring in his trousers.

'I seen you.'

'What?'

'I seen you jerking off in phone boxes. Lots of times.'

'I dunno what you're on about.' He was stammering and he felt a hot blush flame his cheeks.

'I been watching you. You talk to yourself while you're doing it and then you come all over the phone. You're weird.'

'I never.'

'Yes, you did.'

'You're mad.'

There was a heavy awkward silence.

'I'll do you for a tenner if you like.'

Malcolm paused from his crushing sense of humiliation to take in this new direction. 'Haven't got a tenner.'

'A fiver, then.'

'Haven't got a fiver, neither.'

'You're sad.' This was so patently true that Malcolm felt it needed no comment.

'Well, then, would you like to stick it in my mouth? I won't swallow, though.' This last bit was said rather aggressively.

Malcolm's heart was pounding so loudly, he wasn't sure he'd heard her properly. He looked quickly around at the empty street. 'What?' he finally spluttered as he played for some time to digest the full import of what she was offering. Being offered sex was an alien concept to Malcolm and needed some thought. The hard swelling in his crotch was becoming uncomfortable and he squirmed to ease it.

'Well, do you want to or not?' She was kneeling on the ground in the shadows and he found himself moving into the alleyway towards her, fumbling ineptly with his belt. With a final quick glance out into the street, he moved deeper into the dark and she took his belt from his tremblingly incompetent grasp, undid it deftly and slid down the zipper. Fingers not his own took firm hold of his ravenously rigid cock and freed it to curve boldly into the night air.

Malcolm gasped at this public obscenity. He'd never done this in company.

'Oooh, you're full of surprises. Who'd've thought you'd have such a nice big dick, eh?'

And then the unimaginable happened and she enclosed it in her warm, moist mouth and sucked it.

Malcolm cried out. This was a pleasure undreamed of, so intense that it was almost painful. He quivered from head to foot with anticipation and desire. Then suddenly he was stabbing into her mouth with rapidly spasmodic jerks, out of control and urgent. Breathing harshly, clutching at handfuls of her lank, thin hair, he beat hard and fast into her full, scarlet lips and deep down her throat, causing her to gag. As his fervour gained momentum, his breathing became more stertorous and his thrusting stabs more jagged.

When he groaned, she moved her mouth away and took him firmly with both hands. Quite suddenly the wet, white fountains flew out of him high into the air, splattering over her washable nylon coat. With one final sharp jerk, he drained himself dry and wilted, sagging into himself and breathing heavily.

'You got a nice cock,' she said admiringly. 'Meet me here again tomorrow night and I'll do you properly for a fiver. You ain't never done a girl before, have you?'

'You talk too much,' he gasped at last, not wanting to admit the truth of her accusation.

'See you tomorrow, then,' she returned, undaunted, and briskly trit-trotted off down the street.

Malcolm remained a moment gathering his thoughts. He'd just stuck his dick into a tart's mouth and he couldn't believe how wonderful it had felt, all warm and tight and wet, and now he was on a promise of going the whole way, if he could find a fiver.

He went without food the next day, saving both his lunch- and dinner-money and drinking only cups of coffee. He couldn't get it off his mind and he was sweaty with nervous excitement all day. He wanted to tell someone, to boast that he'd scored, but there was no one to tell. He never really talked to the other blokes at the warehouse. They were all into football and beer and girls, and stuff he could never get his head round. Besides, they'd think he was pathetic, never having done it with anyone and feeling so excited about a whore.

He tried to pass the early evening by watching the telly but he couldn't concentrate. He'd smoked two packets of cigarettes already and was buzzing from

26

endless cups of coffee on an empty stomach. At last it was midnight, and suddenly he wasn't sure he wanted to do this. He panicked and decided he wasn't going to go after all. Instead he got undressed and climbed into bed, lying there in the dark, unable to sleep and shivering, his prick rigid, berating himself for his cowardice but certain suddenly that she hadn't meant it at all but had only said it to wind him up, taking the mickey out of him with no intention of keeping her word. Having convinced himself it would have been a waste of his time anyway, he fell into a fitful sleep. In the morning, he put the fiver he'd saved under the clock on the mantlepiece and left it there.

The next few days were miserable. He felt completely inadequate and useless. He couldn't believe he'd let the opportunity of a lifetime pass him by and kept yelling at himself for the fool that he was, and kicking things in his fury. The lads at work avoided him, not sure if it was just unexplained bad temper or if he was finally losing his marbles completely. Either way, he wasn't safe to be around.

It was a week before he got confident enough to go out again. He knew she wouldn't be there and somehow the wank in the phone box was ruined now that he knew she might be watching, but he wanted to reclaim the streets and make the night his own again. He was bitterly resentful that his one solitary pleasure had been stolen from him.

He returned to the shadowy alleyway where he could still feel the sucking warmth of her mouth around his cock. She wasn't there, of course, but his lust was hotly and solidly aroused by the vivid memory and he took out his angry dick and masturbated swiftly, muttering his dirty talk and squirting his come at the wall, pretending she was there. He wanted to see it land on her face.

'You didn't come. Where was you?'

Startled, he spun around; then, mortified that she

27

might have been watching and listening, he took to his heels and ran off down the street. Once inside his bedsit, he ranted and raved, swearing at himself and slagging her off for the cheap, easy, dirty little trollop that she was. By now he was furious and his fury lasted through the next day and carried him into the evening until he could bear it no longer and he stormed off into the street, full of rage and frustrated desire.

He waited in the dingy alleyway for nearly half an hour, smoking cigarette after cigarette, aroused and aching with thwarted lust but determined not to miss another opportunity. And then she was there in the alleyway with him, wearing the same leopard-skin nylon coat with the fake fur trim and white plastic boots.

'There you are, you dirty little bugger. Have you been playing with yourself again?'

'No!' he hissed vehemently. 'I been waiting for you.'

'What for? You don't want me, you pervert, not even for a miserable fiver – and after a free French, too.' She sounded surly and resentful.

He thrust the fiver that he'd saved into her hand. His palms were sweaty and he was incapable of speech.

She stared at the five-pound note in her hand, took stock, then pulled him deeper into the alleyway. Away from the street, in the moonlight, she opened her coat to reveal her complete nakedness beneath; then she took his hands and placed them on her breasts. He could barely contain his need. As he squeezed them clumsily, his inexpert prick emptied its wet load inside his trousers. He almost wept, but his hands were still kneading her tits and he was transfixed by the feel of her naked skin, so satin-smooth and shining palely in the steely grey light.

He began to mutter. 'Filthy slut,' he accused as he massaged her spongy tits. 'I bet you do this with everyone, you dirty little whore.'

'Usually costs a damn sight more than a fiver,' she

retorted sharply, pulling his head down to her chest and pushing his bespectacled face against her breasts. He found his mouth close to a nipple, so he took it between his lips and began to suck, while his other hand continued to rub and circle her other breast. He explored the sensation of the hardening nipple as it responded to his lips, losing himself in the discovery of her anatomical differences.

She was not slow to understand his need or appreciate his games and, as he indulged his searching mouth, she responded to his provocation.

'You're just a sad wanker, anyway. Good with your own fist but I bet you wouldn't know what to do with a real pussy.'

At the sound of the filth from someone else's mouth, he felt a steady resurgence inside his trousers.

'Have you ever been inside a nice wet, slippery pussy?' She was reaching for his flies.

His naked, swelling prong fell into her hand and continued to rise inexorably until it curved proudly upwards, like a scimitar in the silver light. He unglued his mouth to speak. 'How would you like a real man with a real hot, hard dick up your cunt for a change?' He was proud of himself now, upright and solid before her, and he pushed it against her bare belly and rubbed sideways, grinding against the pubic bone.

This new game was having an effect on her. Mixed with her sense of superiority and feeling a bit sorry for him, she was, for the first time in her life, in command and, for the first time in her life, her body was responding with a craving of its own. Sex had never been a pleasure for her before, but the crude language and his inexperienced ineptitude awoke a new warm tingling between her legs, which felt nice and made her like him a bit more.

* * *

'How does that feel, eh? Does that burn you, you trashy whore? Does that make you juicy?' He rubbed harder against her belly.

'Name's Jenny, for your information, wanker, and are you going to park that disgusting hot rod at all tonight, or what?'

Malcolm was carried away on the tide of his success and no longer hesitated. Pushing her hard up against the wall, with his hands pushing on the bricks and his knees bent, he let instinct take over.

She stood with her legs apart, as accessible as she could make herself, wondering at the wetness and very pleasant hollowness that had awakened in her cunt.

She guided him with her hand to the entrance. He pushed and shoved unceremoniously, aiming in the general direction of, rather than into, and eventually landed, more by her sense of direction than his own, inside the outer lips and against the slippery tightness of her secret, mysterious cave. He kept shoving and, by force of the angle of entry, rubbed hard against her clitoris, stimulating trickles of hunger down her legs and all through her pelvis.

She stopped breathing as he fumbled and pushed, arousing her response further with every stumbling thrust and, finally, with a sharp hiss, he fell deeply into her greasy, clinging tunnel, sliding and sliding until he was fully enveloped. She closed on him with a muscular grip and pushed down.

With a throaty groan he began to force himself upwards, taking the weight on his knees and, having nothing else to grip on to, she clenched and squeezed with her cunt-muscles as he began the rhythm of the ages, pushing in and out with the base of his root hard against her pleasure-button. His full length crashed against her cervix and fire blazed within her. She surrendered and opened as he gave himself over to the warmly encased, delicious friction. They were both blissed out by the mounting, rising heat of pure pleasure.

Gradually her orgasm broke within her like a flower coming to blossom. She scarcely understood what was happening as the new billowing warmth pervaded her senses and left her gasping and trembling with a satisfaction she had never dared hope for. She cried out with a high, thin wail.

Then she heard him muttering as he thrust up into her, faster and faster, 'That made you yell, you bitch. My long, hard cock made you yell. Now take my come – it's coming, it's coming. I'm going to fill you with hot come.'

'Fill me, fill me! Squirt it in me!' she cried and he did, great spurts of cream pooling into her as jab after jab released his inhibitions with the vigorous spasms of a triumphant ejaculation.

They collapsed against the wall with his head resting upon her shoulder, his glasses steamed over and his wilting cock languid inside her and happy to stay there.

'What did you say your name was?' he mumbled against her neck.

'Jenny. What's yours?'

A girl actually wanted to know his name. 'Malcolm.'

'Well, Sad Malcolm, if you want to do that again, I'll be here tomorrow night but it'll cost you another fiver.'

She wrapped herself back in her coat, heaved herself off the wall and strutted perkily away back into the street. A little dazed, Malcolm could have sworn he heard a thin, childish voice singing in the distance as she disappeared. He thrust his hands into his pockets and sloped off along the street, grinning broadly. Something crinkled under his hand. He pulled it out and looked at it in the watery moonlight. It was his fiver. He stared for a minute, not comprehending; then he let out a jubilant whoop. At the current rate of exchange, they could go on doing this forever. Malcolm leaped at an overhanging tree and swatted it with his open palm. The sound of his laughter rang eerily in the deserted midnight air.

The Birthday Party

*T*he annual event of the twins' birthday was a grue-
some task and Fleur knew she would end up with a
crashing headache. That was why she had booked them
to sleep over with their father for the night. Meanwhile,
here they were with all their little friends, screaming
about the house, rushing in and out, flapping wildly in
their Batman capes and masks, vigorously saving the
world and shrieking with childish delight.

There were twelve of them in all and the table was
covered with the scattered debris of the party they had
all pigged out on. She was good at that and always
made a real effort with the food. After all, that was what
parties were all about: that and the presents. Along with
the ice cream and jelly there had been fairy cakes,
sausage rolls and a huge chocolate birthday cake with
five candles on each half. Games had been organised,
with prizes being fought over, and the mild hysteria of
the present-opening ceremony had been successfully
kept within manageable bounds. Now she was just
chaperoning their play until all the parents came to
collect them; then the twins would leave with their

father and she could clean up in peace and take her pounding head to bed.

It had been a scorchingly hot summer and today was no exception. Even with all the windows open she was melting with the humidity and wondered how on earth the children could dash about so frenetically without seeming to notice the heat. The icing had been softening on the cake and the neatly piped words HAPPY BIRTHDAY JESSIE AND JACK had drifted into each other. Never mind. They'd been happy and now it was all over once more and their little tummies were full of cakes and jellies and ice cream, just as they liked it.

One by one the children began to leave; then David came and collected the overexcited twins and finally, with a huge sigh of relief, Fleur was alone with the detritus and the mess. She flopped down gratefully on to the sofa; the sweat trickled uncomfortably down her arms and breasts underneath her damp shirt, and her thighs were sticking together. She hated this kind of heat, so suffocating and exhausting. Anything at all was too much effort. She stripped off her wet shirt and skirt and lay motionless for a long while on the sofa, putting off the task ahead. It was better being naked but, even so, she still felt sticky and claustrophobic. After a few moments she drifted off to sleep and allowed herself the luxury of a much-deserved rest.

It was the heat that woke her half an hour later, although her headache had diminished to a dull heaviness behind her eyes. Reluctantly she lifted herself from the sofa and thought about clearing up. Her bare breasts jiggled as she bent forwards and she noticed again with pride that they were just exactly the right size. Not too large or heavy but large enough for a good grasping handful, rounded, yielding and pliant. After feeding the twins they were not quite as high as they had been, but the large brown areolae and nipples still pointed upwards and she found the faintly silvered radial marks

34

from breastfeeding not unattractive. They proclaimed her fulfilled motherhood.

Her stomach was flat, though no longer concave; she still had hip bones, and her firm, smooth, strong thighs were unmarked by childbirth. Because of the hot summer, her skin was tanned and darkly golden and there were no silly white marks. That was one of the advantages of having a secluded back garden.

She looked at the dark mole inside her collar bone. There was another on her opposing hip. She thought of them not as blemishes but as adornments, for her skin was otherwise silken-smooth and supple. She was at her best with a glowing tan and felt healthy and alive.

Lethargic with the stifling heat, she wandered aimlessly into the kitchen and opened the fridge door. The blast of chill air was a welcome relief and brought her nipples stiffly to attention. The tub of ice cream had not been replaced in the freezer compartment and was beginning to melt. She removed the lid and would never remember what possessed her to do what she did next – the relentless heat, probably. She plunged her hands into it and took large scoops, then began to rub its delicious coldness all over her breasts and stomach. Ooooh, that was better. More scoops, covering her breasts and smeared thickly across her belly, and she closed her eyes, blissfully indulging in its coolness on her hot skin.

'I'm so sorry; I'm intruding.' The pleasant, slightly amused masculine voice startled her and she jumped in alarm, turning her full frontal ice cream-smeared torso into his apologetic gaze.

Eyes wide, she was momentarily rendered speechless and it was he who broke the silence.

'I'm Glen. I've come for Emily.'

'She's gone,' she finally spluttered, pulling the frayed ends of her brain together with a mammoth effort, aware of the ludicrous nature of her situation. 'Her mother took her.'

'Typical,' he muttered, his eyes twinkling. 'She asked me to. She does this all the time.' His head had not moved but his eyes were raking her now-melting iced coating. He pulled himself together. 'I'm so sorry. I've caught you at a bad moment,' he said but his eyes were sparkling. He turned away and made to leave.

'Just a moment, Glen,' she heard herself say. 'Would you like some refreshment? There's plenty left.'

It must have been the heat. She must have become fevered. But in mitigation, she reflected, she had noticed the stirring movement beneath his trousers and, while he had been gazing fascinated at her besmeared breasts, she had been watching the bulge swelling and protruding revealingly. It had to be the heat. She could think of no other excuse, but he was very attractive, kind of hung loose and elegant, without tensions, a little predatory with a lean langour. Something had happened between them and she wasn't going to stop to analyse it.

'There's ice cream, for a start.' She walked up to him, challenging him with her eyes.

He returned her look and she knew she had not been mistaken. Somehow, she did not feel stupid standing there in just a pair of lacy white briefs, smeared all over with raspberry ripple ice cream, her rounded golden breasts bouncing like fresh ripe oranges with the tight little stalks chilled and frosted. She caught the appreciative glint in his eye and felt a shock wave race through her loins, stiffening her nipples even harder as she realised that he was enjoying the sensation of his own manifesting arousal. She presented her torso seductively and, the next thing she knew, he was licking the ice cream from her upthrust breasts, beginning at the nipples, sucking hard, then twining his tongue around the soft curves of her smothered breasts.

'Mm, raspberry ripple – my favourite,' he murmured as she tried vainly to suppress a moan.

Pursing his lips tightly around the stiff little stalk, he

pulled, lengthening it between his lips and tongue, cleaning off every last drop of ice cream. A thrill shot through her, contracting her cunt with a sharp spasm of desire. He licked across the valley between her breasts, sweeping it in long lapping strokes, using the full length and breadth of his tongue vigorously, and then sucked all over the other breast. As he placed his hands on her hips, he knelt down and with long, ravishing strokes and nibbling with his lips, slurped his way across her belly. The sliding, sucking tongue sent tremors of pleasure coursing through her veins and drenching her knickers with her own juices.

Once finished, he looked at her stark, golden naked-ness appraisingly. Standing up, he smiled down on her petiteness from his lanky height and, grinning, said, 'I didn't know ice cream could taste so good.'

The protruberance in his trousers was pushing out at an angle, forming a peak beneath the straining cloth.

'You don't look comfortable,' she said. 'Why don't you remove some clothing? It is incredibly hot.'

Slowly and with dignity, he undressed, removing his shirt and tie and placing them over a chair – a tidy man. He removed both his shoes and his socks and placed them under the chair. He knew a thing or two, this man, she thought with a tingling shiver. Most men would have left their socks until last and ended up looking ridiculous, but not him.

He was revealed as having dark hair on his legs and forearms, and lightly covering his chest, tapering away to a single line down his hard, flat stomach. He unzipped his trousers and lowered them, together with his boxers; he folded them and placed them over the chair also. In one swift movement, she whipped off her panties and kicked them away across the floor. Then they were naked together, his sinewy lean, dark hard-ness confronting her glowing, succulently rounded soft-ness: strangers, except for his appetiser.

'It's Fleur, isn't it?' he asked.

'Yes,' she replied inanely, not quite knowing where to begin and trying not to look too eagerly at the straining erection curving rock-hard up against his navel, the engorged veins pulsing.

'We're both pleased to meet you, Fleur.' He grinned wickedly.

They were standing in front of the open fridge door and an unaccustomed mischievousness overtook her. She reached in and took out an aerosol can. With a twinkle in her eye, she aimed carefully and squirted frothing whipped cream all over his upright penis. After reaching into a small jar, she then placed a glacé cherry right on the tip.

He laughed at the ridiculous sight of his thickly lathered dick crowned by the sticky, glistening red cherry. Gleefully, she knelt and enjoyed the hors d'oeuvres, first plucking off the cherry and chewing it, then curving her strong tongue around the solid mass and sucking with her cheeks, maintaining the pressure as she wound and sucked up and down the creamy length of him, licking and lapping until she had removed all traces. His prick leaped in her mouth, twitching and bucking, and he groaned softly.

Wickedness made her creative. There was a bowl of ice cubes melting inside the fridge door and she took two and placed them in her mouth. Before he could resist, she bent down once more and placed her icy mouth around his hot cock.

He cried out with the shock and his legs began to tremble. After a second or two of hesitant stillness, his hips began to move as she slid her mouth up and down the full length of him, juggling with the ice cubes, allowing her lips to glide firmly over the ridges of the glans and teasing her tongue into the tiny aperture on the top. The ice cubes melted and ran down the smooth, solid shaft into the pubic hair, dripping on to his thighs. He pushed into the clinging mouth and retracted to sink deeply again, almost choking her as he penetrated to the back of her throat.

Adjusting as necessary, she controlled his rhythmic stroking with the suction of her tongue and cheeks and held him firmly, twining her tongue lithely around the smoothly gliding shaft thrusting into her mouth. When she felt his urgency begin, she gently removed herself and stopped him with her hand held under his swinging balls. He was breathing heavily but allowed himself to subside slightly as she reached behind herself once more to a bowl on top of the fridge.

This time, she returned with a banana, and peeling it quickly, she bent her knees and shoved it unceremoniously inside herself. He grunted with the shock of this sudden brazenness and, with trembling hands, blindly took the aerosol she handed him. And then she was on her back on the floor offering him banana dessert.

He looked at the can in his hands, obviously bewildered and bemused and on fire with lust. Chocolate sauce. In a rapturous daze he looked at the banana protruding from between her spread legs and lasciviously squirted chocolate sauce all over it. He was ablaze now and greedily licked and lapped and slurped with softly grunting animal sounds as she writhed and moaned on the kitchen floor. He drew the banana from her pussy with his mouth and ate it, tasting her cunt-juice mixed with the chocolate that was smeared all over her sodden vulva. When he had finished, he pushed his tongue into the empty space and searched her crevices and depths, pushing and probing insistently, reaching for every morsel. Her hips were moving against him but, before her desire rose uncontrollably, she wriggled away again and he lost her for a moment.

* * *

He was finding it hard to keep up and his breathing was ragged. What the devil was she up to now? Well, what was sauce for the goose was sauce for the gander. He got to his knees and watched her disappear through the doorway into the other room. She waited for him by the massacred table, laughing, enticing, taunting him, with a bunch of grapes in her hand, but he knew the rules of the game now and was determined to be her match. As she hung the grapes over the hook of his rigidity and chewed them off one by one, gently cradling the tightened, serrated bag of his balls in her mouth, he prepared himself with a whole bowl of strawberry jelly and, pushed her backwards onto the sofa before dumping the jelly on her stomach.

He rubbed it all over her jutting breasts and flat belly, tweaking her nipples with gooey finger and thumb until she cried out. Then he rubbed his own body against hers, slithering and sliding up and down in the gelatinous mess while she laughed at his audacity. He pushed his aching dick up against her pert breasts and prodded at the nipples with little sucking sounds. Then he cupped her breasts with both hands and pushed them together before slipping his engorged erection between them, using the jelly to lubricate. She watched the swollen dome poke up between her breasts then disappear and reappear again, infused and angry. He could see her pupils dilating and guessed that her crotch was throbbing. Intoxicated and inspired, he leaped up again and strode over to the devastated table, coming back with what was left of the chocolate sponge.

They were both drunk with the merriment of their wildly wanton lust and, with shrieks of childish delight, they threw handfuls of cake at each other and smeared it wherever they could place their hands, licking it noisily and gluttonously from each other's buttocks, nibbling and nipping at the yielding flesh of the full moons, their tongues digging deeply into the crevices for every last crumb. He daubed it all over her cunt and she slopped it all over his prick and then, simultaneously, they set about eating it off each other. She sucked and dragged and tasted his pounding, pumping rod while he tickled and flicked and pulled on the tiny erection of her clitoris, licking her chocolate-box clean and vigorously scooping with his tongue along the sticky slit and back again to the eager bud until their mutual climax arose between them, surging hot and urgent and breaking in violent spasms of bucking, plunging release as he spurted the final course of his thick creamy semen into her mouth and she exploded against his tongue, releasing sweetly salty cunt-juice into his mouth.

The multiple-cresting waves of their abandoned passion were slow to subside, throbbing away finally to a sated whimper. Neither had ever been so uninhibited before and they blamed the heat, which couldn't possibly be natural. They collapsed in a heap of hysterical giggles and ruefully looked at their splattered, bedraggled ruins, still sticky, incredibly messy and thoroughly mingled with sweat.

'You can't go like that.' She giggled at him. 'You'd better have a bath.'

'Please.' He grinned, and kissed her laughing mouth softly, savouring the faint taste of his juices on her lips. 'You do a great party, Fleur.'

Together in the foamy bubbles of the tepid bath, it was a real pleasure to soap each other with the slippery liquid gel, gently, soothingly and lingeringly, without desire, discovering the details of each other in mutual admiration. They continued to chuckle over their unrestrained midsummer madness and he remarked that maybe his ex-wife's unreliability had its positive side after all. Any future children's parties would now be infected by the memory of this one, and would for all time call forth a fit of reminiscent chuckles. It would be a deliciously wicked memory to shock their grandchildren with when they were old and feeble – though of course neither of them could possibly realise that they were destined to share the same grandchildren – and for the rest of their lives there would be ample opportunity to catch each other's eye at children's parties, causing them both to dissolve into a fit of uncontrollable giggles. It would brighten up the sunset years that they did not yet know they would be spending together.

With the long, sultry summer evening stretching ahead of them, refreshed and relaxed without the children, they conversed pleasantly over a drink, after which it seemed natural to retire to the bedroom, where languour and sensuality inevitably conspired. They lay in comfortable silence, lazily aroused, her legs draped in abandon about his, and he slipped easily and fully into her, tightly enclosed in a perfect fit. In close embrace, without urgency, sliding effortlessly in and out and rocking gently, they succumbed to the drifting sense of dreaminess as the pleasure lifted and bathed them on a new, slowly expanding tide of ecstasy, surging and uplifting them upon gradually breaking waves of intimacy.

When Fleur awoke in the morning, Glen was still there. Thirty years later, he was still there, still slipping effortlessly inside her cosy, snug fit and conjuring up the ever-fulfilling delights of their mutual desire.

Real Men

*T*he catcalls and wolf whistles rang down from the scaffolding and Harvey smiled and stopped to watch. It was a regular daily ritual as the office girls spilled out on to the street for their lunch-break. Sometimes he would half-heartedly join in but mostly he didn't bother. The other blokes only did it out of habit anyway, to wind the girls up, but really to show off their manliness to each other – which wasn't something Harvey needed to do. He took off his hard hat and wiped the sweat off his brow with the back of his hand. Leaning over the rail of the scaffolding, he noticed one of the girls separate from the group and walk closer to the building site. Standing directly underneath them, she began to unbutton her blouse.

The whistling stopped abruptly and there was a hushed silence.

'What's she doing?' enquired one of the blokes pointlessly, as it was pretty obvious what she was doing.

Harvey was curious to see how far she would dare to go.

When she reached the final button, she pulled the shirt wide open and displayed her naked tits for all to see.

'That's what I've got,' she called up to them. 'Now get yours off and let's see what you've got.'

'Bloody hell!' he heard one of the lads splutter. 'What the fuck does she think she's doing?'

'Calling your bluff, I'd say!' Harvey yelled down to him.

'Well?' she called up, still flashing her boobs. 'Too hot for you? What are you, then, men or mice?'

There was a long silence and a lot of shuffling and coughing.

'I think it's mice, love,' Harvey called down to her gaily. 'There's too much there for anyone up here to handle.'

There were mocking hoots of derision from the gathered crowd of women below. 'You're all piss and wind!'

'Why don't you shit or get off the pot?'

'All mouth and no trousers – typical men!'

Harvey grinned to himself and thought, good for them. He'd never been quite comfortable with the whole game and had sometimes wondered what the girls thought about it. He doubted if the lads would ever play it again with quite the same cockiness, and chalked that one up to the girls.

Harvey knew he didn't quite fit in; he wasn't quite, somehow, 'one of the lads'. He thought it was because he wasn't too bright and couldn't keep up with their banter. He took everything very literally and fell too easily into the predictable booby traps. When they sent him for a left-handed spanner or a can of striped paint, he went for them. He didn't hold grudges and took it all with a good-natured grin. He didn't let it get to him – but neither did he ever feel he belonged.

He was used to it. It had been the same at school and it was the same at home with his brothers and sisters.

'Harvey's thick,' they'd explain breezily to their friends, and he'd heard it so often that he believed it himself, so he kept himself locked away in a private

44

space and got on well enough with everyone. He was a hard worker, pleasant-natured, willing to share a joke and even-tempered. People accepted him without much bothering to enquire into who he really was.

Physically, he was beautiful, with a magnificently powerful body, not particularly tall but superbly moulded with strong, hard muscles like sculpted granite, sinews like ropes and pecs to die for. His belly rippled under the light golden skin, and his neatly trimmed, waving blond hair, swept up and off his forehead, tapered thickly down his neck, revealing a gentle, open, pleasant face with an engagingly frank smile. His hazel eyes always had a slightly bewildered and vulnerable expression but they sparkled easily and often with a ready sense of fun. On his right thigh at the hip there was a tattoo of a green crocodile with a red eye. He was fascinated by them. They were primal, inviolable. Nobody messed with a crocodile.

Harvey had no idea he was beautiful and would have scorned the very idea.

The outdoor work as a building labourer suited him perfectly. It was never boring and made use of his strength and energy without taxing his brain, just as he preferred. His thoughts were his own, he knew his place in life and most of the time he was happy.

As he had no real friends, Harvey's social life was a bit lean. He went clubbing and partying sometimes with his sisters and their friends but had no girlfriend of his own. When he was still at school, he had had sexual encounters with several girls, usually quickies 'behind the bike-sheds'. For some reason, they threw themselves at him and opportunities kept presenting themselves, but he hadn't rated it much and didn't go seeking it. Sometimes, though, he did get a bit lonely and would have liked someone he could be comfortable with to share all the things he had locked inside.

The gang at work was expanding as the plumbers and

plasterers came on to the site and among the new group there was a Turkish bloke that Harvey hadn't met before. His name was Yusuf but everyone called him Joe, and he looked like a darker version of Harvey: the same strong, stocky body; the same frank, open, gentle smile; the same sweep of wavy hair, only black; and the same good nature – except that Joe was bright and gave the lads back as good as they handed out, which drew Harvey to him like a magnet. Joe was not naive and knew his way around. Harvey liked the look of him and, without knowing why, he wanted to know more about him.

The first time they were alone together was in the loo, having a pee. Harvey always noticed other blokes' todgers – not in any pervy or obvious way. He just noticed them the same way other people might notice eyes. He liked them, and they were all different. He couldn't help observing a major difference between him and Joe. His cock was of about average length but had an unusually thick girth; it was broad and fat with a long, concealing foreskin. It hung over his balls neatly.

Joe didn't have any foreskin and his long, brown prick dangled loosely. Harvey wanted to look some more – it reminded him of a horse or an elephant, or that whale he'd once seen on telly, with the huge waggling, dangling penis flapping about above the water that had made everyone gasp and giggle. Joe's drooping, dangling, dark length with the bare knob was fascinating and Harvey had to be careful not to stare.

More sophisticated about such matters, Joe had noticed Harvey noticing him and stored the knowledge away for another time. Meanwhile, he began to watch how the other blokes treated Harvey and tried to find out more about the man. He in his turn was attracted to Harvey's fair hair and golden, muscled perfection. Everyone Joe mixed with was olive-skinned with black hair and a moustache. The sight of a smooth-skinned blond was a rarity and he found it a welcome relief and very pleasing.

Joe was into men. It was the way where he came from, where the morality concerning girls was so strict and sexually forbidding. Men took their pleasure among themselves quite freely, though discreetly. You didn't need to be gay, but Joe preferred men to girls. He waited and watched before he decided.

It was clear that Harvey was a bit of an outsider and a loner, and no one seemed to know or care what he did after work. Joe took the trouble to position himself next to Harvey in the lunch-breaks and they struck up a conversational matiness. Joe discovered that Harvey had very little excitement in his life and thought perhaps he could help to change that. One day, feeling comfortable enough, he invited Harvey to come clubbing with him and some mates over the weekend. Harvey didn't even notice that the invitation was unusual. He found their friendship natural and agreeable and was not at all surprised that they should want to extend it beyond work, so he said yes without thinking about it.

The club they went to was full of men, and Joe explained that he found such places more fun, that he and his mates preferred the company of other men to girls, and with an easy gear-shift Harvey realised that he felt the same way but had never noticed.

Making the next step was a little more difficult. As the evening progressed, he saw men holding hands and even kissing each other, and he noticed that when they danced together they wiggled their butts and flaunted themselves. Even the way they were dressed was sexier than most men usually dared. On a trip to the gents, he surprised two blokes doing something to each other that had never entered his head and he rushed out of the loo without using it. Outside the door, he had to stop for a minute while his racing blood and pounding heart slowed down. He suddenly couldn't breathe and had to go outside into the cool, fresh air to try and think straight.

Thinking was not easy. All he knew was that the muscle bulging and swelling in his trousers was suddenly ravenous in a way he'd never experienced in his life before and he didn't understand.

'Harvey?' It was Joe, come looking for him. 'What's wrong?'

'They were wanking in the bog – not themselves – each other.'

Joe approached the moment gently. 'How do you feel about that?'

Harvey looked at him with troubled eyes and took a deep, gulping breath. 'I've got a hard-on!' he blurted. He was almost weeping in his anguish.

Joe put a consoling hand on his arm. 'Is that so bad? It happens to me all the time. Didn't you know that was how you would feel? It's better this way. It's right for us.'

Harvey looked directly at Joe with new eyes, disconcerted but curious. 'You do that – with other men?'

'Yes.'

There was an enormously long silence while Harvey struggled and Joe waited. Finally, Joe had his reward. 'Do you want to do that with me?'

'Yes.'

Now when they looked at each other, it was all different. Their eyes met searchingly. Harvey's entire internal structures were moving and shifting and Joe waited for them to settle. Then Harvey moved his head a little, just a little, but forward in Joe's direction, hesitated, then turned away. Joe took the evasive chin with his fingers, turned the face back and moved towards it until their lips touched. As they held the almost-kiss, Joe delicately extruded the tip of his tongue and lightly traced the edges of Harvey's trembling mouth, parting the lips and pressing a little more firmly until Harvey responded with his own tongue and the tips came together.

It was electrifying. Harvey was quivering from head to foot, his whole body charged by the sparkling tingles of a new and delicious desire. Separating and gasping for air, he placed the palm of his hand on Joe's jaw and stroked the cheek with his thumb. His fear had turned to wonder.

'Everything makes sense now. It all fits. This is what I always wanted, only I didn't know.'

Joe turned his head and nibbled gently on the caressing thumb. 'Come on. Let's go home to my place.'

In the cab they were silent, but out of sight of the cab driver's gaze they were holding hands, their fingers twining and confirming the breathless anticipation that bound them together. All of Harvey's nerve-ends were aquiver and Joe had become intensely attractive.

Once in the flat, they undressed each other slowly and appreciatively, their two stocky, powerful bodies so alike, one mocha, one golden, superbly honed and toned, the two different penises thrust hard up against the taut navels in their two different styles, Joe's long and curving and circumcised like a rearing horn and Harvey's thick and fat and straight and hiding coyly inside its helmet.

Harvey didn't know where to begin so Joe led him, teasing his tongue around the nipple-buds and sucking upon them, caressing the solid curves of Harvey's pecs and buttocks with both hands and kneeling to take Harvey in his mouth and glide up and down wetly upon him.

Harvey was holding his breath. He did not want to miss or forget one single sensation or tingling thrill that was coursing through his veins and into his cock, pulsating throughout his newly-awakened body and making him feel both soft and melting, and hard and potent at the same time.

Joe stood up and led him to the bed. As they lay together, it was Harvey's turn to pleasure Joe. He looked at the upstanding, curved rigidity, able to stare at last, and found it immensely desirable. He admired the smooth, silky skin and the pointed dome. He felt within his own organ the hungry ache of the snaking veins and the tightening balls.

Knowing what Joe craved, he placed his hand firmly round Joe's cock and watched avidly as the loose skin moved fluidly over the solid muscle. Without thinking, he licked the oozing moisture from the eye, then slid the glossy head inside his lips, surprised by the size of the mouthful. Joe groaned and this encouraged Harvey to gulp more fully, pushing the full length all the way down his throat and then back again, to play with his lips on the tip and discover the spongy ridges with his tongue, carefully covering his teeth.

After some minutes, Joe placed his hand on the fair head and said, 'We can do this together. Let me show you.'

Rearranging their bulk, he turned Harvey on to his stomach, got him to his knees and placed himself behind with his cock between the hard buttocks. Reaching for the lubricant, he whispered, 'It won't hurt – just relax.'

Harvey was more than willing. Already relaxed, he expanded, opened and received. Joe slathered the cream upon them both and entered Harvey carefully and tenderly. The tightness created a barrier for only a moment, then suddenly yielded invitingly and, as Joe buried himself deep in the engulfing cavity, Harvey knew himself penetrated and filled, his erection stimulated internally by a sensation more intense than he would have dreamed possible, and he thought he was about to explode.

Then Joe placed a greasy hand around Harvey's

screaming prick and the rhythm began, slowly and steadily at first until the hunger took control, and then they were plunging and thrusting and grunting in unison. Harvey's mind felt totally obliterated by the almost unbearable, ever-expanding shock waves of pure pleasure within and without, which threatened to blow him apart. He came with a spouting, splashing gush of hot spunk that drew from him an unrestrained cry of joy as he spewed fountains of cream onto the sheets. Then Joe removed his hand and grabbed both hips, spurred to his own expulsion by the ferocity of Harvey's and, with one hard, deep, thumping lunge, released torrents of come into Harvey's arse.

They lay for some time next to each other, their fingers trailing lightly across the sweaty, gleaming skin. Joe traced the contours of the crocodile. Harvey leaned up with his head on one elbow, his other hand lightly fondling Joe's gorgeous belly-hair.

'Cocks are best, no doubt about it: but don't tell the blokes at work or they'll all want some.'

Joe smiled at his naivety. 'They all think their own cocks are the best; that's the trouble. They're not like you, none of them, and they'll never know what they're missing. You're special.'

'No, I'm not. I'm thick.'

'Only where it counts.'

It was a mere second before Harvey got the joke; then he nearly fell off the bed laughing. The shift taking place inside him had always been there, waiting for him: and now that he knew who he was, it was going to be hard for anyone to take advantage of him any more. Besides, he had Joe now and that made everything different. Harvey felt like a man for the first time in his life.

He was on fire now, his body alive and vibrant. When he went to the club with Joe the following weekend, he was wearing a new sleeveless red top, aftershave, and blatantly advertised his sexuality. As they danced, he felt eyes upon him and he waggled his pelvis alluringly, to Joe's huge amusement.

A bloke standing at the bar attracted his attention. The outer shell of one earlobe was completeley covered in silver earrings and his tight leather jerkin displayed several tattoos on his chest and upper arms. His number one haircut gave him a slightly menacing look and his eyes were fixed burningly upon Harvey with a predatory stare that made Harvey's skin tingle and spark.

Joe leaned in to him and whispered, 'You've scored with Bruno, you lucky sod. I can't get anywhere near him. He only likes blonds.'

Harvey suddenly felt hot. There didn't seem to be any rules and he felt faint and unsure of himself. Suddenly he needed a pee and a breath of fresh air. He ducked out and made for the gents. As he pushed open the door, someone came in close behind him.

Bruno didn't waste any time. He grabbed Harvey's swollen crotch and rubbed. Harvey's surge of desire misted his vision. Without thinking, he moved his hand towards Bruno's trousers and unbuckled the belt. Within seconds they were both unzippered, trousers lowered around their hips and hands fondling and stimulating each other's erect cocks.

Bruno was huge and dark, like a stallion; the infused dome protruded angrily from out of the withdrawn foreskin. Harvey thought, with a thrill of pure lust: I can have as many of these as I like, all different, all unique and all hungry for me.

Other men came and went around them but nothing interrupted the steady rhythm of Harvey and Bruno briskly pumping each other to climax. Harvey's eyes were fixated on Bruno's snake-eye. He had yet to see another man come and he was panting and gasping with anticipation and his own erotic compulsion. Bruno groaned heavily and thrust his big cock urgently against Harvey's grip, and then Harvey felt the semen travel up under his fingers and watched it race out the slit and shoot high into the air with several dwindling leaps of arcing froth.

The sight of it brought his own orgasm to fruition and then, there he was in a public place, with a stranger, in front of other men, crying out his pleasure and spewing gouts of semen into the air for all to see, with his trousers dangling about his knees. He felt liberated and defiant. He didn't give a damn what he looked like and completely forgot that a similar sight the previous week had filled him with panic.

Joe was waiting for him at the bar with a grin and another drink. He slapped him on the back and laughed. 'Welcome to the club. Now that you know what your balls are for, you'll be able tell the eunuchs from the real men.'

Holy Orders

*V*irginia was in her forty-fifth year and, true to her
name, still a virgin, but this was right and proper
and exactly as it should be, for Virginia was, in fact,
Sister Virginia. She had entered the Holy Order of the
Sisters of Mercy at the age of eighteen, still innocent,
naive, sheltered and with no life experience to speak of.
She would not have survived well in the outside world
for she was childlike in her simplicity and trust.

Sister Virginia had never had a relationship with her
own body. She had simply never noticed it, taking it
completely for granted and not having it called to attention through illness or incapacity. She did not even know
what she looked like, for she hadn't really looked at
herself; she still bathed in the old-fashioned way in a
light cotton shift, dressing and undressing quickly and
discreetly with no mirror to reveal her below the neck.
Apart from the basic daily necessities of survival and
cleanliness, she had no communication or contact with
her own flesh, covered as it always was from head to
foot in the disguising robes of her calling – now only
knee-length, in the modern way – with a bit of hair
showing under her veil.

She could have been completely shapeless, for all she knew, for she did not notice other people's bodies and had therefore never compared herself. However, she was not at all shapeless. Unbeknown to her, she was buxom and softly rounded. All her energy was consumed by her devotion to her calling and in this she was single-minded and dedicated. No one could have been more committed to a life of prayer and service than Sister Virginia, with her unsullied purity, sincerity, naivety and absolute trust. She took everyone and everything at face value, believed only in other people's good intentions, had a rare and unassailable faith in human nature, knew absolutely nothing at all of the mechanics of procreation – which never crossed her mind – and was protected by her innocence and her sequestration from disabuse or disillusionment.

All the sacred vows were safe with Sister Virginia; she obeyed without question, had no physical appetites or emotional needs of any kind not supplied by the church, and no personal ambition. The church took care of all her requirements, occupying her fully with useful tasks and absolving her from any need to think for herself or make any decisions. She never doubted its absolute rightness, never questioned its authority, was uplifted by its rituals and was happy, contented and fulfilled.

Nothing gave Sister Virginia greater pleasure than attending Mass and, as she was best suited to practical tasks, it had for some while been her special duty to prepare the church each Sunday for the visiting priest. She made sure the missals were neatly placed in the pews, the altar was ready, the flowers arranged and the vestments properly laid out for Father Maximilian; then she put it all away again afterwards. She adored Father Max, with a child's total faith. Not only was he the earthly representative of her Lord and Master, and not only did he minister the Holy Sacrament which filled her with bliss, but he also looked like an angel, with his soft silver hair framing his gentle, kindly, fatherly face like a halo, and his long, flowing robes. He was her best shot at an image of what God would look like and sometimes when she prayed it was a face like this that she saw.

One particular Sunday, after Mass as usual, when all the other nuns had vacated the church and Sister Virginia was fussing about her tasks, she heard a voice from within the vestry. It sounded urgent. She trotted over to enquire the matter and was arrested at the door of the vestry by a sight she had never in her life expected to witness. Father Max had removed his sacramental robes and was standing in only his white vest and underpants. Seeing him thus would have been shocking enough for Sister Virginia: but what she could not understand was the strange, hard, smooth, huge bit of gristle that was protruding from the gap in his pants. She had no idea whatsoever what this was but she could hear him muttering, 'Get thee gone, Satan, get down and leave me alone. Away with you, you Devil's torment. I would be free of you.'

Sister Virginia's heart went straight out to Father Max. He was clearly undergoing some dreadful anguish, and that thing looked painful. She desperately wanted to help. She was also aware of a peculiar response within herself at the sight she was witnessing. Her mouth was dry and her heart was pounding in her ears. There was an uncomfortable wetness between her thighs; she felt hot, and she could not tear her eyes away from 'Satan'. Father Max dropped his cassock but there was a large peak jutting out in front of him which looked very odd, and he was groaning.

What Sister Virginia did not know was that Father Max had spent his life struggling against the temptations of the flesh, not always successfully, and found the delicious sight of all the nuns with their pure, shining faces, taking the host upon their moist, pink, adoring mouths, with their eyes closed in ecstasy, too much to bear altogether. And there was one particular nun, although middle-aged, whose cherubic face was framed by pale golden curls, whose adoring eyes were huge and beguilingly blue, whose lips were pouting and pink and receptive, and whose bosom was generously ample. Sister Virginia's simple, trusting innocence was a trigger that fired all his aching, unspent, repressed lust and desire in a way that caused him perpetual torment. He loved the Church and was sincere in his devotion to his ministry but he wished with a passion that the bishop would send him to a monastery rather than this exquisite, delicious, agonising torture among the worshipful nuns every Sunday.

As he groaned, Sister Virginia wrung her hands in sorrow for him and breathed softly, 'Oh, Father.'

He swung about aghast and looked hard at her, wondering how much she had seen or heard. She was staring at the protrusion under his cassock.

'I am so sorry you are suffering so much, Father. Are you in pain? How has Satan been tormenting you? Is there anything I can do to help?'

He stared at her in shocked disbelief. Could this innocent cherub – whose great pools of blue were so tempting to him – be, in reality, a wanton slut offering to fornicate with him? He recovered himself and realised that in fact he was looking at the personification of an innocence and purity he thought long gone from the world. His lust rose with a swift stiffening and lurched upwards. Animal instinct took over. He knew she had seen his reaction, for she was staring at it avidly.

'Sister, before you stands the unhappiest of men, a deeply troubled and unworthy wretch. Since you have witnessed my distress, I will confide in you. Satan has been tormenting me for some while now and, no matter how hard I pray, I cannot gain release. This is the weapon that he is using to tempt me and I must find a way to free myself from its grip.'

'Excuse me, Father, I did not mean to spy, but was that Satan's weapon that I saw just now underneath your cassock? Was that the torment? It did look very painful.'

Something inside Father Max fought for a grip at this unsuspecting and frank revelation of what she had seen, and lost the battle. He gave in to temptation. 'Yes, Sister. I'm sorry that you have witnessed this but that obscenity is indeed the product of the devil that I would be rid of.' He seized his chance. 'I know this is a great sacrifice for you but, as you are a true child of God, I do believe that you can help.'

'I will do anything at all if I can be of service.'

Father Max sent up a swift prayer for forgiveness and proceeded, his loins ablaze with a greedy desire at the sight of her rapturous devotion. Her huge blue orbs burned him up with a devouring lust that rendered him insensible. 'I do believe, Sister – if you could bear it – that if you took the evil thing in your healing hand and held it for a moment in prayer, it might help. Yes, I do believe it would help immensely. Is that too much to ask, Sister?'

In her desire to assist, Sister Virginia did not examine the feelings that were stirring within her nor question her deepest motives. She licked her lips and moved forwards a few paces, hesitant but willing. He lifted his cassock just sufficiently to allow access to her touch, then took her hands and placed them underneath until she felt the solid, pulsing rod of the devil's scourge. She quivered at the touch and slowly gripped it firmly in both hands.

'Hold it very hard, Sister, and squeeze the torment from it.'

She shut her eyes and prayed fervently for his release;

a strange aching wetness seeped into her underwear and her breasts felt sharply tight. She felt a sudden rapid and violent vibration between her clutching fingers, a sudden jerk, and something warm and liquid spilled upon her hand. Instantly the piece of gristle subsided into softness. Enraptured, she removed her hands and whispered, 'It's gone, Father; oh, Heaven be praised, it's gone away.' She looked at the white cream dripping over her hand.

Father Max thought fast. 'Gadarene swine,' he said swiftly, taking a cloth and wiping her hand.

'What, Father?'

'You remember when Jesus released the possessing demons from the boy into the Gadarene swine, and they rushed over the cliff and were destroyed?' This is the demon being released and now I am made well and very, very grateful. Sister, I do not know whether this will be the devil's last attempt to entrap me thus but you have been a truly devoted servant of God and I thank you. Can we keep this little secret to ourselves? I would not like the Reverend Mother to know of my ordeal in my struggle against Satan. Nor do I believe that anyone else could offer me the healing relief that you have, Sister. Go with God's blessing, child.'

Sister Virginia prayed and prayed with increased ardour for the following week, delighted beyond words to have been the instrument of such a powerful healing and anxious beyond measure that Father Max should not have to undergo this distress any longer. In response, something peculiar was also happening to Sister Virginia. Everywhere she looked, she saw the shape of Satan's scourge. The church steeple reminded her of the lofty spire protruding from Father Max's underpants. The candles on the altar began to look like the spike of the devil and, whenever she saw this, a hot flush would rush through her that she took for holy devotional ecstasy. She was grateful and began to glow.

The following Sunday after Mass, she knocked timidly on the vestry door. Father Max was waiting for her. He was dressed quite properly, but with a gasp of horror and a twitch of warm expectancy that she did not acknowledge, Sister Virginia saw that Satan was back.

'Oh, Sister, how glad I am to see you. I have been greatly improved and released from torment since your gentle ministrations last week and I wanted to thank you.'

Father Max knew that lying was a venial sin but with all the other weight on his conscience, he decided he could live with this smaller one.

'This is the first time Satan has tormented me since last Sunday and I think it is because of performing the Mass. You know, they say that the closer you are to God, the harder the devil works. I am sure that is why he has chosen this moment to return, sadly, more powerful than ever. I am in such anguish, Sister. Just look at this obscenity.' She could not look at anything else. 'But I have been given a sign of what must be done to exorcise the demon. It will be like a Sacrament, if you would be willing to perform a task of monumental self-sacrifice. I hardly dare to ask such a thing of you.'

'You can ask whatever you require of me, Father. I will do anything to be of service to you.'

Father Max wished she were less innocent or would stop talking like that. His craving was inflamed by her sincerity and the absolute knowledge that she had no idea of what she was saying. He was unable to go back, now, for his lust was ablaze and had obsessed him every moment since first she had so trustingly touched him. At the sight of her tender, pouting, pink lips receiving the Host as he placed it upon her moistly eager tongue, he had thought he would come on the spot but was sufficiently disciplined to desist until after the Mass. He sincerely did not wish to profane the Holy Sacrament, which he loved performing – as he genuinely loved all his priestly duties – but this carnal fire between his legs would not be quenched, no matter how hard he prayed. He was a man driven, compelled by a raging lust that would not be assuaged by his own manual relief, no matter how frequent. Guilt, shame and fear of being caught were only adding fuel to the furnace he was burning in.

'Sister, you know how the body and blood of Christ are transmuted by us upon ingestion to become pure spiritual communion. I have been inspired by a vision to perform an exorcism of a similar type of transmutation, with your help, to be at last completely rid of this demon. It is a great sacrifice for us both but would you take the scourge of Satan in your pure and cleansing mouth? Together we will pray for my release from this anguish.'

The only thought in Sister Virginia's mind was the gift of being able to offer healing. The thudding, pounding pleasurable sensation that wet her mouth and her nether parts simultaneously and sent rippling tingles all over her skin was not registered in her conscious mind, and so she had no objections to his unorthodox request if he thought it would help – far from it. It seemed logical.

She felt the now familiar flush of a rosy glow in her pelvis and between her legs and the stiffening of her untouched nipples, and accorded it to devotional longing and ardour. It felt so good that she was sure Father Max's rather unusual command must be right and proper. This was, at least, what she wanted to believe.

She knelt in front of him and he lifted his cassock to reveal the uplifted sword of Satan, hard and angry and demanding. It jumped at the touch of her soft mouth and she had to place her hand around it to steady it towards her lusciously pursed lips.

Father Max groaned loudly. 'I can't stand this any

61

longer!' he said in agony, and her heart went out to him. She gripped him hard between her lips, covering her teeth instinctively, and licked him without intending to. He gave a strangled cry and the same thing happened again: a couple of rapid thrusts, a violent jerk and the spilling of warm, thick cream which went down her throat in several mouthfuls, tasting slightly of the sea.

Only, this time, something else happened. Just before his release from the possessing demons, Father Max had rubbed his foot against her in a very personal place – quite accidentally, she was sure, with his mind on his anguish – and something had happened to her that made her feel faint. Waves of pure ecstasy had arisen from her groin and spread like a fire throughout her whole body, wracking her with a pleasurable thrill such as she had never dreamed possible. Her mind went completely blank at the same moment that she swallowed the demons and she dissolved for a while into a kind of trance. She thought it must be the transmutation of his possession, and surrendered gratefully to the blissful sensation.

'There now,' said Father Max gently, as he raised her up on her feet. 'That was the state of grace that you just experienced, a sacred gift for your devotion, not often granted. This has been a most propitious moment, Sister Virginia: one that only you and I can share, for no one else who has never experienced it could possibly understand.' Of this he was certain. 'By the way, Sister,' he added, almost as an afterthought. 'The starch in these vestments is giving me a rash on my neck. I wonder if you could bring some Vaseline with you next week to soothe it?' She would do anything he asked.

Sister Virginia was a new woman. She had experienced a state of grace, vouchsafed to very few, and her whole being was aglow with a new vitality. The other nuns were astonished. She sang, she laughed, she chattered, and she worked with vigour and joy. Nothing was too much trouble for her and she gave herself to any new chores with gratitude. She offered her services to anyone who needed help and was glad to perform any little act of support or assistance.

Everyone could see that it was a state of bliss that she had entered and, although they were astonished, no one questioned it, for it was assumed to be the reward for her years of devotion and her simple faith. The only thing that nobody knew was that her mind, her dreams and her prayers were full of Father Max and towering images of 'Satan'. From time to time her body was puzzlingly hungry in a way that she could not identify, feeling as if she needed to empty her bladder a lot more often than usual but without achieving much relief.

She looked forward with trembling anticipation to Mass on Sunday and arrived extremely early to prepare the church. She did not normally see Father Max before the service but today she knocked gently on the door as he was preparing himself. He let her in and she gave him the pot of salve for his rash.

'Oh, Father, I just wanted to know. Has Satan been tormenting you this week?'

'No, my child: not since last Sunday, praise be given.' He prayed to be absolved. His heart was genuinely troubled but his body was addicted. Guilt, secrecy and Sister Virginia's blue-eyed compliant innocence were a powerful drug.

'Let us pray with all our hearts that he does not arise within me during the Mass. Please come to me after the service and we will pray together.'

Her heart leaped. He still needed her. She radiated with adoration and rejoicing as she received the Sacraments and Father Max was in a sweat as he lifted them to her mouth. He fervently prayed that his aspiring lust would remain tucked inside his underwear and stood behind the altar as long as he could reasonably do so. Fortunately, the vestments were capacious and his unholy spire was unlikey to be detected, but the fever in his veins and in Satan's unsheathed sword was undeniable, unquenchable, undiminished and crippling. He knew it was time he addressed the problem in a proper and professional manner, but it would have to wait until tomorrow. Today he was burning, and it made him stumble in the prayer and splutter. He pretended to have sneezed and recovered himself but, in his heart of hearts, he did not welcome this intrusion into the performance of his priestly duties. He knew he would have to take responsibility – tomorrow.

Once they were alone together in the vestry, Father Max paced up and down like a caged animal. 'I am sorely tried, Sister. It has never been worse than this. I fear I am possessed of something more powerful than you and I alone. I have prayed and prayed for guidance and I am bewildered, lost and afraid.'

Her heart was breaking for him and she felt an inappropriate urge to put her arms around him.

As if he read her mind he cried out, 'Would you comfort me, please, Sister, like the Holy Mother? I am in such unbearable pain.'

She took him in her arms and he embraced her fiercely, crushing her ample bosom against his chest, and then he placed his mouth on hers and kissed her roughly and passionately, grinding against her rosy pout voraciously. She responded in like manner, enjoying his bigness and power hard against her soft body.

He broke away abruptly. 'Thank you, Sister; I needed your comfort. I am grateful. But it has not helped. Look at this evil scourge of the devil I must suffer. It must be beaten and beaten into submission. It must be plucked and purged. It must be plunged into the mighty depths and purified in fire.'

He thought he might have gone a bit far but she was sobbing and gasping and trembling, wringing her hands and pleading, and he felt success within his grasp.

'Oh, please don't torment yourself like this, Father. It is not your fault. Let us pray for help. I cannot bear to see you suffering like this.'

He took her arms and looked deep into her great, swimming, blue pools. Unable to resist, he risked all. 'There is one final, enormous favour that I could ask of you, Sister, but you are much too good, much too kind and much too gentle to undertake such a monumental task for my sake. I take it you are a virgin, Sister?'

'Oh, yes, of course, Father.'

'And you have never been tempted to break your holy vows?'

'Oh no, never, Father. I never think about it. The holy vows are easy to keep.'

This had not been his experience and he envied her her certainty and simplicity.

'Sister, do you know what virginity is?'

'Well, I'm not sure, Father, but it has something to do with husbands and children.'

'Do you know where in your body your virginity is kept?'

'I'm not sure that I do, Father.'

'It is here.' And he placed his hand over her mount of Venus, the pagan goddess of physical love, tucking the fingers under just a little and cupping her. The warm glow spread again throughout her, creating a hungry sense of void and she gasped at the touch. He removed his hand.

'That place belongs to Our Lord and must never, ever be touched or entered by a man or any instrument. That is your virginity, and it is your sacred gift to your heavenly husband.'

'Yes, of course, Father.' Sister Virginia had been sure that the lovely tingling glow that had burst upon her with such intense pleasure had been holy and was glad to have this confirmed.

'But there is another place on your body, not quite so holy, which could finally complete the releasing of my demonic possession in a way that would not interfere with your virginity or your vows. It would be a powerful act of supreme healing that I truly believe would exorcise Satan's hold over me forever. Do you remember how it became calmed and disappeared upon the act of swallowing and ingesting?'

'Yes, Father.' She would never forget. Her blood felt hot, and where his fingers had touched was throbbing and wet. She was panting.

Father Max's demonic obscenity was as hard as forged iron, his demon's spike demanding immediate sheathing and the unburdening of its clamouring possession. It was pressing hard against her and making her quake.

'Comfort me, once more, Sister, with your compassionate gift of healing.' He held her close and placed his mouth again upon her tempting rosebud, which she opened in hungry response.

This time, they did not pull apart. The mounting fervour of desire took them both in its unholy grip and toppled them from consciousness with a passion and demand that could no longer be denied. Father Max was a basically decent man and compromising her vows did not sit easily with him. He knew that chastity and virginity were not the same but, in the grip of this inordinate craving, unable to stop the tide of their mutual lust, with Sister Virginia plastered yieldingly against him, responding to his caresses and ardour with a clutching, pleading, aching hunger of her own, sophistry or not, he chose the lesser of two evils.

66

'I promise I will not hurt you in any way. Will you trust me?'

'Oh, Father.' She was beyond all care or control, clearly in the grip of a passion she did not understand and could not command.

He lifted her skirt while she attempted to wrap her legs around him. He removed her heavy stockings and her puritanical bloomers. He took the pot of Vaseline and rubbed it liberally about her posterior tightness. He removed his own underpants and smeared the Vaseline all over his angry, aggressive, purple-infused, satanic monster. Then, turning her away from him, placing her on all fours before him so that her full, soft curves writhed and churned against him, he steadily and slowly inserted himself into her anal orifice.

She moaned and cooed and pushed back. Once the ring of tightness was penetrated, she expanded and opened like a full-blooming flower. Feeling the clinging grip around the base of Satan's spike, he pushed eagerly into the forbidden cavity. At the same time, he reached his hand forwards and found the swollen, erect bud of her arousal. She shivered and cried out softly. Never one to linger, he juddered swiftly several times and, with an uncontrolled lunge, splashed the essence of his possession out of himself and into her virginal body, vibrating hard with his finger. She arched in a spasm of rapture, cried out joyfully and flushed rosy from top to toe in the grip of a sharply peaking, violent orgasm that she would never identify as such.

He showed her the result of their success. 'It is gone again, Sister: quite left me and gone, releasing me and leaving me whole again. I believe this time it will never return. I shall never forget your gracious kindness to an old man in his suffering. May you be richly blessed. Here, now, put your clothes back on.' He quickly reclothed and covered himself, turning his back discreetly while she found her discarded underwear.

'And did you experience again the state of grace?'

'Oh, Father, it was beautiful. Quite beautiful.' Her face radiated beatitude and he felt ashamed of his deception. He kissed her softly and dismissed her.

'I am fully healed now, Sister. That was a most powerful exorcism and I will never forget your blessed sacrifice on my behalf. You will be missed.'

He handed her the Vaseline pot, which she placed in her pocket, and glowing and radiant she returned to the convent.

During the following week, the Mother Superior called her in to see her. Her face was troubled.

'Sister Virginia, Father Maximilian will no longer be taking the Sunday Mass.'

Virginia felt a crushing blow beneath her heart.

'He has had words with the Bishop and decided to withdraw to a monastery. There will be a new priest next Sunday, and I have decided to let Sister Angela take over the duties in the church. You have been exemplary in your service, Sister, and we will find another task for you which is commensurate with your abilities and your willingness.'

Sister Virginia felt saddened and bleak not to be seeing him again, but also glad that this must mean that Satan was no longer tormenting him. She felt sure that if he was, Father Max would have returned for her healing favours.

'May I ask you something personal, Sister?' The Reverend Mother looked anxious and torn.

'Yes, Mother.'

'Are you a virgin, Sister?'

Sister Virginia's face lit up with such rapture and naked sincerity that it was impossible not to recognise. 'Yes, of course, Reverend Mother. How odd. Father Maximilian asked me the same thing just last week. He asked me if I had found my vows easy to keep and I told him that I had.'

The look of sheer relief that crossed Mother Superior's face was lost on Sister Virginia.

It took some time for the strangely empty, hungry feeling down below to wear away but after a while, all Sister Virginia could remember was the beautiful, blissful state of grace that she had been so blessed with. She did not expect such a gift to occur twice in one lifetime and neither did it. She radiated a huge and generous motherly warmth all the rest of her days, which she showered upon her fellow sisters, and was much loved in return. She lived and died a virgin, never dreaming for a moment, at least not in her conscious mind, that she had had experience of sex. Heaven forbid. But the sight of a church steeple, especially with a tolling bell, always gave her a cosy sense of fulfilment and pleasure.

Pandora's Chest

*T*he old trunk had been up in the attic as long as Pandora could remember. Even as a child she had been fascinated by it, but every time she had enquired about it, her mother had clucked her tongue, shaken her head and ominously muttered such admonitions as, 'best left', or, 'never wise to meddle with the dead', which had only stimulated her curiosity all the more.

Now that the house and its contents were all hers and with Russell away on a business trip for a few days, Pandora could hardly wait to climb the stairs to the dusty old attic and unearth the forbidden secrets. Girded with a gin and tonic, warmly wrapped in her favourite weekend cardie and jeans, she cleared away all the jumble of furniture and junk stored in the attic and created a space around the old trunk. She was clutching the brass key which she had retrieved from her mother's jewellery case. It slipped easily into the rusty lock; she turned it with a loud click. Dust flew off the lid as she opened it wide and let it fall backwards.

The open trunk appeared to contain piles of old clothing. It had come from her great-great grandmother, so she presumed they must be Victorian. On the top there was a thin, black, leather-bound book with a small brass clasp, locked. There was another teeny weeny little key on the ring for that. She inserted it and twisted and the book fell open in her lap. The pages were crisp and smelled mothy and slightly stale. At first sight it looked like a diary but there were no dates and no name inside it. The handwriting was round and clear and carefully formed like a child's, written in black ink. It began on the first page without introduction.

Mr G visits regularly once a week, always with the same requirements which must be performed exactly as commanded or he will demand that his money be returned, which causes nuisance and embarrassment. I hope we do not lose Lavinia as she is the only one equipped to service his particularity. Upon arrival, he must be scolded scathingly for his lateness and disobedience. He will be escorted forcefully up the stairs, undressed to his vest and long johns and locked in the linen cupboard for exactly half an hour. However much he cries and pleads for release, it must be denied him. He whimpers a great deal and is terrified of the dark. The door must be opened upon the stroke of thirty minutes by Lavinia, dressed as a nanny, who then kisses and cuddles and comforts him, opens her bodice and presents her breast to him. He climbs into her lap and suckles her milk like a child. Lavinia has recently had a babe and is lactating plentifully. I do believe she prefers this work to the usual because of her recent labour, so the arrangement works for all concerned.

As he is guzzling at her breast, she must extract his penis from inside his pants and pull upon it with the tips of her fingers and thumb. Only thus will he allow it. As she pulls and tweaks his erection, she will tell him what a fine upstanding young

71

boy he is and how he will one day become a strong, upright gentleman and please all the ladies. Still feeding at her breast, he squirts his semen into the palm of her hand. He then stops suckling and falls asleep in her lap for several minutes. For this service he pays the extra guinea willingly and never stays longer than one hour.

Costume required: a long black dress, buttoned double-breasted across the bodice to open easily. A starched, frilled white apron and cap, black shoes and stockings. Lavinia or someone with breast milk.

Pandora gawped at the book in shocked disbelief. Could this be the diary of a Madam – well, not diary exactly, more a client notebook, and what the dickens kind of a brothel was she running? Not your average house, certainly.

She started to unpack the trunk and, sure enough, there was the black dress and fresh white apron and cap as described, with the shoes and stockings. Lavinia, however, was long gone. She could hardly wait to read on:

Mr L-S likes to visit on the first Sunday of each month. I do not ask why it must be a Sunday but he always appears at midday after attending church. He must be shown to the Ruby Room, which has the necessary arrangements. He will undress himself alone and wait, lying naked upon the floor (which must be prepared with a rubber sheet and Indian blanket). The girl enters and, as if she cannot see him, washes her armpits and private parts with water from the jug and basin, then stands astride him. Lifting her petticoats and squatting over him, she voids her bladder upon his penis. She then takes the glass-topped table, places it over him as he lies beneath, masturbating, crouches above him and defecates upon the table as he watches from underneath. It will bring him to climax. He has strictly admonished that no one must ever touch him under any circumstances or he will never return. For this I have chosen Fanny, as she has no inhibitions about such things, being brought up in the countryside, and finds it easy work. Several of the other girls would do as well but Fanny has the most favourable combination of qualities. To begin with, she has extraordinary bodily control. She is always able to perform prodigiously. She is as fresh as a daisy, charming and feminine but quite without shame. He likes the girl to be wholesome and not at all slatternly.

Costume: a starched, white, lace bodice and several layers of frothy, frilly white petticoats. A rubber sheet and special blanket for the floor. I pay the housekeeper extra on these days.

Pandora was feeling quite steamy and sticky. Surely people didn't behave like this? But there they were: the pure white petticoats and bodice and, horror of horrors, the rubber sheet and Indian blanket. Pandora wasn't sure whether to laugh or shut the trunk. But she couldn't stop reading now:

Mr T does not accept any responsibility for his pleasures. He must be able to believe that it has nothing at all to do with him but that he is the helpless victim of the depravity of others. I should not say here, but I have it on good faith that he is a preacher and a missionary. For his appointment, he brings flowers and likes to take tea and converse as if he is on a parish visit. The girls (there must be two, one very young) invite him upstairs to look at their collection of butterflies. They will go to the Gold Room. He is overcome with the heat and sits on the bed to recover while they fuss and comfort with kind words of concern and offers of sal volatile. They lie him down and, as they do so, they tie his hands and feet to the bed rails with stockings so that he is unable to move. He will cry out for help but is to be ignored. The younger girl begins to undress herself, performing slowly and seductively before his eyes, while the other teases him all over with a feather duster to arouse him. The naked girl will then perform an act of auto-eroticism (or simulate one) while the other, with liberal amounts of butter and using both hands, masturbates him to ejaculation. He must be able to see his own cream spurting. As he deflates, protesting loudly, they untie him and leave the room.

He is a good reminder of the wisdom of demanding payment before enjoyment, as he will come running down the stairs with accusations of blasphemy and debauchery and rush from the house in disgust. He does not visit regularly and cannot be anticipated. Any of the girls will do, though Annie has been an exotic dancer and is both nubile and adept at the art of erotic undress.

Costume: Whatever the girls are wearing as normal but with a jacket and skirt for the taking of tea. The stockings and feather duster are beside the bed in the cabinet drawer. One of the girls must bring the butter from the tea-tray.

The duster was there – speckled brown and white owl feathers on a wooden handle – and the plaited stockings, made of silk, kinder to the skin. Pandora was more than hot and steamy now; she was decidedly frisky and wishing she had not waited for Russell's absence. Although, thinking about that, she was no longer sure of Russell's adequacy. They had known each other all their lives and had slipped comfortably into a companionable marriage without passion. He was familiar and safe and their sex life, while not unpleasant, was predictable and infrequent.

Neither of them had noticed it fall into routine as they had never been particularly imaginative or demanding of each other: and anyway, because of his long business hours, he was so often exhausted or stressed. They were good friends and she had thought the sex satisfactory – until now. Now, she was beginning to wonder if she was missing something, but all this was way out of her league and, she suspected, not even in Russell's ball park. She read on:

Mr P likes to play ride-the-horsie. He will undress to his combinations and affix a tail. A buxom girl with broad hips will bridle him and they will cavort, trotting and galloping throughout the house (exceedingly noisily!) as she sits upon his back and whips him on with a riding crop, until he is exhausted, when they will return to the Emerald Room. On some days, he prefers to be a dog, in which case they go straight to the Emerald Room where he eats from a plate on the floor while covered only in a coat made of goatskin and wearing a collar and lead which can be tightened to control his misbehaviour, particularly if he lifts his leg. She walks him, barking, through the house. Either as a horse or a dog, he has not so far had any little mishaps on the carpet but he likes us to believe that he might. The girl will be dressed in a tight, black leather corset and riding boots, with her breasts bared and her privates accessible. He will take her from behind on all fours on the floor, either barking or neighing, and may occasionally nip her buttocks. Betsy is the best girl for this as she has the generous proportions required and great patience.

Mr P makes an appointment before he visits and he pays an extra guinea for the public inconvenience.

Costume: a leather corset which leaves the breasts and nethers bare and thigh-high riding boots. For the horse, reins, bridle, and a crop, and a collar and chain and goatskin coat for the dog. These are kept in the garde-robe in the Emerald Room.

There they were, all folded neatly: corset, boots and animal accessories. Pandora felt goosebumps as she unfolded them. She was not even going to mention these to Russell. Whatever would be next?

Mr K is never here for long. He is in and out in a flash, every week, Monday at six promptly. He is very particular and must not be kept waiting. He always asks for Harriet as he says she is inventive and precise. Poor little Harriet has little else going for her and I would probably let her go, but for him. She must take whatever seasonal fruit Cook can provide from the kitchen and hide it in as many different places as she can think of upon her body, then, draped in seven flimsy veils and a red feather boa, she hides herself under the covers. Mr K gives himself exactly fifteen minutes to expose her, extricate the fruit from its cavities and complete his business. Disrobing her veils, leaving the boa wrapped around her, he eats the fruit he finds while she eats him and finally he ejaculates very quickly into her mouth. He insists on paying over and above the normal fee if he fails to find all of the fruit in the time allotted and is never here longer than twenty minutes.

Costume: fruit, seven veils and a red feather boa.

The veils were diaphanous and brightly coloured, reminding Pandora of a magician's scarves. She had visions of them unravelling in an endless stream from out of Harriet's fanny, with fruit lodged in the knots, and giggled at herself. This was not doing her any good at all. Late as it now was, Pandora could not get her nose out of the notebook:

Father B is a real gentleman, courteous and kindly at all times. He was once a monk but has been defrocked. In my active days I would have been happy to service him myself. He pays a reduced rate on account of his advanced age and reduced circumstances, and he always offers it upon arrival without needing to be reminded. He has Florrie, who has the face of an angel. It is a mystery to me how she has maintained her air of innocence but it makes for good business. They use the Opal Room. Florrie will be dressed as a nun, fully covered, and kneeling at her *prie-dieu* saying the rosary. She has memorised it especially. While she prays, with her eyes closed and face upwards, he undresses until quite naked, then, kneeling at his own *prie-dieu* he takes a whip which has tiny metal pellets on the end of each strand and prays for forgiveness as he thrashes himself raw. The pellets draw blood. As he prays, his erection swells and hardens and, with cries of 'mea culpa', he flagellates himself thus to ejaculation which he spouts all over Florrie's enraptured face, all the while berating himself as a sinner and defiled wretch, unworthy of God and deserving of hellfire. The poor man is tormented but satisfied, and Florrie is never hurt. She offered herself to him once but he deflated on the instant. Too impure to enter the holy sanctum of a woman, apparently.

Costume: one nun's full regalia with wimple and rosary. Two *prie-dieux* and a whip, kept in the Opal Room.

And there at the bottom of the trunk was the traditional nun's clothing, black dress and white headpiece with black veil, heavy black shoes and stockings and the inoffensive-looking rosary beside the whip with the wicked metal pellets. Pandora shivered. It was astonishing what people did for pleasure. She was staggered at the imaginative variety of human sexuality and began to feel quite inadequate. Hide-the-fruit took her fancy and she wondered if this would be the one she suggested to Russell.

Poor Russell. He had no idea what was about to hit him. She did not know whether she dared. He was due back the following evening and it would have to be then or she would lose her nerve altogether. It had to be while she was still inspired and aroused by the notebook. It continued:

Mr Y has simple pleasures. He likes to watch two of the girls performing upon each other but they must both be slender with small breasts and dressed as men. Mabel and Alice are the right shape and very accomplished. They are also intimate friends. They look most elegant in formal dress with cravats, fob watches, waistcoats and tails. They begin slowly, caressing and kissing, then remove their waistcoats and shirts and progress to licking and sucking each other's breasts. Mabel then removes all her clothes while Alice unbuttons her flies to reveal the dildo she has strapped upon her. She does not remove her trousers. Although he is quite content to see the dildo enter Mabel's fanny and watch her writhe, pinioned upon it, he will pay the extra guinea if Alice spreads Mabel's buttocks and inserts it into her rectum while Mabel stimulates herself manually. Sometimes I think they really do enjoy themselves and the orgasm is not always feigned. He, meanwhile, with the aid of a velvet glove, masturbates while sitting in his armchair watching them.

Costume: two formal men's suits, one velvet glove and a dildo.

They were there too, neatly piled together and Pandora looked long at the dildo. She was not sure she was quite ready for that.

The rest of the notebook contained information about housekeeping and grocery lists along with details of the property, and it was clear that it was all in preparation for handing over the business. Pandora wondered what had happened that it had all ended up in the chest in her attic. There were more financial and legal matters which were of little interest to her. She picked up the dildo and put it down again. It needed two, she decided. Finally she settled for the red feather boa, which she was not quite bold enough to wear down the stairs but trailed behind her.

That night she masturbated but her own hands were not satisfactory. Where the idea came from, she would never know, but there was Teddy sitting on his shelf in the corner, all soft and silky and unsuspecting, and there was the red feather boa she had liberated from the trunk. She felt incredibly lewd but highly aroused. Wrapping the boa around her nakedness and luxuriating in its tickling softness, she took Teddy and frotted him across her breasts, teasing the nipples to stubs with his paws and responding with tingling thrills of sensuality to the furry caress.

He paddled about awhile on the upper slopes of her double D-cup mountains, then slid eagerly down the foothills to the lower valley, where he dived nose first into the underbrush and played up and down the wet rift with glee. Held by his ears, he rubbed his nose joyfully among the crevices until the whole valley erupted in his face with a series of quakes which shot off the Richter scale and left both him and Pandora gasping and panting.

Oh, bugger, thought Pandora. It's never going to be the same again, and Teddy's OK for a one-night stand – but he's not my ideal man.

The next morning she awoke late, ravenous for a huge, greasy cooked breakfast and still raunchy. Russell was not due until late evening, so, emboldened by her success and fired up by the images conjured by the notebook, she dressed herself in the luscious froth of the white Victorian petticoats. The boa was still draped around her neck and her heavy globes were bare and hugely pendulous, swinging freely and flagrantly over the hot stove as she fried her eggs and bacon. She felt liberated and wanton, and loved it.

And that was how Russell caught her. Letting himself in, earlier than expected, he came up behind her as she hummed and sizzled, happily unaware of his presence. He paused in the doorway, gob-smacked and uncomprehending. He had never seen her like this and wasn't sure he was in the right house. Initially horrified and appalled, he was taken by surprise when his usually well-ordered groin blazed alive and surged into throbbing rigidity. The overwhelming rush of lust took the blood from his brain and he felt faint.

She turned and, seeing him there so unexpectedly, screamed and dropped the plate on the floor. Her huge breasts wobbled and jiggled and flaunted themselves brazenly in his face. Russell uncharacteristically lost control for the first time in his life. He ripped off his trousers and jocks and pinned her back against the kitchen table with a hearty shove. Still in shock, she let herself be hoisted up on to it. This man with the stiffly angry dick protruding from under his shirt was no one she knew.

Once her backside was on the table, Russell was

incapable of restraint. He was rock-hard and burning. Lifting the frothy white skirts, he plunged. Still highly aroused herself, Pandora was dripping wet. Her cunt clamped itself about him gratefully and they collided with a blind crash. Russell found himself assaulted by the succulent, globular boobs and sank upon them, sucking and pulling at the nipples and burying his face in the bouncing mountains of naked flesh.

'God, I love your tits!' he cried.

Pandora nearly stopped dead in mid-coitus. He never spoke like that. He wouldn't say things like that. He'd never told her that. Did he mean it? He must do. She felt a bit unhinged by this disclosure. Her tits had always been something of an embarrassment and this was a whole new idea she would have to adjust to. It blew her away and she gave herself up to the rampaging lust.

The result was totally unexpected. Normally he was very controlled, waiting for her response and helping her a bit before allowing himself his carefully-timed arrival, but this time was like nothing normal. His fires raged and he was grunting like an animal. As his unbridled desire built to a frenzy, it stoked her into a corresponding blaze and they erupted together tumultuously with wild, unrestrained shrieks that must have given pause to the neighbours. Gasping and astonished, he blurted, 'Jesus! What's happened to you?'

'I might ask you the same question,' she panted, trembling. 'Do you really like my tits?'

Even the language was new. This wasn't how they spoke to each other.

'I love your tits. I always have. I can't get enough of them.'

'Why didn't you tell me?'

He was silent for a moment. 'Out of respect, I suppose. I didn't know it could be like this.'

'Bugger respect. Give me this any day.' She felt like a

81

slut but she meant what she said. There was no going back now.

She showed him the diary. He read it as avidly as she had, shocked and disgusted but, nevertheless, from that moment on they exercised an astonishing degree of undreamed-of sexual creativity and it was surprising how often Russell was home in the evenings instead of being with a client. The costumes all got tried with recycling and combinations, and hide-the-fruit became a regular favourite. Pandora could conceal whole bananas beneath her boobs, and when Russell hid the cherries between his toes he discovered the exquisite delights of having his digits nibbled and suckled and titillated. Lychees in the ears elicited the toe-curling pleasure of ear-licking, and plums under the arms led them to the unsuspected thrill of nosing about in armpits.

When they went on holiday to the Bahamas, the licentious and wicked thrill of sex in the sea or the open air kept them in a permanent state of hot passion. There was new fruit to experiment with and they amazed themselves with the winning discovery of sugar cane up the bum. There was, of course, the added factor that Pandora no longer bothered with a bikini top and when he saw the huge globes sun-ripened and swinging free, Russell was totally incapable of keeping his hands off them.

'There's a moral in here somewhere,' Pandora suggested one day.

'You must be joking,' Russell chuckled. 'There's precious few morals round here any more.'

'No, you clown, I mean the Madam's notebook. Without it we'd never have discovered this. We'd have lived dreary, boring, dull, predictable lives with little pleasure.'

'So the moral is –' he grinned at her '– if the sex is hot, always keep a diary. You never know what good it might do.'

'You've got a salaciously filthy mind.' She leaned over to kiss him. As she did so, her mountainous breasts flattened against his naked chest – and they were off again.

Ladies' Day in the Hammam

*T*urkish coffee with *loukoum*, always the same. I enjoy my regular habits. Not that I come here very often, but it is a nice once-a-year treat to come to Paris and visit the mosque for a completely self-indulgent laze about in the luxury of the beautifully tiled steamy *hammam*. It's a total blob-out: no pressures, no stress, someone to pamper you, if required, with a good vigorous rub down, hot rooms, wet rooms, washing rooms, sleeping rooms and a café, all surrounded by the complex delicacy of the Islamic patterned tiles.

I love the stained glass and the ornately decorated tiles. Such a treat for the eyes, so multi-coloured and intricate, they create a sumptuous atmosphere of sensuality and decadence. Before I begin in the steam-room I always treat myself to the little sugary cakes and *loukoum* with strong black coffee, lightly flavoured with cardamoms, to get into the mood.

This year, my boyfriend was unable to come with me. Normally we would have attended the baths together on a mixed day. There are stricter rules about couples, however, and we're obliged to wear a little cloth around our hips to cover our loins. A bit put out at first, by his absence – for the baths are always a good way to get into a romantic mood and create the atmosphere for long, slow and sensually satisfying sex, which is not always available in our busy, work-dominated lives – I had eventually decided it might be fun to attend a women's day without the compromise of male presence and, now that I was here, I actually did feel more expansive and quite glad of my own company. In this exotic and heady place, where the air is thicker and everything moves more slowly, there's no sense of time or the hustle-bustle noisiness of the world outside. It's complete bliss and makes a wonderful change to have nothing but pleasure on your mind.

I gazed idly about the café and could not help noticing the woman who entered with flamboyant energy, like a summer tornado; She was obviously a great favourite with all the staff. She laughed and chattered with them in voluble and fluent French, her arms full of shopping bags from designer shops on the Champs Elysées, and she was clearly a regular.

She radiated warmth, size and good cheer, and every effort was being made to accommodate her. She seemed to occupy twice the space she actually did. Sitting down largely and effusively at the neighbouring table, she busily rearranged her many bags and seemed to include the whole room in her enthusiastic activity. She must have been about forty and in the full bloom of her ripeness: buxom, expansive and luscious. She was draped in a flowing, expensive, black woollen cape, and her small dainty hands were manicured to perfection with shapely, ruby-coloured nails. There were rings on every finger. Her abundant, mahogany-brown hair fell heavily on to her shoulders and her smooth skin was coffee-and-cream. Her laughing eyes were a liquid chocolate brown and the tastefully made-up features open and expressive. Everything about her spoke of opulence. As she sat down, her cape fell open to reveal a full-skirted, ruby-red, velvet dress, low-cut across her fulsome and bountiful bosom. She reached down to her bags and no one could miss the deep and sumptuous cleavage. Her presence was huge and radiant.

Once settled, she took out a cigarette case and a gold lighter. Unable to coax a flame from the lighter, she leaned over the table and asked cheerfully for a light. It was inevitable from that moment that we would get into conversation. This presence was too all-inclusive to avoid and, besides, she was such fun. She gave her name as Solange and it transpired that she spoke very good English in a heavily seductive and fruity accent, in a voice that was redolent of all the good things in life. This was a woman who took her pleasure seriously. For some time we chatted about the comparative merits of shopping in Paris or London, and every now and then she would lean over and tap me on the wrist with her perfectly manicured, bejewelled fingers. Her touch was light and teasing, and mildly flirtatious.

When we'd finished our coffee and cakes, my new acquaintance suggested that we should visit the *hammam* together as we were both unaccompanied and company would be more fun. I agreed readily and, gathering up all the shopping bags with a great deal of bustle and noise, we went through to the changing rooms and collected towels. We had both brought our own washing equipment and, wrapped in the large, soft, fluffy towels, we padded barefoot through to the inner room where a number of other women were enjoying the facilities in slow-moving, unhurried langour, lounging about, washing lazily or soaping each other.

There were no dress rules on women's day, and everyone was uninhibitedly naked. It put me in mind of the *hammam* in Turkey where the women were astonishing. Typically large, always publicly covered and reticent, away from prying male eyes they were shamelessly and outrageously abandoned, combing each other's hair, shaving each other's armpits and pubes, and washing each other intimately and thoroughly in the ever-flowing hot water.

I contemplated the variety of womanhood about me and remarked silently on the contrast between the two of us, so oddly matched; I, blonde and pale, with long, lean lightly golden limbs, flat stomach and firmly upstanding breasts, and she brunette, with her ample cappuccino curves, her dimpled, generous arse and her heavily bountiful, bosomy succulence.

We chose our mattress-beds and, organising ourselves, yielded to the pleasurable indulgence of doing absolutely nothing at all, reclining in the hot, steamy luxuriance of the marble-tiled *hammam*; the only sound was the water, pouring in a continuous stream from the taps into the marble sinks set into recesses around the walls.

After relaxing for some while in easy silence, Solange asked if I was ready to be washed. This took me somewhat by surprise as I had never considered sharing my ablutions, but I quickly realised it was perfectly normal for these women, just the way it was always done. I stood up with my hands against the wall and my body available, as I had seen the other women do. With handfuls of a richly scented shower-gel, smelling of perfumed purple fruit, she began on my shoulders, with long, smooth strokes up my neck and across my back, soaping under the armpits, massaging along both arms with long, firm strokes and kneading gently between my fingers. Then she rubbed her way in sweeping motions down my back, into the waist and circled all over my neatly rounded arse. With a little shock, I felt her hand separate my buttocks and wash underneath them in a place I have always considered most private. Then, beginning inside the crease of the inner thigh with a new dab of gel, her hands ran strongly down one leg, swooping up and down, rubbing behind the knee, down my long calves and ankles, lifting the heel, then the ball, and gently massaging between my toes. The other leg received the same careful, thorough strokes, slowly and attentively.

She came around the front and began again on the shoulders; with the same long, slow strokes, she moved down to the breasts and circled all over them, lifting each gently to soap under the crease, over my flat belly and down to the mons – blonde, like the rest of me. She took another handful of soap and lathered the pubic area generously; her hand efficiently washed between my legs, and I felt the sudden sharp, unwelcome tweak in my breasts as my nipples suddenly contracted and stiffened to two hard little points. This did not seem appropriate and discomfited me.

The entire experience was unforgettably delicious. She was careful and thorough, without becoming too personal, and the sensation of being pampered was undeniably blissful. I closed my eyes and allowed the unfamiliar indulgence to massage both my body and mind into a state of trance.

I have never been particularly aware of women sexually, but a new and prickling excitement was flooding my senses and causing me some alarm. Although her touch was impersonal and discreet, she herself reeked of a ripe, fruity, pervasive sensuality. She was luscious and, in her richly suggestive presence, my own appetite was awakened and I began to feel the tingles and trickles of a fiery arousal. I became aware of my cunt: alive with a pulsing energy. The fluttering caress of her expert fingers was sending shock waves rippling across my skin and up and down my spine. She oozed sex and it permeated all my senses. As I closed my eyes I breathed her essence, nearly suffocating in the eroticism of her.

Lightheaded and dizzy with desire, I could not believe she was unaware of my response, although I was careful to reveal nothing overtly. My breasts had contracted sharply and the naked nipples were standing up like bullets. My skin was flushed and I felt faint. I wanted to drown in her.

When the washing was completed, I knew it was my turn to reciprocate. With an enormous effort, I pulled myself together, took a deep breath and a handful of gel and tried to concentrate on washing her as expertly and impersonally as she had me. I was pleasantly surprised by the feel of the deliciously yielding, smooth elasticity of her flesh. The roundly curved shoulders and back tucked unexpectedly into a narrow, surprisingly small waist, then out again to the ripe fullness of the flowering hips. Not to be outdone, letting go of my Englishness, and not without some curiosity spurred by desire, I parted her full globes and placed a soapy hand between her buttocks, washing the narrow space with the edge of my palm. Almost unwittingly, I felt my finger run over the tightly pursed anal rose and only just resisted the sudden temptation to linger. Withdrawing my hand, I quickly took another squirt of gel and finished the legs, pleased by the unexpected daintiness of the ankles and feet. Coming to the front, I almost wallowed in the fecundity of her breasts and belly; then, to compensate, denying my quivering temptations, I briskly soaped her soft private parts.

We set aside the gel, giggling girlishly, and gleefully threw bowls of hot water over each other to rinse away the froth, then retired to the ante-room and lay, naked and exhausted by the heat, on the commodious beds. We dozed lightly for some while but my aching need for her was keeping me from sleep and my awareness of her closeness was so powerful that I could barely keep my hands to myself. The craving was unbearable.

I was only a litle surprised and hugely relieved when, after some long while, Solange leaned over and whispered to me, 'Why don't you join me here on my bed?'

My joy was unbounded. Without hesitation, I willingly went over and lay down beside her. It seemed natural to cuddle close against her succulently warm, slightly damp flesh, my head nestled into the capacious bosom where I could smell the wholesome, peachy smell of her fresh skin. Closing my eyes, I surrendered myself to her erotic sensuality.

I did not know whether there were others present or not in the room. It did not seem to matter. Dreamy and drowsy, in a surreal state of disconnected bliss, I felt comforted as a gentle hand caressed my breast. My nipples stiffened again in response but the hand was undemanding. It was gently and searchingly exploratory, enjoying discovery. It circled my firmly rounded breast, cupping the fullness tenderly and squeezing the nipple lightly between finger and thumb.

A finger travelled to the other breast, then traced around the areola and fluttered across my erecting nipple. The back of the hand drifted lazily down to the concave stomach, then softly explored the hollow of the curve inside my hipbones. Unhurried, it glided down over the hips and thighs, then ran lightly up the golden smoothness of my inner thigh to the place of all delights enclosed between my legs.

Quivering, I responded to the gentle stroking of the fair down on the outer lips by separating my legs sufficiently to grant her hand freedom. I felt wanton. The hand stroked and stroked until I ached for something more; then, a probing finger parted the lips, entered my moistness and played in the ready slipperiness, finding every fold and every corner and creating sensations I had barely dreamed of.

I felt totally discovered in a new way, delighted in and fully appreciated. I offered myself gladly to the undemanding touch and rhythm of the cherishing finger. My pelvis retracted, tightening and clenching the muscles to encase and encourage its intrusion.

In response, it pushed its way deeper in and rapidly vibrated against my love-spot. I thought I would die.

Having increased my wetness, it withdrew to the tip of my hard and swollen clitoris. Pressing and circling, it searched out the excited extent of it and, after drawing moisture from inside the thrusting cavity, began to rub with intent. With slow, purposeful strokes it moved harder and quicker, encouraging up a warm, spreading glow throughout my loins and belly, which, slowly increasing, reached a peak and broke over me in a long, slow, languid, gratifying swell.

Gratefully, I turned and placed my mouth around the large, brown nipple, sucking gently, like a child, my face buried in the bounty of her luxurious flesh. With satisfaction, I felt the nipple harden and tighten to a bud and I raised my hand to encompass the other.

Overwhelmed by her freely given, unsought generosity, I longed to return the gift. New to this but with intense pleasure, I moved my mouth lower and played over the lush belly with my lips. Her skin was silken. She gave a deep, moaning sigh. She was no stranger to this and she clearly enjoyed her sensuality without restraint. With my hands on the gloriously spreading hips, I wriggled myself down between the sumptuously fleshy legs and explored the dimpled belly button with my tongue, prodding and sucking, then ran the tip of my tongue down the central line of the fruitful belly to the furry mound.

As I stroked along the full thighs with my fingers, digging just a little, I licked and nibbled the creamy inner thigh and she moaned softly. Sensing with delight the gratification I was providing and wallowing in this new experience of melting softness, I released all inhibitions and responded to the pleasure of giving pleasure. I parted the ripe, coffee-coloured lips with my thumbs and ran the digits swiftly and lightly up and down the swollen, downy ridges, then slowly lowered my face and placed my virgin tongue into the swollen, welcoming, wet depths.

The groaning deepened and, thus encouraged, I ran my tongue strongly upwards to discover the hard tip of the eagerly waiting clitoris. Fascinated by its tiny erection, I took it between my lips and sucked the soft flesh, flicking the tiny nodule with the tip of my tongue. I felt the body beneath me shiver and heard a small cry of delight. The delight was not all hers. I was discovering a wealth of sensations and pleasures from a whole new angle and the abundance of it was joyous. I penetrated my tongue to its full length into the tight, moistly quivering cave and explored every crevice of the folds and angles, seeking out the pleasure-spot. I could taste the sweet sea-taste of the juices, and smell the light muskiness. I found it not at all unpleasant, but stimulating.

By now my own arousal was increasing again and I was beginning to crave the sensations I was creating. Sensitive to my responses, she lifted my head from between her legs and gently suggested that we try a new position. I allowed her to lead. Turning her body heavily and manoeuvring mine into position, she deftly placed us both so that we were lying side by side, facing upside down. My anticipation at what was about to occur was so intense, I felt the moisture trickle down my thighs as the ripples of hot current flowed freely through my pelvis and into my cunt. From now on we would be in tandem and it became impossible to concentrate, so I yielded entirely to instinct and the complete annihilation of all thought.

Beginning at the base of my vulva, she ran her tongue up the slippery slit and I felt again the trembling, mounting ecstasy of orgasm. I was eating her honeyed cunt in similar fashion and felt her corresponding response. She licked again, and again, and again, each time harder and more insistent. Finally, teasingly, she sucked hard on the clitoris, pulling it tightly with her lips; then, relenting, she began to caress it with the fluttering tip of her tongue, rhythmically now, getting faster.

In response to my burgeoning climax, the intensity of my caresses was also increasing upon her fully erect button. We were mindlessly unaware that we were shuddering and moaning, and the mutual passion increased until the mounting orgasm broke in molten waves over us both with loud, joyfully mingling cries as, flowing out from our sacral centre to the tips of our fingers and toes, our enthralled bodies were wracked by the cresting, climaxing tide.

Elated with my achievement, I collapsed upon the sated body of my companion, who placed a dainty, trembling hand on my head as it rested in the angle between her thigh and her pubis; and in the steamy, embracing warmth, we gently subsided.

As we drifted off into a contentedly drowsy oblivion, I sent a silent thank you to Solange. It is a special gift to be able to bestow such a glorious new experience simply by the power of your presence. Had it not been for this unreserved sharing of her femaleness, I may never have fully appreciated the generosity of my own womanliness and femininity, an awakening which would enrich my other relationships. Without guilt or shame I felt expanded by this new knowledge of how generously a woman gives herself and I was grateful. Such an awakening is not the lot of every woman.

Feeling satisfied and complete, I drifted off into a deep and nourishing sleep. When I awoke, Solange had gone. I never saw her again but I would never forget her, either. There must be something in the air in Paris.

May Day

Young Sally Semple was all a-twitter and a-fluster. It was May Day and she had been chosen to be one of the May Queens. Her plain, gauzy white dress was spread out on the bed, along with her coronet of spring flowers and she was gazing at herself appraisingly in the mirror. Her cheeks were flushed and her black eyes were bright and sparkling with excitement. The maypole that had stood for hundreds of years on the village green was freshly bedecked with garlands and ribbons and she would be on the end of one of those ribbons for the maypole dance. She knew what the maypole stood for, as the girls had been instructed in the ancient ways and rituals of the old religions and had been taught to respect the symbolism of the fertility rites of spring.

Fertility. It was a titillating word, full of earthy secrets and ancient mystery, conjuring up a shivery sense of longing that was somehow linked to the maypole. She ran her hands over her smooth, round belly and wondered at its creative potential.

Sally was just seventeen and ripe. Still a virgin, she knew in her waters certain stirrings and desires which unsettled her and made her tremble, but for what she could not say exactly. Her body was fully woman, with sumptuously rounded curves and softly swelling fecundity. She was not a modern shape. Her hips flared invitingly and her cleavage was deep and buxom: a true country wench. The flush of her young cheeks accentuated her black eyes and luxuriantly wavy black hair, and her dimpled rosy-lipped smile suggested a juicy plum waiting to be plucked. Her skin was flawless and milky white.

She knew she was luscious. She could feel the flow of her sensuality coursing through her entire body. She looked at the womanly shape in the mirror and ran her hands down over her voluptuous curves, caressing the breasts and exploring the smoothness of her thighs.

The image of the maypole sprang to mind unbidden, tall, bold and erect, and with it came a rush of power and a ripple of goosebumps. Her breasts contracted sharply and she gazed fascinated as the nipples hardened into little fruit-stalks. Something was missing. Words appeared in her head from nowhere, causing more tingling ripples. Cock. The crude hardness of it made her gasp aloud and the blood rushed to her cheeks. Cunt. Hard and soft together, secret and forbidden. His cock, my cunt.

She was shocked at herself and giggled guiltily but the tingling ache within her was somehow delicious. 'Oh, Sally Semple, you are wicked,' she upbraided herself, and quickly dressed in the simple, softly draped, long white frock which was cut very deep and tight across her bosom, pushing her bouncing, unrestrained breasts up under her chin, the small, off-the-shoulder puffed sleeves revealing her bare white arms. Pinning the wreath of pink and yellow spring blossoms into her thickly waving hair and slipping into the satin slippers, she quickly distracted herself from the lewdness of her thoughts and, laughing at herself, she ran down the stairs, out the garden gate and across the field to the village green where people were gathering.

It was a perfect day, sunny and bright but not too hot, promising a glorious summer, and she could hear the music of the fiddles and the flutes drifting across the fields. Her heart danced and her feet flew across the meadow. She joined the other girls, all giggling and twittering, around the maypole, and her friend Daisy whispered eagerly, 'Have you seen the morris dancers? Look! Over there!'

Sally looked to where Daisy was pointing and could not believe her eyes. These were no ordinary morris dancers. They were punks and skinheads, dressed all in torn black denim and leather, with silver chains, piercings, tattoos and huge buckles, their feet shod in large boots laced up to the calf and their muscled, sharply etched biceps bare in the sleeveless jackets. You could see the hair on their chests, peeping over the buttons and they all had knives tucked down the sides of their boots.

Sally shivered. Her skin prickled and the blood raced in her veins. She glanced surreptitiously up at the garlanded maypole and back at the solidly male and potentially threatening presence of the morris dancers and quivered from top to toe. One in particular caught her eye. He had a stiffly starched Mohican stretch of brightly blazing copper-gold hair down the centre of his head and he was standing slightly apart, idly tracing something in the dust at his feet with his stave.

The music abruptly changed to something very bright and lively and the dancers got into formation and readied themselves. Suddenly there was a clashing and banging and whirring of staves and bodies and feet as they sprang into action and it was nothing like anything she had ever seen before. She watched, breathless and mesmerised as they appeared to half kill each other with the challenging, crashing staves and their faces were intently focused and alive with passion. She had never witnessed anything so powerfully, aggressively masculine in her life and could not tear her gaze away.

Following the ferocity of the baton dance, they took out swords and short knives and were tearing at each other in a carefully choreographed frenzy of warlike violence. Sally felt a rush of dampness between her legs and her nipples were once again pertly visible under the filmy bodice of her frock. She didn't care. This was riveting her to the spot.

Coming out of her trance, she became aware that the girls were moving around the maypole and it was time to twine her ribbon about it. It suddenly felt a wickedly erotic thing to do. Her feet automatically moved into the steps that they had rehearsed and she noticed the morris dancers, now finished, ambling across the green to watch them. She looked up at the gaily bedecked, proud-standing maypole and took up her ribbon, drunk on the sensuality of the atmosphere and laughing brightly. Daisy waved at her, her blue eyes sparkling, and they danced as they had never danced before, their feet twinkling and skipping as the maypole gathered its adornment.

They danced for the morris men, leaning on their staves, smiling slyly as the bevy of girlish blushes and giggles twisted and twined in a flutter of delicate maidenly pink and yellow and white froth, ravishing them with their virginal and untouchable femininity. She was filled with a rapturous anticipation as the ribbons took them closer and closer to the pole and when they reached the end and touched it, she and Daisy collapsed in a fit of hysterical giggling into each other's arms, tears of mirth running down their blushing cheeks.

Then it was over and she could not face the menacingly masculine presence of the black-clad, be-leathered morris dancers with equanimity, so she and Daisy, hand in hand, still giggling, dashed off to the central marquee, where they joined in the treasure hunt which had just begun. Together they raced off enthusiastically towards the woods and meadows where the treasures had been hidden. In the trees, they separated and she could hear the cries and shouts of the others as they all careered about among the bracken and ferns, trying to gain advantage of each other for the coveted prizes. The woods were full of fluttering, shrieking, white-clad nymphs and village youths in a fluster of spring-drunken May Day fever. In her rush and hurry Sally did not look carefully enough where she trod and, without warning, she tripped over a tree root and was tumbling tipsy-tilty, over and over, down a mossy bank.

She landed at the bottom a little dazed and feeling rather foolish when she heard a concerned voice from above, 'Are you all right? You haven't hurt yourself, have you? Hang on, I'm coming down to get you.'

A fruity, mellow voice, not local but roughly countrified. At the top of the bank, clutching the branch of a tree for support was the morris dancer with the copper-gold Mohican. Sally decided she was hurt enough to require his assistance and obediently waited as he began to clamber down the slope. His heavy laced boots were hindering his progress over the gnarled old tree roots and, the next thing she knew, with a frustrated yell, he had slipped and slid down the bank, off balance, and landed right on top of her.

There was a moment of bewildered stillness as they both registered their plight and gathered their wits. Feeling with pleasure the hard, male potency so suddenly and intimately upon her, Sally was breathing heavily, and he opened his eyes against the close-up view of her softly swelling bosom rising and falling against his face. He paused, and in that pause Sally Semple made her mind up. She looked at his unexpectedly gentle features, the worried sky-blue eyes and the fullness of his wide mouth, sensual lips slightly parted as he tried to catch his breath and she succumbed to a searing rush of hunger.

She looked him straight in the eye with all her passionate lust naked in her face and as he recognised her invitation he gasped and looked back at her incredulously. She put her hands behind his head and pulled the red-gold coxcomb deeper into the sumptuous receptivity of her cleavage. Hardly daring to believe, he began tentatively to kiss the deliciously curving, gently heaving mounds and she discovered why her nipples contracted and hardened to suckable points. As he enclosed them with his mouth, she sighed, and as he plucked her stiffened fruit-buds between his lips and tongue, pulling a little, it sent a thrill spiking deep into her womb. Fertility, she thought with pride, and pushed her chest towards his seeking mouth. His hand had cupped her full globe and freed it from the dress and the air was playing coolly over her bare skin and saliva-wet nipple.

She sighed and surrendered, sure now that her time for fulfilment had come and glad of it. He looked up and they gazed at each other searchingly for a moment. She drank in his virile power and strength and thought of the maypole. There was a hardness pressing against her yielding belly and she closed her eyes to enjoy the sensation, wanting it deeper, closer, rejoicing in the stirring movement of its swelling as it unfolded stiffly, digging itself insistently into her pelvis through the folds of her dress. She wanted rid of the dress. He drew his face towards her and kissed her ready-ripe mouth. She traced the inside of his lips with her tongue and he drank of her more firmly, entwining his tongue around hers and mingling their mouth-moisture. There was a corresponding rush of juices dampening her loins and a ravenous ache began deep in her centre, creating a void which craved filling.

Overwhelmed by curiosity, she ran her hand down between them to search out the rigidity of his maleness and placed it over the solid, straining bulge. She trembled all over at this first touch of manhood and wanted it urgently for herself. Wantonly, she unzipped him and released the swelling penis into the naked flesh of her hand. With a whimper, she took it and squeezed, stunned by its aggressive hugeness. She pushed him up so that she could look at it and watched in awe as it leaped in her hand and strove upwards.

How will I ever get all that inside me? She licked her dry lips and tried to calm her pounding heart. Then she slid the skin downwards as the hot pulsing brute pushed into her hand, and was fascinated by the magical appearance of the glans and the tiny slit which, with a tremor of anticipation, she instinctively knew was where his fertility would emerge to seed hers. She pushed his trousers further down over his hips and stared in fascination at the pale golden fuzz covering his tightened testicles. Rising in a greedy curve up his navel, the implied menace of his rod was somehow softened by the densely curling bush of pale gold which she found rather endearing and which made this monstrosity somehow more approachable.

As she traced lightly with her fingers underneath the balls to the base of his gilded shaft, it jerked sharply, lunging upwards and a contracting spasm overtook her pelvis. With a molten rush of desire, she thrust her hips towards this monster that she craved. He responded by peeling down his trousers to his ankles, where they were held by the laced boots; he yanked off his leather jerkin, then carefully took her dress and lifted it over her head.

She arched her back as it floated easily away from her, exposing her ample breasts and rounded belly, her pubis still covered by the virginal white panties. She lifted her hips to allow him to remove these, exposing her maidenly black bush, and all the while she traced with her mouth and tongue the golden hairs on his hard, sculpted chest and massaged the grandly tumescent object of her lust with her enthralled hand.

He raised himself up on his hands and watched her writhing hip-bones grinding against his erection. Glowing palely opalescent and luscious upon the green mossy bank, drunk with desire, she appeared as a goddess of the woods, generously offering the gift of herself to his virility. He was overawed by her naked beauty and his lust rose swift and urgent as he drank in her nubile loveliness.

The organ in her hand lurched and stiffened and the words came unbidden to her mind again. She let them emerge from her mouth, trying them aloud. 'Cock. Cunt.'

He gasped in obvious astonishment at this obscenity.

'I want your cock in my cunt.' His rock-hard prick lunged greedily at the shockingly crude sounds emerging from out of her innocence. With her hand she placed his engorged tip inside her wet, softly swollen labia and thrust herself at him. Not yet fully convinced, he resisted for a moment.

'Your cock in my cunt,' she whispered again hoarsely, knowing it inflamed him, and with a groan he yielded and sank his twitching cock into the clinging, slippery, sucking deliciousness of her aching cunt, which closed tightly about him in welcome.

She felt the sudden sharp tweak of the tearing hymen announcing her entry into womanhood, and thought, with satisfaction, good, that's over.

His eyes flew open and he went very still. Raising himself above her, he looked into her eyes in consternation.

She did not want his concern. 'Just fuck me,' she commanded, and so he did, gratefully sinking into the tight, sucking cunt and slowly withdrawing against its silken clutch, to sink again with a low groan. He moved with a steady, considered rhythm, aware now of his full

101

responsibility and determined to arouse her total response before surrendering to his own. She was moaning and writhing, falling easily into rhythm with him, thrusting and retracting her hips in strong, steady motion to match his even stroking. Encouraged, he began to gain speed, lifting her knees over his elbows to achieve deeper penetration. She cried out as he hit against the cervix and, gritting her teeth, drove hard into him, sending electric shock waves through her core. She drove again and he finally surrendered to her lustiness and ardour. With a cry, he plunged himself deep into her with unrestrained vigour and they began to roll over and over each other on the mossy bank.

Now she was on top, riding him, breathing harshly, head thrown back and breasts bouncing and swaying freely, his hand pressing the tiny swollen erection of her clitoris and stimulating electrifying currents of fire which spiralled out and threatened to drown her. Then he was on top, his trousers still trapped around his ankles, slamming and thumping hard at each other with guttural grunts and cries of, 'Fuck me, fuck me, harder, harder!' which almost caused him to lose control.

He wanted her pleasure to be utterly satisfying and willed himself to wait for her. Before long, the steady, inexorable rise of her first orgasm rushed up from her core, crested and broke mightily, the climactic peaks exploding from deep inside and blazing out along every nerve-ending, ravishing her with hot surging waves of ecstasy and covering her with a rosy flush from head to toe. She cried her rapture aloud as peak after peak raged through her, gradually subsiding with a long tremulous sigh as she sank, fulfilled, against him.

Now he could allow himself the release of his own pleasure and, in response, she rose again to meet his urgency, eager to experience the fullness of union. The fiery serpent uncoiled at the base of his root and he pounded hard and fast as it rose until, with one final juddering lunge, he spewed the gushing fountains into her eagerly receptive fecundity. Again and again, with noisy celebration, he erupted convulsively and violently, and she sucked and clenched her muscles tight around the thick, pumping sperm, drinking it in to where it belonged.

They collapsed in sated exhaustion, his weight still pleasantly upon her and his deflating member still nestled inside her moist warmth. He had never met any woman like her, and she was certainly a woman now – although, notwithstanding that he had been party to that, he knew it was none of his doing and all of her own. It flickered across his mind that he would find it hard to leave a woman like this.

At that same moment, she knew with intuitive woman's certainty that there was going to be a baby and she was glad. That was exactly the sort of thing that should happen on May Day.

Soldier, Soldier

'*H*ands off cocks and on with socks!'

He was awake in an instant. It was Sunday
morning and he'd had a good lie-in after last night's
overindulgence, but this was their secret code, their
personal 'call to arms'. It meant she was aroused and
ready for action. He knew she'd be standing at the
bottom of the stairs, giving him time. Inevitably he felt
his own private soldier begin to rally to her battle cry
and he slipped his hand under the duvet and placed it
lightly over his unfolding cock. He liked to feel himself
becoming erect and now he was definitely responding
to her challenge, unrolling slowly up over his thigh,
steadily swelling and finally present and correct against
his navel, like the good soldier that he was.

'Did you hear me, you disgusting little wanker, you
self-abusing obscenity? Are you standing to attention,
all polished up and ready for inspection?'

She was coming up the stairs and he was fully erect
and stiff as a ramrod, as ordered.

'You revolting, incontinent tosser, Corporal Smeg, I
hope you're ready for me!'

Then she was standing in the doorway stark naked,

breasts pert, with the baton under her armpit and the sergeant's cap with the polished peak perched aloft her golden curls. She whipped off the duvet and exposed him with his hand around his cocked weapon.

'I thought so, you unspeakable excrescence! About face and take your punishment!'

He turned over on to his stomach. She took the baton in both hands and ran the leather strands of the whip-end through one palm. His engorged organ was pulsing against the mattress.

'Punishment detail for sordid, filthy habits begin!' And she brought the leather strap down on his upturned buttocks. 'One! That's for the state of your weapon!' His prick stiffened and lurched. 'Two!' She thwacked him again, raising blushing welts. 'That's for your grossly overenthusiastic privates. And three!' Another thwack, while his aching cock pushed hungrily against the sheet. 'And that's for your fumbling manual incompetence!'

He shuddered with a spasm of desire that electrified his groin, his arse ablaze and his lust surging through his loins.

'About face, Corporal Smeg!'

She climbed on to the bed and, as he turned back, lowered herself over his face. He grabbed her taut buttocks in both hands and pushed his tongue into her pink, wet folds, licking noisily at her honeyed cunt.

She moaned and began to writhe as he flicked hard against her button. 'That's it, Smeg,' she whispered hoarsely. 'Prime the switch.'

He lapped up and down the slippery slit, driving his muscular tongue deep into her juicy tunnel and tasting her sea-sweetness.

'Enough!' she commanded, lifting her buttocks off him. 'Now get fell in,' and, as he obligingly raised his pelvis, in one swift movement, she impaled herself hard upon his aggressively upward-thrust sword. 'Are you ready for action, soldier?'

'Ready, Sarge,' he concurred.

'Is your weapon polished and primed and battle-hardened?'

'Hard and smooth and cocked, Sarge,' he replied.

'Then go, go, go!' she cried, and began to pump up and down on the solid spike which drove deep into her clinging cunt and pounded hard on her pleasure-spot, sending ripples of streaking shock waves around her belly and down her thighs.

'To arms! To arms!' she shrieked and, flipping her on to her back, he thrust his arms under her knees and pushed her legs, dangling them in mid-air, back up by her shoulders, plunging even deeper and thudding harder against the neck of her womb. After a while she went very silent and he knew that this was the signal for her imminent explosion, so he drove faster and faster until she rasped breathlessly, 'Finger on the trigger – now!' He reached down, placed his thumb on her hard little bud and pressed firmly. She came instantly, with jerking, violent spasms and cries of 'Now! Now! Now!'

Stimulated by her climax, he felt his own mounting and kept driving hard into her until he cried, 'I'm going to shoot!'

She responded jubilantly, 'Fire your weapon! Shoot it in me! Shoot your spunk inside me!'

So he forcefully unloaded several rounds in thick, creamy jets of fiery release.

They collapsed, spent and sweating, on to the bed and lay there subsiding until she said, 'OK, soldier, fall out. Time for breakfast. What do you fancy?'

He withdrew wetly. 'Soldiers dunked in egg yolk.'

'Now there's a good idea,' she quipped. 'Must try it some time.' He chuckled and slapped her delectable rump as she sprang up from the bed.

Although still a corporal, he was due for his third stripe, and he wondered what she would do then. Her father had been a sergeant and it was his cap she wore for their sex-games. He supposed that as he went up a rank, so would she. As he became a sergeant, she would become a sergeant-major. He grinned.

As army wives went, she was pretty special. When he came home from exercises, hardened, weary and remote, she was silent and patient, asking for nothing and waiting for him to slowly return to the real world. When he was away on more serious business, 'classified', even from her, she had a full and busy life of her own, working for a children's charity and organising craft exhibitions of the wives' handiwork. She was incredibly resourceful and, as they had no children of their own, during those times when they were together, she was always hot and receptive and full of creative ideas for new games which kept their marriage exciting and alive. She sensed and adapted to his every mood and fulfilled his every need, without having to be asked – no mean feat for a soldier's wife.

He had never been unfaithful to her. He didn't need to be; she was all he had ever desired or loved. He knew the regiment was due to be sent away again soon, probably into one of the unpleasant trouble spots, which was why he was on leave and at home with her. They were both determined to make full use of their precious time together.

She returned with breakfast on a tray. Sliced, buttered toast – 'soldiers' – soft boiled egg, and strong tea you could 'trot a mouse on'. She was smirking secretively and looking at him sideways. He wondered what she was up to.

'What's on your mind, Debs?' he queried.

'Eat your breakfast,' she said, her eyes twinkling.

As he dunked his soldiers in the runny yellow yolk, she rested her hand lightly over his now idle privates, cupping the balls gently, lightly stroking the undershaft and the furred ridges of his scrotum. As they ate and drank, her tender caresses were reawakening a response.

Knowing they had all day together, he yielded to the pleasure of his resurrecting arousal and the sensuality of her touch. She leaned forwards and as he glimpsed the curving silhouette of her firm, full breast exposed by the gaping kimono he felt a renewed surge of desire. Reaching inside the gap, he cupped her naked breast in his hand. The kimono fell away to expose the tight bud of her nipple and he bent over and took it between his lips. She stroked the back of his neck with her fingertips.

'I've had an idea,' she said, kissing the top of his head. 'Look, Steve, I know how close you and Torch are, and I know the next tour is not likely to be a bunch of laughs, so I just wondered ... Why don't we invite him over one evening and ... have a bit of fun ... together ... you know, the three of us. Would you like that?'

Torch was his best mate, also a corporal and still single.

He sat bolt upright on the bed and leaned back against the wall, pausing to think about this bombshell she'd just dropped. He knew what she meant. They could be months without female companionship and this time, as always, some of them might not come home. But the three of them? How did he feel about that? His cock stiffened and lurched.

She noticed.

'That's a "yes", then,' she quipped and leaned over to take him into her mouth, gliding her tongue smoothly from the base to the tip and sucking firmly.

He groaned. The thought of a threesome had never crossed his mind but he was willing to bet it had crossed Torch's, who, he knew, was quietly in awe of Debs and had once called her beautiful. As she continued to pleasure him with her mouth, the idea she had planted inflamed his lust and resulted in a quick, sudden eruption of his juices down her throat, and he knew the answer was a definite 'yes'.

She planned it carefully. On the designated evening

she left him alone downstairs to greet Torch while she prepared herself. Torch's eyes had lit up hungrily when he understood what they were offering him. He'd swallowed hard and licked his suddenly dry lips, nodding briskly once, and nothing more had needed to be said.

His nickname hailed back to their early days as young squaddies, before they'd got their stripes, to an incident that was hilarious in the retelling but had been anything but funny at the time. He was a typical soldier, built like the proverbial brick shit-house, a great solid block of pure muscle. Ironically, he was softly spoken and shy – a gentle giant who knitted balaclavas for relaxation. They were both fond of him and his loyalty to them was unquestionable. He was utterly dependable in a crisis. She felt somehow reassured whenever they went away that Steve had someone like that looking out for him. And here he was, stiffening his resolve with a neat whisky – his second.

Both men were in jeans and T-shirts, superbly fit and muscle-hardened by their training, bulging solidly in all directions. They were in peak condition at all times and the sharply etched pecs and biceps straining under the T-shirts never failed to arouse her. She was strongly attracted to men in uniform, the authority of it making her feel safe and protected. In her secret heart, although she was fully aware of the reality and risk of what they did for a living, and how much it cost them, she was very turned on by the thought of all that tough, brute power and the sheer, raw courage it took do do what they had to do.

Sometimes, when Steve came home stinking of sweat and gun-oil and engine-grease and worse, her lust for him almost made her swoon. At times like that, he took her standing up, impersonally, hard and swift from behind, just for release and not really noticing her. She loved it. At other times he was so tender, almost reverential, exploring every curve and crevice with delicate, searching intensity, almost as if he was terrified he might lose a bit if he didn't concentrate.

The games they played were a bonus. He was several different people in one and all she had ever wanted. She loved him to distraction. Her offer to include Torch was not created out of boredom with her marriage but from a genuine desire to include in their pleasure someone they were both fond of, and in recognition of their exceptional circumstances, living on the edge.

As the two men waited in erotically charged anticipation, uncertain of how to proceed, she appeared in the doorway and they both gasped. She was fully made up with a scarlet mouth, her blonde curls piled high and wild, her curves tightly corseted and shapely in a black basque, with suspenders and stockings perched on high, black stiletto shoes. The mounds of her firm, full breasts burst over the tight lace, which only just concealed the nipples, and her softly curling blonde bush was nakedly exposed beneath, as were her taut, high buttocks. In her hand she held the multi-stranded short leather whip, which she was lightly swishing against her leg.

Torch choked and spluttered, dropping his glass on the floor.

'Naughty, naughty,' she whispered huskily. 'You're on punishment for that. Get your trousers down.' He hesitated. '*Now!*' She swished the whip sharply against his muscled thigh.

He unzipped his jeans and dropped them, exposing his huge, solid erection as it sprang upwards to freedom.

'That monstrosity is obscene. Get yourself in hand, soldier!' she ordered, and he placed his fist around it. 'Prime your weapon!' He slowly began to massage himself.

She turned to Steve, whose eyes were riveted and the bulge in his jeans looked tightly uncomfortable.

'And you, Corporal. How dare you turn up for duty dressed like that? Strip!'

He whipped off his T-shirt and jeans and the sight of their two perfect bodies and straining, swollen erections made her knees go weak. Waves of hot lust almost overwhelmed her. She noted with a quiver that neither of them had been wearing any underpants. Her eyes took them in, raking their corded, granite-like, curves; the rippling six-packs; and the chiselled power of their arms and legs. She knew they could sustain physical exertion for hours and her mouth went dry. She nearly lost her command and had to breathe deeply to regain composure. Her cunt-juice was wetting the insides of her upper thighs and she could scent the perfume of her musk arising.

'On your knees, arses high!' she croaked out, and they both dropped to the ground with their tight, hard, concave cheeks towards her. She dropped her voice.

'I hear you haven't been getting enough, you slacker,' she said to Torch and landed the whip forcefully across his arse, watching it draw the livid welts over the solid contours. His back arched against the smarting and his dick slapped hard up against his navel. 'And you, Corporal, you've become very greedy, you gluttonous little pervert.' She brought the whip down on Steve's bum with all her power and she heard him suck his breath in with a hiss.

Two cocks were thrusting against the air and greedily seeking targets. Two dew-drops of moisture were leaking from two engorged domes. They were breathing heavily.

'And since you both seem to be enjoying it so much, have one more for your disgusting obscenity.' She hit them both once more, the welts criss-crossing scarlet and angry, and in her efforts her breasts overflowed out of the corset, revealing her nipples which were puckered tight and long.

'About face!'

As they turned around, she stood astride in front of

them with her hands on her hips, her nipples jutting and her pelvis awash with surges of heat and hunger. Juices trickled down her thighs.

'Now, eyes on the target.' She dropped to all fours, the stalks of her nipples silhouetted below her, her wasp-waist pinched and her luscious buttocks, edged with black lace, flaring into their faces, exposing her dripping wet, swollen pink fanny, which she pulled apart with her hands, tempting them with the secret, sucking red lining of her cunt as it throbbed and pulsed in wet expectation.

'Ready! Aim! Fire!' she commanded jubilantly.

Torch invaded her savagely from behind with a lunge that knocked her forwards. Ramming himself hard into the cave of his fantasies and, gripping her hips, he beat himself upon her like a piledriver. Steve pillaged her mouth rapaciously, thrusting so deep she choked, and she tightened her tongue and cheeks around him, allowing her lips to glide up and down the silky rod as it pumped vigorously back and forth. Simultaneously fucked both fore and aft, she had never felt so full and surrendered to the ecstasy of not knowing one end from the other. Sensation claimed her as she yielded to the rhythm of their pistons sending shock waves of searing heat in every direction.

Torch was moaning deep in his chest, and Steve was grunting with short, sharp, brutish violence, both gripped in the obliterating compulsion of their lust.

Torch came first, with a frantic increase in speed and she placed her hand beneath him to dig her fingertips hard into the undershaft behind his balls and feel the rippling muscular surge of his ejaculation. The added sensation took him by surprise and he yelled his pleasure loudly, firing his load in sharp, stabbing spurts. It brought her orgasm to fever pitch immediately, following him with a long, wavering cry as the thundering waves crashed hotly and convulsively over her in response to his final deep, aggressive lunge. She wanted to see Steve gushing and, sensing his surge, she reached forwards under his bouncing balls to stroke the spasming muscle as it fired, quickly removing her mouth to watch. With a strangled cry, he shot great gouts of creamy, thick come high into the air to land warm and sticky all over her breasts, dripping down the valley between.

They fell into a tangled, sweaty heap on the floor. She took each of them by the hand and they were silent a while. Finally, she muttered appreciatively, 'Bloody fine piece of teamwork. You're both confined to barracks for the next twenty-four hours.'

'What for?' Steve was plaintive.

'Oh, I dunno, whatever it takes. Lewd and filthy perversion, probably.' She turned and gave each of them a big juicy kiss on the lips. 'I'm not letting you two out of my sight.'

Strangers on a Train

*U*nusually for a Monday morning, the Underground was running smoothly and the trains were frequent. Kate gratefully found herself a seat. She was annoyed because she'd awoken late feeling frisky and hadn't had time for a nice, cosy early morning wank, and to top it all she'd forgotten to buy herself a newspaper. In her carefully correct, navy-blue suit and buttoned blouse, with her smooth brown hair neatly pinned up and legs chastely crossed, she looked the picture of conformity. With nothing to read and still with a lingering sexual awareness, she casually checked out the potential of the crowded carriage. They all looked pretty normal and dull, as usual. There was rarely anyone of interest and, generally speaking, she preferred the newspaper, but today she began to wonder, since it occurred to her that she must look just as dreary to them, whether she might be quite surprised to know what was going on in other people's heads. Were they as dull on the inside as the outside?

Mark was sitting opposite her with his newspaper unfolded on his knee. Although young, he wore a con-

114

servative dark grey suit and looked the typical public school product with his wary, guarded self-assurance, light grey eyes, conscious composure, and fair hair, which he flicked back habitually, falling over one eye. Mark was a puritan. He liked his pleasure laced with guilt and his regular daily pleasure was to use his time on the Underground to dream up all sorts of different smutty fantasies with which to steam himself up for a quick, furtive wank in the bog before starting work. The one he was preoccupied with this morning was his favourite.

He pictured himself at a dinner party, a very grand affair, with solid silver tableware, a large bowl of flowers in the centre of a circular table and food served by waiters and waitresses in crisp black and white uniforms. About twelve guests in full evening dress sat around the table, all important public figures, some titled. He was seated opposite an elderly dowager and her faded, balding, aristocratic husband. The conversation was stiff and formal. He had unfolded his starched linen napkin and placed it in his lap and was now toying with his consommé. He almost didn't notice the light touch on his lower leg as a shoeless foot traced up inside his trouser leg along the line of his calf. Startled, he stifled a gasp, then gathered himself, taking another mouthful of soup. In dismay, he felt his groin lurch and begin to unfold uncomfortably against the constraints of his underwear. He was a white cotton jockeys man, an old-fashioned sort of chap. The foot ceased and he breathed a sigh of relief.

Rather inappropriately, his swelling member twitched and uncoiled, and he felt it escape through the gap in his Y-fronts and begin to emerge into the freedom of his trousers. Unsuccessfully willing it down, he calmly took another mouthful of soup and wiped his mouth with the pristine napkin. The dowager lady was asking him about roses. What did he consider the most efficient way of pruning? He concentrated on the answer as he felt the foot return, only now it twined itself about his leg and tickled the inside of his ankle. His prick leapt in uncalled-for response. The prim maiden lady on his right was ardently dismissing his opinion regarding the roses, and the dowager lady's husband had suddenly become eagerly engaged in the debate.

As the conversation required his attention to the right, he was unable to turn and discover the identity of the wanton tease sitting on his left. Was it a man or a woman? He couldn't tell. His independently minded penis pushed hard against the cloth of his trousers, out of his control, stiffening to full pride. At least it was out of sight, under the table. He wished it would go. Then, with a shock, he felt the light touch of a palm flutter across the thrusting tip and his prick hardened and clamoured for attention. He was trying to reply to a question concerning the best way to rid his garden of slugs when he felt the flat palm again rub across the head of his twitching tumescence, and struggled to keep cool and stay with the slugs and snails. The waiter took the soup plate, which was soon replaced by prawns. Between the courses, and now into the various merits of fertilisers, he felt the zipper of his trousers swiftly released and his naked cock sprang free.

He could not believe this; above the table his dicky bow and smile were carefully composed and correct, and underneath his eager dick was exposed and erect. Fingernails ran themselves playfully up and down the length of him and, involuntarily, his pelvis retracted with a jerk. To cover the movement, he quickly coughed and wiped his mouth with his napkin. He looked around but they were all intent on peeling their prawns. Recovering his poise, he wished the fingertips would not trace his quivering shape so lightly and teasingly. He could not control the desire to thrust much longer. He knew there would be a dew-drop and, sure enough, a skilful

116

finger found the tip of him and moistened the smooth head in tiny circling motions.

Trying to suppress a groan, he was now being drawn into the best place for holidays at this time of the year. Hadn't he just been to Tenerife? Tenerife. He grappled to think and resisted a sigh as the hand, finally, mercifully, enclosed itself about the full length of him and squeezed. Tenerife, Tenerife, where the hell is Tenerife? Please don't do that. As it pushed down hard into his groin, allowing him to stretch upwards against its grip, his fork pierced an unshelled prawn which shot off his plate. Unnoticed, he quickly recovered it and strove to remain relaxed as the strong hand slid firmly up and down.

He was upward-thrust, proud and straight, as the skin glided silkily back and forth over the long, smooth rod, and he stuffed his mouth full of salad in order not to moan. The slithering hand moved quicker and quicker and he no longer knew whether he wished it would stop or wanted it not to. The maiden lady was looking at him expectantly and he begged her pardon, what was the question? When was the best time of year to visit Tenerife? Ah, let me see. Faster and faster the hand was moving and the inevitable climax began to stir. Faster and faster, tighter, quicker, rubbing, keep smiling, spring, yes, spring, no summer, what?

It was inconceivable that no one could see the swift, smooth strokes pushing and pulling, pumping up his now uncontrollable urge for the unthinkable act of spilling himself under the dinner table. Not now, not here, I don't want this, I can't help this, please don't do this, please don't, please do, don't stop, faster, faster, I musn't come, I can't do this, I have to come, not here, oh, please, oh, God, I'm coming, I'm coming, oh, no, oh, no, and he felt the heat of his urgency surging up from the base of his shaft as the snake of fire uncurled, and knew he was losing control but, keeping his manner cool and relaxed, desperately expressionless, tried to hold on to Tenerife. Yes, we had a *lovely* time. Yes, it was *great*. (Here it comes. Oh, God, please no!) Oh, *yes*, we would go a*gain*!

And the fiery serpent raced up the long, solid length of his traitorous member and exploded out of him as the hot, creamy jets of his semen gushed in fountains into the space under the table. Again and again, shockingly, wickedly, emptying in great spurts into the air below their social stuffiness. The dowager smiled and said they preferred Mauritius themselves: wasn't Tenerife just a *tiny* bit clichéd these days? Beads of sweat sprang up on his brow and his upper lip, and his heart was thumping wildly. Coughing again, he dabbed at his mouth with his napkin. Yes, she could be right.

Astonishingly, they were all completely oblivious to his torment as they heartily attacked the boeuf bourguignon. He felt the anonymous hand carefully take his voided softness and tuck it back inside his trousers, into the opening of his obliging Y-fronts, and deftly zip up the flies. A final friendly pat on his spent groin and it was gone. He looked blankly at the prim lady as she expounded now on weather patterns and allowed his pounding heart to subside. During a cessation in the conversation, his opinion no longer required, he finally turned to confront the mystery persecutor on his left. The plate was empty and the chair pushed back. Whoever it was had gone.

Mark flicked his hair back nervously and coughed. He was nicely hard inside his jockeys and looking forward to that sneaky wank.

Susan was a romantic, though she looked like a frightened mouse. Sex was never far from her mind and she wore suspenders and stockings under her staid, plain work clothes every day because you never knew when 'he' might appear. She had a packet of condoms in her handbag for the same reason, which had gone past their use-by date, but deep inside she wanted to believe it would be true love and he would be gentle and respectful. She hadn't found him yet but she could dream, couldn't she? Meanwhile, as she kept herself chastely pure for Mr Right, her mind was never far from the unrelieved hungers in her body, especially riding to work on the Tube first thing in the morning. Every day was going to be the day. She knew exactly what he would be like. He became clearer and more real each day. She played it again in her mind:

He wore a dark green Armani suit over a black woollen polo neck – no tie – and his shiny blue-black hair waved luxuriantly down to his chin. His penetrating eyes were deep sapphire blue. He looked more Celtic than Mediterranean, with pale, opalescent skin, a straight nose and a clean, though not square, jawline. His shapely mouth curved up slightly at the corners and there was, of course, the hint of a dimple in his chin. He was, tall, naturally, neither solid nor broad but elegant and lean, with square shoulders. He got into the empty carriage and sat opposite her. Susan felt herself sweating lightly with anticipation. He looked up and their eyes met. His were direct and clear and he saw the true person behind the unassuming façade. She thought she was going to swoon. I can't let this go without a fight, she thought wildly. She strove to think of a strategy but, finding none, succumbed to hopeless despair as the train finally arrived at her station.

As the doors opened, they both rose together. He gestured to her to alight first but at the step she panicked and stumbled and they collided into each other. He caught her before she fell, gripped her arm firmly and pulled her to her feet.

'I do beg your pardon.' His voice was deep and warm and very slightly accented. At the exit they were separated by the crowds and she did not dare to look back as she rode up the bustling escalator. Her heart was pounding as she fought to regain her composure. Eyes closed, trying to collect her scattered thoughts, crushed by disappointment and self-recrimination, she nearly died when she heard the mellow voice again: 'Would you like a coffee?'

Her searching, questing, hazel eyes looked straight into his clear, confident sapphire blue and she knew that coffee would be a complete waste of time.

'Your place or mine?' she asked in a husky, throaty drawl, and he chuckled.

He found a café where they whiled away the hours in intimate conversation, getting to know each other and careless of the world. He wooed her gently. They spent the whole day together, in perfect harmony, each knowing that this was their destined moment but each wanting to delay the inevitable consummation and enjoy the delicious anguish of restraint.

'I don't want to rush this,' he begged her at last. 'I think we have plenty of time. I want to be sure.'

There, it was out in the open. Looking deeply into the troubled sea of dark blue, she fell in and drowned, lost beyond sense. 'Yes,' she whispered. 'We have all the time in the world.'

Sighing, she leaned back and watched him as he examined her longingly with his caressing eyes. She noticed the flawlessness of his pearly skin. He could not look away from her. She was available, open, given, and totally his in this moment. He reached out one long, strong, sensitive finger and lightly traced along the line of her jaw. Tilting her chin up with the finger, beseeching with his eyes, he quickly dropped a brief and fleeting kiss on her softly parted, eager lips. She dissolved and flew apart. Alone together in their invisible bubble of shared communion, nothing more was necessary, and they remained at the table, not touching, savouring the perfect sense of arrival and belonging.

Eternal minutes passed before he stood up and

reached out with his hand. She took it, standing, and silently, hand in hand, they walked back to the station. It felt so right, the strong, reassuring hand around her small, feminine one. It felt like home.

'I don't want to leave,' he admitted at the station.

'Nor I,' she replied.

He smiled ruefully. 'What happens now?'

Hopelessly surrendered and incapable of rational thought, she bowed her head, then raised it, laughing. 'Your place or mine?' she finally blurted, this time for real.

His place turned out to be a large, bright studio flat in Little Venice, overlooking the canal. Several long shuttered windows let in the daylight and the primary-coloured furnishings were bold and cheery against the white decor. Spacious and modern, it was unpretentiously masculine and energetic. Under an enormous Matisse there was a huge, more than king-sized divan bed, covered in brightly coloured cushions and a red-and-black cotton throw. The floor was polished pine. She avoided looking at the bed and tried not to think of its history. From here on, it had no history but the one they created together.

There was little point in further delay. They both knew it but were both unwilling to pass the point of no return. There was risk. There was the possibility of spoiling the magic. There was a mutual desire to preserve the preciously delicate promise.

'Glass of wine?' he procrastinated.

'Please.' Welcoming the delay.

He took a bottle of champagne from the fridge and skilfully popped the cork with his strong thumbs, pouring the foaming bubbles into long crystal glasses. She watched silently. She could feel her heart beating faster and repressed an involuntary quiver as her skin tingled with anticipation. Her mind still blank, she was utterly acquiescent to whatever might follow. He raised his

121

glass in toast and she responded in like manner. He removed his shoes, pulled up a big, soft cushion, dropped it at her feet and sat upon it, leaning his head against her knee. Quietly awed, she reached out a tentative hand and began to stroke the thick, dark velvet. They drank their wine in companionable silence, neither needing to speak, wordlessly bonding, both understanding the tremulous need to pause yet awhile.

He finished his wine and put down the glass, rose to his feet, removed her glass from her trembling fingers and, taking both her hands in his, pulled her to her feet. Ever so gently and slowly, he drew her towards him and she sank into his powerful embrace with a soft cry of release. Her body shook and she could feel the corresponding frisson from his. There was a coiled tension within him, controlled and tamed, that she longed to free from its restraints.

She lifted her face to his and he bent and placed his open mouth upon hers. Blood racing, hearts pounding, dissolving out of time and into each other, they drank and drank, their bodies clinging and electrified. In a blissful, timeless eternity, they lost sight of separateness and became one sensation. In silent communion they began to undress each other, fumbling but unselfconscious, still seeking with their mouths. He was enchanted by the change of character between her outer and under garments, unclipping her suspenders with a smile, and she was glad she had had the foresight to adorn herself for this.

Unclothed and revealed, they stood naked before each other, drinking now with their eyes. He gazed at her with admiration. She looked back at his firm, spare masculine perfection and his proud maleness, visibly ready and attentive, and everything within her melted.

He put out his hand. She took it and together, eyes locked and hand in hand, they moved toward the sundappled divan. Sinking among the cushions, they remained a moment in close embrace, long limbs entwined, lips seeking and desirous, tongues probing and sucking, unable to drink deeply enough. With the palm of his hand against her cheek, he leaned back and looked at her. Tracing the lips with his strong, gentle fingers, he murmured, 'I want this to last. I want this to take a very long time.'

And they did take a very long time. Kneeling up on the bed, they explored the curves of each other with tender, stroking hands, discovering every delight and tracing with their lips every delicious line and mark, knowing each other intimately. There wasn't a corner, a mole or a freckle untouched. There wasn't a caress ungranted, a sensation unrequited. She lifted her arms as he ran his tongue around her hardened nipples and stretched up to wallow in the luxuriance of his wonderful hair. She rubbed her breasts against it, ran it through her hands, and bent to bury her face in it as his tongue explored the hollows of her navel. She loved the angle of his hips, that precious curve from the thigh to his flat hard stomach and licked and sucked all around its smoothness, deep into the belly button and down the line of his navel hair to his groin. She ran her nails rakingly down his back, and he kneaded hard into her buttocks and nibbled up and down her neck.

At some point he had produced a sensually perfumed body oil smelling of musk and, with indulgent, luxuriating strokes, he rubbed it all over her torso and she over his. Breasts and bellies together, they slipped and slithered up and down and around each other in the aromatic oiliness and she felt the straining hardness of his virility pressing and rubbing all over her breasts and stomach, and prodding at her thrusting nipples.

I want to put this off as long as possible, she thought. I want to wait; I want to go on forever. He clearly felt the same for he delayed and delayed, restraining his desire until he felt hers ready to meet it, then teasingly held himself apart as he kissed her mouth with aching, quivering, hungry longing. They no longer knew whose body was which, all sensation blending and merging as they sank beneath the tide of their pleasure. Every other possibility fully exhausted, he finally paused and knelt above her. He placed his hands under her back and raised her up to kneel in front of him.

Eyes closed, head flung back, breathing rapidly, she knew the moment had come and, kneeling high on the supporting bed, she spread her knees apart and granted him access. With his mouth upon hers, he drew himself closer towards her until their bodies were lightly touching at all points. The dark fur of his chest tickled her breasts and she arched them out against his muscled leanness. Embracing each other and lips fast, he slowly, gently, lovingly approached her sanctum with his sceptre and eased himself smoothly into her. She shuddered and cried out, long and joyfully as, with a low groan, he sank to the hilt into her clinging warmth, filling her void, and every nerve in her body leaped up to greet him.

United at last, they paused before beginning the long ascent to each other. Darkness enclosed them both and they found within it an intimacy of being and oneness that neither had ever known. As one, they rocked and plunged and tossed on an ocean of desire. Blissfully unconscious, relinquishing the world and losing themselves in each other, they moaned and uttered and cried out as the flames of their craving blazed through their conjoined loins, surging and soaring, vanquishing, uniting them, enthralling them in all-consuming passion. As one, celebrating loudly, their voices mingling, they arrived together on the fiery crest, wave after convulsive wave crashing ecstatically over them. Time stood still and eternity waited as they dissolved and disappeared beyond self into oblivion.

Subsiding, collapsing, they remained joined, and he

lay heavily upon her, both of them suspended in the new sense of fulfilment, hardly daring to return. He wept, with deep, wracking sobs, upon her belly. Her own tears streaming silently, she tenderly stroked his beloved back with her fingertips and knew it would last forever.

Susan brought herself to with a deep sigh and felt her suspender pinching her thigh, her knickers sticky and her clit throbbing painfully. Reality was cruel, she thought in despair, and heaved herself up to fight her way through the crowds to her unrewarding and pre-dictable day in the office, where the best she could hope for was Dennis with his wheeze and his adenoids and his clammy hands. He was always after a quick grope and the awful thing was that if she went on feeling the way she did now, he might just get it, out of sheer desperation. Susan knew he was probably the best she could hope for.

Stanley was hidden behind his book but he was not reading it. Although he was middle-aged, neatly dressed with thinning hair, soft, pale, formless features, metal-rimmed spectacles and a professorial air, the books Stanley read on the tube were rarely innocent. They looked like classical tomes of great portent but they were in fact classical tomes of pure filth. Today, for example, he was rereading *Fanny Hill*. He had always fancied himself in a period setting. His mind wandered to his own college as it might have been in another age.

He could see himself in Victorian dress and a picture began to form of a dark, polished room such as a college don like himself might live in, with a single bed, walls lined with books, a desk and a large open fireplace. The window overlooked a vine-clad courtyard. Someone was emptying the ashes out of the grate. Of course! He had a housekeeper: had her in every sense. Quick, casual, easy sex, non-relational, no finesse – just the way he liked it.

He entered the room and noticed the figure bending low over the grate. The circular orbs of her perfectly rounded breasts were sharply outlined against the tightly stretched bodice and his groin flickered. He walked into the room and flung his overcoat on to the bed. Turning, he was confronted with the seductive flare of her curvacious buttocks, the abundance of her bending hips swelling out lusciously from the narrow, corseted waist.

His lust rose, swiftly stiff and hard, and a rapacious hunger gripped his loins with uncontrollable urgency. Completely overpowered by this unexpectedly ravenous need, he lost control and fumbled frantically with the trouser buttons to free his suddenly swollen, insistent organ. Completely possessed by the demon of his compulsion, he lifted her petticoats and skirts and found, naked to his view, the thickly furred, invitingly soft, pink folds of her pudenda. Gasping, blindly driven, he rammed himself into it, pushing hard against the initial resistance until he felt it gradually yield and suck him deep into its tight, clinging warmth.

He heard a sharp intake of breath as she fell forwards, grabbing desperately at the mantel, but he couldn't wait. Grasping her voluptuous hips with both hands, he thrust hard at her with short, sharp, pounding blows and within seconds felt the rush of his seed surge up the driving length of his greedy root and explode violently into the hot, sucking depths. Receding rapidly, he quickly withdrew and hung there for a moment, limp, wet and dangling, catching his breath. Then, hastily tucking himself away and redoing the buttons, he grabbed his overcoat from the bed and fled from the room, leaving her with skirts aloft and arse bare, to recover herself as best she may.

Stanley removed his glasses and wiped the mist off

them, glancing about himself discreetly to see if his flush had been witnessed but he was, as usual, invisible. No one ever noticed him. He crossed his legs and tried to ignore the uncomfortable erection which was almost permanent these days. He'd wait until he got home then he'd do something about it, standing in the open window and daring the prudish old biddie next door to challenge him. He knew she watched him from behind her net curtains but she'd never complained.

Regis liked it in public, secretly, taking risks. His favourite time of year was the Notting Hill Carnival when he could get it several times if he was clever. He sprawled arrogantly in his seat, taking up the space beside him as well as his own, because no one had the balls to ask him to move. His cigarettes were tucked up his black T-shirt sleeve, turned inside out, and his dreadlocks hung to his shoulders in a loose tie. His long legs were encased in tight black leather and the bulge in his groin was blatant and deliberately displayed. The slender girl with her hair in Topsy twists and her purple stretch boob-tube advertising her full breasts caught his eye. Her legs were smooth and bare in her mini-skirt and he raked her all over with his hard, black eyes. She felt him looking and glanced up. His gaze did not waver. He looked her directly in the eye, undressing her and she looked right back, undaunted. Regis's cock uncurled and he shifted in his seat to ease it. She giggled, and when she got off at the next station she gave him the finger through the window.

He had to have her. He had to dominate her and wipe the smug smile from her face. As the train moved off, he daydreamed his revenge.

It was Carnival day, late August, and hot. His sleeveless top revealed his rippling, polished ebony biceps. The crowds were dense and suffocating. Regis was aroused and erect as he always was on this day because he knew he could get it any time, in a doorway or up an alley. Everyone was hot for it on Carnival day, dancing and throwing their pelvises at each other, breasts and chests on display and high on the heady atmosphere and pulsating sound of the drums.

He caught sight of her on the other side of the street, with a group of friends, dancing and wiggling her butt, her full breasts straining against her tight crop-top and her chocolate belly naked and sinuous. She was laughing and singing, her head thrown back, without a care in the world.

Regis insinuated himself through the crowds, found a gap in the parade, dashed through the musicians and dancers and forced his way towards her. His prick was solid and ready to burst. He squeezed his way up behind her without attracting her attention and allowed the crowds to jostle them until he was pushing against her back. They were both wedged in tightly but she was oblivious to anything but the loud music and the colourful spectacle. Swiftly, he unzipped his flies and released his angry cock, pushing its hardness against her bum. He shoved it between her thighs under her mini-skirt. She squealed, taken by surprise and not quite sure what was happening. Before she could get herself together, he rubbed rapidly back and forth against her soft thighs, feeling the tip pushing against her panties.

She grabbed him suddenly, her fist closed tight around his overexcited knob, vibrating rapidly, and her backside pressed against him, which doubled his pleasure and brought him to an unexpectedly early conclusion. With a quick, shuddering, triumphant release, he came into her palm as he shot his load through her legs. She looked down to see the spurts of thick, creamy spunk shooting from under her skirt and dribbling over her hand. Turning her head to confront him, their eyes met and they glared at each other.

'Where's mine, then, wanker?' she challenged him.

He ducked away through the crowd and vanished. That'll teach you to laugh at me, he crowed to himself.

Regis wasn't feeling quite so comfortable any longer, so he got off the train for a change of scene.

Meanwhile, unaware of the fun other people were having all around her, Kate was taking a good long look at the tourist standing nonchalantly guarding his luggage. He looked newly arrived and out of place. His curly blonde hair hung over his face, hiding it, but his body was solid, sun-ripened and muscle-hardened. His powerful, bulging calves were visible between his baggy, knee-length, khaki shorts and his big desert boots, the hard sinews etched and thickly covered in fuzzy pale gold. He looked Australian and she hoped he would not speak. He looked up and she felt a flicker of disappointment. He was nothing to look at: eyes too small, mouth too big, too young. Not to worry. She didn't want him for conversation. She had other plans. He looked ripe for a quick, hard bang. No frills, no foreplay: just cock-in-cunt, straight up, wham-bam sex.

She could see him emerging from the sea with his surfboard under one arm, shaking the salty drops from his shaggy locks. Laying down his surfboard and stripping off his wetsuit, he rubbed himself vigorously with a towel, then, naked, flung himself down upon it, stretching full length on his back to soak up the burning heat of the sun. As she watched from her vantage point behind an upturned boat, he reached down to his crotch and lazily scratched beneath his balls, readjusting his tackle and making himself comfortable. Then, one arm on the sand and one flung over his face to cover his eyes, he relaxed, ready to doze. To her gratification, as she watched, his prick began to swell and rise in the sun's warmth, nudging its way up his navel and pointing straight up past the belly button to the six-pack. Fully extended, it lay flat against his belly, hard and full.

She felt her own heat surge through her loins, creating an aching emptiness and sudden, urgent, undeniable need. She'd been sunbathing and was clad in just the narrow string of her bikini bottoms tied high on the hip. Her firm, proud, upturned breasts and long shanks were all-over golden.

Arrogantly, she strode barefoot across the white sand, hips swaying and pert breasts jiggling, stood astride him, blotting out the sun, and asked in a low, fruity drawl, 'Fancy a fuck?'

Without waiting for a reply, pulling the strings of her bikini untied and whipping it away, she lowered herself on to him. Greedily, she took his hard cock in one hand, opened her wet swollen lips with the other and pushed him into her throbbing, hot cunt. Already juicy, she sank down hard and wriggled her hips, feeling a sharp thrill as he thudded against her pleasure-spot deep inside. He instinctively raised his hips to achieve full penetration and held himself there with the strength of his hard-honed fitness. She tightened her cunt muscles and gripped him. She knew it would be quick and, without further ado, retracting, sliding easily back up the slippery length of his prowess, she thrust herself at him.

She rode him hard and fast, driving, driving, grinding her clitoris against his groin, banging his shaft again and again deeply upon her sex-spot, sending waves of hot excitement around her loins, and quickly felt the volcanic surging rise to a peak. Within seconds, in a molten rush, she climaxed in sudden, explosive, savage bursts, releasing cunt-juice, and emitting a deep, throaty animal growl. For just a second she collapsed, sated, her long hair draped over his smooth chest; then, in one easy motion she withdrew, lifted herself off his wetly gleaming, still proud cock, scooped up her bikini, and strode off with a satisfied lope across the sand.

Glancing back over her shoulder, she saw him kneeling up on the sand, the protrusion of his unfinished business jutting out in front of him and his hand around it. Well, she thought, smiling smugly, that makes a nice change.

Coming back to herself, she looked again at the callow features and thought, God, I'm losing it. If that's the best I can manage, I think I'll become a nun. The painful ache in her cunt thought differently. I know, she decided, with a flash of inspiration. While I'm in this state I'm going to indulge myself. I'm going to treat myself to a bloody vibrator. As she arose to leave the carriage, she glanced cursorily around it one more time, thinking, what a lot of starchy, stuffy, lemon-faced prudes we all are. She was suddenly overcome by a fit of bold rebellion.

'What you lot all need,' she declared to the startled faces, 'is a good shag.'

As she got off the train she heard the emotionless tones mechanically announcing, 'Mind the doors. Stand clear of the closing doors.'

'Oh, get a life!' she snapped.

Sweet Revenge

*A*ndrea was a cold, calculating, ruthless bitch, and proud of it. She had been brought up that way. Her father had been the same and he was her hero. The powerful head of a multi-million-dollar international corporation, she had adored him utterly and grew up in his image. When the company had forced his retirement under the cloud of a huge public scandal over financial deception and fraud, ruining his reputation, bankrupting him and breaking his spirit, she had been furious and had sworn vengeance. She knew that he had been sacrificed to preserve the interests and salvage the reputations of others, and he had eventually been replaced by men who had been his friends and close colleagues all his life. Once a giant among men, he had shrivelled and dwindled into a drooling, mumbling, disintegrating old age and ignominious death, and she began to plan a merciless campaign of revenge.

Andrea knew that she was gorgeous and oozed high voltage sex appeal. It was her best weapon. She had tied her father around her little finger by flirtation, eyelash-flapping and feminine wiles, sitting on his knee as a little girl, pouting prettily, and she knew exactly how to make herself irresistible. She did not enjoy sex for pleasure but used it only for self-advancement and personal gain.

It was her belief that any clever woman with the right approach could have anything she wanted from any man in the world through the manipulation of his dick and, so far, she had not been wrong. She had the perfect body for such an approach. She was tall and slender, with endless legs and long, smooth thighs, a gently rounded arse, large, firm breasts and a graceful neck. Her thick, honey-coloured hair was sleek and glossy and her green eyes were framed by stunningly dark lashes. With the creamy, translucent skin of the true English rose, she had a deceptively vulnerable smile and her cultured tones were immaculate. She had been privately educated to exude class and superiority.

Whenever she walked into a room every eye was upon her and she swayed and swivelled with a graceful animal magnetism, perverting every business meeting she attended to her own ends simply by her presence. She only had to cross her legs to secure an agreement. A very wealthy woman in her own right, she knew how to wield her sexual power with supreme assurance. Only she could have masterminded and executed the plan of revenge that she had devised.

There were four men that she targeted: the Executive Director, Hereward Compton-Hughes, once her father's closest friend; the Managing Director, Gareth Bainbridge; the Company Secretary, Jonathan Bowers; and the company solicitor, Colin Winterstone. These four had been central to the malicious conspiracy and had gained the most from her father's betrayal. She knew them all personally and had on many occasions dined with them, hosted parties for them, attended meetings with them and even travelled abroad on business with them.

She chose Jonathan, the Company Secretary, first,

because he was the easiest. Although married, he fancied himself a ladies' man and had a racy, rakish reputation. She equipped herself with the latest and most expensive technology for her undertaking; money was no object. It was quite astonishing what was available, and how tiny the relevant equipment had become.

Dressed to seduce, in a black Chanel suit with a deeply plunging neckline and short skirt, genuine diamond brooch and earrings, she 'accidentally' bumped into him in the bar of his favourite restaurant and suggested that they lunch together 'for old times's sake'. Pretending to 'let bygones be bygones, life must go on and, after all, that's business: every dog has its day,' she simpered and charmed.

Her sumptuous cleavage was enhanced by the lacy black bra pushing it up from underneath. The open slopes of her firm, pearly white breasts were tastefully exposed to a depth of several inches when she leaned forward on her elbows, and the hint of lace appeared at exactly the point required by good taste. Her long golden hair was swept up elegantly with one corkscrew tendril trailing down over her right eye. She fingered it now and then, twining it delicately and coquettishly and, by the end of the second bottle of wine, most of which she had poured into his glass, Jonathan's eyes were glazed with lust. She fleetingly brushed against his leg under the table with her stockinged leg and he dabbed at his mouth with the napkin, raking her cleavage with his hungry eyes. He began to brag of his sexual conquests and she knew that she had him.

Eventually, with deliberate seductivenes, she admitted that she had always found him attractive and was so hot for him now that she couldn't bear to wait. She was twining her leg about his and running her long, blood-red fingernail across the back of his hand. He almost fell out of his chair in his eagerness. She suggested the ladies' room, which was spaciously large and beautifully appointed.

In the corridor, she placed her hand over his trousers and squeezed the hard, burgeoning bulge swelling beneath. Click.

Feigning unbridled lust, chewing his ear and panting, she invited him to join her inside. He waited while she checked the occupancy, in the grip of his uncontrolled, egotistic, wine-enhanced passion. It was vacant. She let him in, and as he came through the door he was already unzipping his flies to allow his erection to spring nakedly aloft through the gap, rising high and pleading for action, its double reflected, pointing directly at her, in the large wall mirrors. Click.

She led him into a cubicle, locked the door and took his leaping, straining cock into her hand, surrounding the long, thin, pencil-like spike with her scarlet nails. Click.

He could not wait. He lusted for swift penetration and was grappling and fumbling at her clothing, so she lifted her skirt and gave him immediate access. She wore stockings for this very purpose. He fucked her standing up, pushing her knickers aside and sliding himself straight up into her cunt with no preamble, nipping her tender white neck sharply and painfully. This was a power game for him, like dogs pissing on posts, staking a claim. Andrea was not responsive but he seemed not to notice, thrusting and shoving himself into her aggressively, with what force he could muster in his state of inebriation, splashing into her quickly and wetly with a series of small grunts, thumping hard to ejaculate as if he were trying to hurt her. As he withdrew, limp and shining, she sat down on the loo seat. Click.

Then he adjusted his clothing and left hastily with a quick peck on the cheek and a casual, 'See you around some time.'

Andrea smiled. It would be extremely unlikely. She had what she wanted.

Colin, the company solicitor, would not be quite so easy for she knew that he was gay, although not out, and he was secretive, correct and guarded. She would have to buy what he wanted, very carefully selected. He was a very slick, conservative, beautifully groomed, public school product in his early forties and lived a very private and reclusive life. His career, though, was high-profile and his reputation for corporate litigation ferocious. He was an ambitious status-seeker, always in the limelight wherever there was power, and in court or out of it was a formidable opponent with a mind like a rapier. He could not be easily fooled or caught off-guard, but he did have a weak spot and she knew what it was.

After much searching in the haunts of working boys, she found two very beautiful, intelligent boys and bought them. She dressed them, groomed them, equipped them, trained them and, by pulling a few strings, got them employed as barmen at his private club. One was a beautiful Italian-looking boy with chin-length wavy black hair, flawless olive skin, melting black eyes and a curving, sensual, full-lipped mouth. He had a cleft in his chin. She bought him a bloused white silk shirt and black leather trousers. The other was a blond angel with a pure English schoolboy look: soft grey eyes, a gentle, diffident smile, floppy fair hair and smooth pale skin. His chin was hairless. She bought him a light blue polo sweater and a beige Armani suit. They were both well-spoken, completely broke and compliant.

It worked. After a week or two of casual bar chat, they had hooked their fish and the two of them took him home to an apartment in a quality central location, which she had rented for them.

One of them, the dark boy, undressed Colin, kissing and licking all over his chest and belly as the clothes fell, running his hands up and down the dark-haired, muscled thighs. Click.

The boy took the upthrust erect cock in his mouth, sucking hard along the solidly curving, veinous shaft, cupping the swinging balls with one hand and caressing the globes of the buttocks with the other. Click.

Then the fair boy took over and guided Colin on to the huge bed with the black satin sheets and the two of them slid about together while the dark boy watched. The hungry, lusting cock slid between the boy's buttocks as he knelt on the bed. Click.

Together, all three of them writhed and slid upon the slippery sheets, wrapping their tongues around each other's organs, pumping into each other's hands and pushing and pounding deep into any available orifice until the fair boy came violently into Colin's smoothly sliding, sucking mouth. He then watched from the bedside as the other two continued plunging, ploughing and thumping, the dark boy eventually manoeuvring himself behind Colin, his cock thrust between his buttocks, his hand forward around the man's strangled, engorged tumescence as it spewed gouts of creamy thick fluid into the air to land in sticky white pools upon the black satin. Click.

No one had mentioned how long they were financed for, so all three remained overnight and did not leave the flat until the following afternoon, mission successfully accomplished without Colin suspecting a thing, and with a great deal of pleasure gained by all concerned. The boys reported back and debriefed, gratefully enriched, then vanished.

The Managing Director, Gareth, was a well-known family man, devoted to his wife and children and exemplary in his private habits. His loyal wife was a well-educated, efficient hostess and mother, adoring and supportive, requiring no independent career of her own, and he took pride in his well-organised, much-publicised, home-loving lifestyle.

However, Andrea had been with him once on a business trip in Brussels when a secretary had appeared whom no one had ever seen before, so she knew his temperament and tastes. He did not play at home, so she would have to take this one further afield. It was not long before she got her chance as he was often abroad, being the company networker and a skilled salesman and diplomat. For all sorts of reasons, he liked getting out of the country and spreading his wings. When she learned his itinerary, she flew out ahead of him, took a suite in the same elegant, five-star hotel where he had booked a suite, and waited.

He thought it an extraordinary coincidence when they bumped into each other in the lobby. She was demure and welcoming, greeting him warmly and saying how glad she was to see a familiar and friendly face, as she was here in the country alone 'to tie up family business' and much in need of sympathetic company. It seemed natural that they should dine together, and for this occasion she had bought the classic little red dress which she had poured herself into. It had cost a fortune and had a very deep, wide neckline to fully expose the creamy depths of her two best assets. It clung to all her curves tenaciously, without creasing, and was so short it barely covered her delectable rump, revealing her long, shapely, eye-catching legs, which were clad in black. She adorned it with dangly earrings of black jet and a jet brooch, and wore her sleek blonde tresses free and waving voluptuously over her shoulders. Her mouth and fingernails were matching red. Her hips swayed and her bosom was invitingly soft and lusciously pliant with a deep rift. Every eye was upon her. She exuded expensive sexual magnetism, laced with elegance, quality and class. She was the catch of the evening and knew it would flatter him to be seen with her.

She played extremely cool, untouchable and inaccessible. Gareth was a natural hunter who would relish the power of the chase. He didn't like easy women and was very discriminating, so she remained just out of his reach and did not flirt or cajole. She let him lead, allowing the seductive sensuality of her presence to do the work for her. She sat back in her chair and blew smoke rings indolently from a long, thin, brown cheroot. She gazed predatorily about the room, but focused her interest upon him when he spoke, keeping him the centre of her attention, suavely alluring but promising nothing. The temptation was irresistible and he was the one, finally, who made the move, inviting her for a nightcap, but it was to her room that they went. Andrea had plans and had spent money on this, so she subtly and cleverly manipulated that small detail. She let him seduce her in his own time, staying just beyond reach. His hand brushed her nipple lightly as he handed her a glass of brandy.

She prevaricated a little longer, appearing indifferent and aloof, but only enough to make him feel in control, his appetite whetted.

As she allowed herself to be reeled in slowly, she watched his eyes glittering and saw the tell-tale bulge straining against the cloth of his trousers. Betting on this moment, she had paid money for the outcome. He bent his head slightly as she poured another brandy, lifted her hair and kissed the angle at the base of her neck. She moved away but not too far. He turned her around and placed a hand over one breast. She eased her breast with subtle pressure into his hand, holding the rest of herself apart. Encouraged, he placed his hand inside the dress and lifted the breast from within to see the tight hard, stem of her nipple stiffening between his fingers. He bent and took the nipple in his mouth. Click.

She moved away again, her breast with the glistening nipple still displayed. Then he pulled her into him and raised the hem of her tiny skirt, pushing the solid bulge hard against her pelvis. She feigned a moan for him and pushed him downwards to kneel before her. He knelt to take off her tights and panties; then, after pushing up her skirt, he placed his mouth upon the fine, pale down of her bush and licked beneath it to tease up the hard little bud to stiff arousal. He would be thorough, taking pride in his skill. She spread her legs so that his tongue could penetrate further. Click.

Then she raised him up so that she could unzip his trousers and free the huge, fat, bursting cock that he proudly presented, removing the rest of his clothing to reveal a good, well-kept, trim body. Click.

He stripped her dress off over her head, then kissed the freely jiggling breasts and licked lingeringly around their softly swelling curves, nibbling a little. She felt betrayed by the trickle of desire that filtered down through her belly and into her cunt. She had not intended to enjoy this. He would pay a higher price for giving her pleasure.

His tongue travelled lithely down her navel and, reaching her lower limits, he took the swollen little nodule firmly between his lips and sucked hard on it. This time, she did not mean to moan. Fiery tendrils of hunger were racing through her and she hated him all the more. She placed her hand upon his savage dick as it urgently nudged against her compliant flesh, seeking entry, and she felt her cunt-lips moisten and expand. She lightly stroked the palpitating rod and the dangling balls beneath, then took it with her hand and guided it into her empty, aching, slippery well. He slid it firmly and easily into her. It fitted perfectly, touching inner chords of hunger and firing up a hot response which caused her muscles to clench, and cling to the sharp spear piercing her armour plating.

He thrust slowly and steadily into her, plunging deep and drawing out the sensual pleasure of each stroke before moving to the next. Betrayed by the rippling, electrifying currents, she grew impatient and longed for faster, harder, more violent action. She pushed back at him vigorously, thumping herself against him greedily. He made her wait and eventually she slowed to synchronise with him and they thumped and banged and grunted in unison. She did not want an orgasm with the enemy but before long his insistent, steadily increasing rhythm drew from deep within a rushing, flooding, molten blaze that gripped her in several spasms of hot eruption, blasting her to her nerve-ends and numbing her mind with all-engulfing sensation.

This was not what she had planned. She was gratified to cause him a powerfully pulsing explosion which drew a loud cry as he lunged fiercely to fire his juice into her.

He stayed the night, performing lustily more than once. She took him in her mouth and fellated him and, just at the point when she felt him losing control and yielding to the convulsive release, she placed her fire-bright nails about his gushing cock, removing her mouth to watch, and saw the viscous white fountains shoot high, then land among the hairs on his belly. Click.

She let him out later that morning, saying only, 'I think it would be best if we were not seen together again.'

'Yes, of course,' he replied.

Then she let someone else out, checked out and flew home. She was furious with herself for having enjoyed it, but all the more determined that her campaign of wrath and revenge should succeed.

Hereward Compton-Hughes, now the Executive Director in name only, was an elderly man who had known her father since their student days. His betrayal was the most galling. He was rarely ever seen in public any longer and hardly came in to his office as he was now semi-retired and becoming frail. He was a silver-haired, statesmanlike grandfather figure, the highly respected head of a dynasty with a powerful reputation as one of the founding pillars of modern society. In their heyday, the two men had been lions together, roaring and battling and forging their way ruthlessly through the opposition until they had reached the top, where they only had each other to compete with.

Andrea made a very special appointment with him, saying that her father had left something precious for him that he had asked her to give him. It was a trophy that had belonged to them both but which they had fought over bitterly. Her father would never have admitted he did not own sole right to it, and would not have let it out of his sight, but she knew she could be forgiven for the sake of the ultimate victory that she intended to win via this devious ploy.

It was midwinter, so she wore a luxurious, full-length, silver-fox fur coat and her diamond earrings; her lovely, tawny mane flowed glossily over her shoulders. His office was vast and spacious, more like a living room than a business centre, with a blazing fire and a huge, gold-framed, ceiling-to-floor mirror on the far wall. It accurately reflected his ego. The old man was initially suspicious but she played at daddy's little girl with all the guile and expertise of a lifetime's practice and he soon melted, thinking her putty in his hands.

She flattered his ageing ego with memories and reminiscences of earlier, better days and the mutual exploits of two giants living in the fast lane. She spoke of forgiveness and the enduring comradeship of two good friends, more durable than death. She touched on his sexual prowess and he confessed sadly that it had given him up and left him impotent, although he was still married to a good, honest woman. She flattered his virility and manhood and his reputed success with women, saying coquettishly that she had always admired him, envied them, and had even secretly coveted him herself, finding him an irresistibly attractive man, who was, by the way, still very fine-looking, charming and more than a little sexually charismatic even now. His inflated ego was desperate to believe and, sensing her prey snared, she persevered shamelessly.

She said she had brought him a gift of her own that she had always desired to offer him, and, unbuttoning her coat, opened it to reveal her nakedness beneath. His eyes popped and he was drooling. He squirmed in his armchair and she preened and posed seductively in front of him, reflected in his narcissistic mirror. Click.

'It won't do any good,' he panted at last. 'I'm too old.'

'Don't you worry,' she said. 'I will do all the work. You just enjoy it.'

She played submissiveness, knelt and unzipped his trousers, revealing a half-hearted and rather flaccid attempt at an erection. Click.

She took it in her claret-red nails and began gently and skilfully to massage, squeezing hard and tickling under the loose-hanging scrotum with her nails. As she did so, she moaned and writhed, pressing her breasts and pubic bone against his legs, telling him what a beautiful young man he had been and how desirable he still was. His limp dick tried to swell a little more. When there was sufficient response, she put it in her mouth and, using all her prodigious expertise, she twined and curled her tongue about it, flicking the edges of the squishy dome and teasing the tip of her tongue into the dry little slit. Click.

With one hand firmly around the base, she glided up and down, sucking hard while the willing but worn-out flesh conjured up the last of its resources. After a very long time, he finally gave a long, tremulous whimper and, pumping briskly with both hands, she removed her mouth to watch. At last, with an enormous effort, a trickle of semen flowed languidly out of the strangled knob and over her hand. Click.

He was pathetically grateful, stroking her face and calling her 'a good girl'. She buttoned up her coat, patted the crown of his silver head and left, disgusted but triumphant.

Andrea had exactly what she needed and it had all turned out perfectly, even better than she had hoped, thanks to the advances in modern technology. One week later, blown up, laminated and nailed to a number of public buildings, including their head offices, was a montage of photographs, named, labelled and blatantly revealing all. There were four for each man, revealing each in a compromised position with his sexual companion, either herself or, in Colin's case, the boys, disrobed with an erection clearly visible, the cock either inserted in an orifice or enclosed by a scarlet-nailed hand, in some cases with the ejaculation visibly exploding – or, in Hereward's case, trickling – and a full body-shot standing or lying, naked or semi-clothed, with a limp dick, looking ridiculous. She and the boys were clearly identifiable. This did not concern her. In fact, her bitchery brought her much sympathy and congratulation. Overnight, she became a heroine and role model.

She had sent the story and photographs to the tabloid papers and they ran it on the front page with acceptably muted versions of selected photographs. The implications were obvious and the evidence irrefutable. Four reputations were destroyed, four public figures were mocked and hounded out of business and four fortunes were ruined. Three marriages landed on the rocks, either visibly or in private, and four fine careers plummeted to ignominy. One old man soon died.

Mission very successfully accomplished. Andrea gloated and crowed and toasted herself with champagne. Then she looked for new prey to hunt. She thought perhaps Gareth Bainbridge, now that he was on the loose and vulnerable, might turn out to be a worthy opponent. They had a great deal in common.

Most of the photographs had been taken with a teensy lapel camera secreted into her clothing, or on the boys', but the particularly fine photographs of her and Gareth together had been taken by someone else hidden in her hotel room – at great cost and worth every penny. She felt a fevered flush of erotic anticipation at the idea of 'accidentally' bumping into him now, with this outrage between them. The volatile mix of their mutual hatred and volcanic sexual attraction would be the ultimate explosion. A thrilling spike of pure lust pierced her cunt and the spider's-web of a plot began to form.

Jason's Mum

*E*veryone knew Jason's mum was an actress and
everyone envied him. Everyone knew she must be
nearly forty but no one believed it. She had so much
vitality and zest and was still full of a youthful sense of
fun. Maeve Madigan. They had seen her on the telly a
few times and, although she wasn't famous as such,
every now and then people would stop her in the street
and ask for her autograph, which she gave graciously,
embarrassing Jason deeply. Her presence was huge and
glowing and when they'd been still at school they were
all terrified of her.

She wasn't glamorous exactly, or grand, but she had
authority and command. Although she maintained strict
rules about courtesy and respect – particularly self-
respect – and was fervent about people being responsible
and sensitive to each other, she was in every other way
very liberal. They all responded to her with a kind of
affectionate awe and she treated them as equals, taking
their problems and opinions and emotional upheavals
seriously. She listened to their music and tried to understand it. She enjoyed conversation with them, encouraging their fresh and passionate views on the world.

Luke was Jason's closest mate and had been spending his holiday's with them since he was an innocent, four-teen-year-old, smooth-cheeked schoolboy. The first time he had set eyes on her he had been smitten and now that he was a grown man in his second year at university he still felt the same way. Silently, he adored her. She was – he searched for the right word to describe her special quality – she was ... effervescent – that was it, like a freshly poured glass of champagne. Bubbles, froth, pleasure, substance, subtlety and class, all in one pack-age. She was the perfect woman and although he had had affairs with girls his own age, they never seemed to satisfy. There was not enough there, somehow: just a vapid, colourless promise of what they might eventually become with more maturity and experience. But she was ripe and full; witty, intelligent, expressive and abundant. She bloomed and radiated sensuality.

He blushed to remember an incident some years ear-lier in his torrid adolescence when he had seen the laundry basket in front of the washing machine with a pair of her panties on the top. They had been shiny black silk with a panel of delicate lace over the front where her bush would nestle. Furtively, he had picked them up and buried his face in them, scenting her musk. His erection had been instant and he had gone into the bathroom urgently, unable to contain his lust. He had wrapped the soothing black silkiness around his proud tumescence and had rubbed the panties up and down in a blissful fervour, coming all over them in hot, gushing fountains of thick, white sperm.

For some time, she thought they were lost but he had kept them under his mattress and would repeat the heavily erotic, secret pleasure whenever he got the chance. Finally, when they no longer smelled of her but of him, he had washed them and stuffed them down the back of the washing machine, where she had eventually found them.

He had never told anyone about his feelings for her but he suspected that Jason knew. He and Jason read each other's minds and didn't always need speech. They were both very alike, tall, well-built, fair and gentle, and they were different from most other young people their age, more thoughtful, more sensitive, more philosophical. They both wrote poetry, loved music and hated football. Their discussions on life in general could last well through the night and sometimes she would join them.

Jason had gone off with the others to a rock festival but Luke had not felt inclined. Maeve suggested that she needed an extra body to help with the gardening, as it was a fine Saturday afternoon and she wanted to catch the weather. He had offered to mow the lawn. They were taking a break for lunch, which they ate in the garden, and she had provided a couple of cans of lager. Her luxuriously abundant chestnut curls were piled on top of her head, untamed tendrils twining down her neck and face, sticking to her damp skin and driving him wild with desire. She wore a small loose pair of cotton shorts and her long, shapely legs were hard and tautly muscled from dancing. She wore turquoise canvas espadrilles and a loose cotton T-shirt with the bright logo of her latest show across her boobs. She never wore a bra and the full, circular globes of her breasts jiggled and jaunced under the light material. He hoped she couldn't see his erection, which he tried to restrain inside his underwear.

He always seemed to have an erection these days, but she was very understanding about such things, never mentioning stained bedclothes or the odd renegade condom that had got lost down the side of the bed. Without comment, she provided tissues in each room and never teased or mocked. He didn't know whether she had noticed him or not and was totally unaware that he was drop-dead gorgeous: lithe, rangy like a lion with his

148

long, flowing fair hair and magnetically sexual with a smouldering dynamism and restrained animal power. He was restless and unsatisfied, quietly and languidly passionate and he had the face of a film star, reminiscent of a young Harrison Ford.

She had noticed him, all right, but only to admire from the parental distance of her generation. Sometimes she teased him gently for looking like a seventies rockstar but she was not into cradle-snatching and preferred her men, like good cheese and good wine, well-matured. But right now she had been between men for some time. She registered the swelling in his shorts but delicately refrained from embarrassing him with her knowledge. A lovely young man – one of her 'boys', and she was proud of them all.

She cleared away the meal and returned to the garden where the hose had been left trickling, to water the bushes.

'Turn it off for me, Luke, please,' she called.

He went to the tap and turned it firmly but the wrong way and suddenly a forceful rush of water turned the hose into a writhing python in her hands. She dropped it and it snaked and snarled all over the lawn, drenching her in a torrent of water. He tried to turn it off but the tap was stuck and it wouldn't budge.

'It won't turn off,' he called back, running towards her and attempting to control the whirling live thing on the ground. Her wet nipples were jutting through the soaked shirt and her loose breasts were sharply outlined by the sucking, clinging cloth, bouncing freely with her efforts to grab the hose. Her hair was falling wildly all about her face, wet and curling down her neck. He tried to grab the rearing and plunging hose to tame it and together they battled and fought.

Neither of them knew how it happened. Neither of them started it, but suddenly they were clutching and clinging and tearing at each other, tumbling on the

149

ground in the puddles of water, covered in showers from the now freely slithering hose, their lips firmly fastened together, legs entwined and hips grinding into each other. Then his mouth was upon her breasts, his lips hard around the tight nipples through the soaking cloth and sucking the moisture fiercely from out of her shirt. She cried out with the sudden sharp pain and grabbed his buttocks firmly with both hands, arching towards him in a straining agony of lust and desire, her head thrown back in abandon, breasts thrust out towards to his hungry mouth. She fumbled desperately at his shorts and freed his solid, upthrust cock, sliding both hands up and down the polished virile shaft greedily.

Blindly, he pulled down the light cotton of her shorts and panties and, as they thrashed about together on the muddy lawn, he plunged himself deep inside her, finding her wet and ready. She was tight. He was surprised and delighted. Her muscles clutched him powerfully and he groaned. Then their mutual rhythm got into sync and they were pounding and thumping at each other in unison. Part of him could not believe he was actually inside her at last and held its breath in dread suspense. Another part was joyfully yielding to this unexpected fulfilment of all his frustrated dreams.

The hose rained over them, whipping up their passion. They were covered in mud and bits of grass but didn't notice, heaving and rolling over and over and thudding voraciously into each other; his mouth fastened upon her neck, licking and sucking the wet rivulets running down the trailing tendrils of hair. He drank of her and drank as if it were the last thing he would ever do. Their mutual pumping intensified as the inferno began to blaze, becoming faster and more frenzied, and they tossed and splashed like ships abandoned on a wild, tempestuous sea. Luke's mind was still suspended in a state of disbelief. His climax was resisting this forbidden pleasure. It seemed too outrageous. Restrained by his respect for her age and authority, he could not surrender to the enormity of unleashing his seed into this sacred, taboo chamber, this deliciously clinging cavern of all his youthful fantasies.

As he held back and held back, unable to permit himself the awful, unthinkable, disrespectful impurity, he felt her exploding beneath him; her body arched in spasms of orgasmic ecstasy, her voice loud with astonished delight, her climaxing cunt clenching and sucking all around him, and suddenly he had to let go, erupting with a voluptuously sinful release. With a cry of terrified joy, he fired the full load of his seed in powerful, gushing jets into her forbidden depths. With one final shudder they subsided in the showers still raining down on them from the serpentine hose.

'Oh, no,' she moaned. 'Oh, no. This can't happen. This mustn't happen. This didn't happen.' And she leaped up, adjusting her clothing, and ran into the house. Dazed, Luke gathered himself and slowly set about turning off the recalcitrant hose.

She was cool and distant and withdrawn for weeks afterwards, careful to speak to him politely, but remote. He stood back, hurt and bewildered, but made no comment. Jason seemed by some sixth sense to know what was happening and was quietly sensitive.

Finally, one day at breakfast, while Luke was still in bed, he said to her gently. 'He really cares for you, you know. It's not just sex for him. Think about it. What would be the harm? I think he'd be good for you.'

There was a long silence. She was used to this wisdom in her son, though it always unsettled her.

'He's a baby,' she said finally.

'He's a grown man,' responded Jason, 'with a mind of his own and responsible for his own choices. He's not your son. Don't think of him like that.'

It was left at that. To Luke, he said, 'Give her time and promise me you'll never hurt her.'

'You know I never would,' Luke replied. 'I think I love her.'

'Yes, I think perhaps you do.'

Luke wrestled with himself, wanting to take control and be a man but still in awe of this older, self-possessed woman who had brought up a son on her own and mothered all of them for years. He was aware of her vulnerability and felt strongly protective of her but she would not allow him in, defending herself with cool, careful courtesy, locked away inside. It pained him to see her like this. She should sparkle and fizz and he felt responsible. He also believed in his heart that he could be the cure.

After much battling, he came to a decision. He was going to prove himself a man. He began to woo her.

The next day a huge bunch of flowers was delivered with a brief note to let her know it was from him. It was a simple acknowledgement. *To the most beautiful woman I know. Luke.* She was thrown off balance.

He began to write her poetry, for which he had a flair. At first it was delicately romantic and he would leave it on her pillow. She read it wonderingly but made no comment. Slowly it became more personal and more sensual and eventually, when he saw that she was not protesting, he let loose his true feelings and expressed his love and his desire in poetry that was raw and wild and beautiful. She was deeply disturbed to find herself so adored and very moved by his ability to allow her into his deepest secret feelings. Slowly, she melted and began looking at him guardedly. He had become new to her.

He was unaware that he had touched a hunger deep inside that no man had ever satisfied. His ability to express his true passion in such beautiful, rich and sensual poetry triggered a response in her heart and she began to dissolve towards his adoration. Then he sent her a note in a card with a single rose. *Please let me take you out to dinner.*

She carefully chose her most plunging and figure-hugging dress, allowing herself to be seductive and alluring. She wore a light floral perfume and underneath her dress she put on her stockings and suspenders. He was too young to know about such things and she worried that she was being outdated and old-fashioned. Her vivacious, sparkling face was framed by a profusion of cascading chestnut curls. She was beautiful and he was elegant, in his loose-fitting, pearl-grey, satin shirt with the Chinese collar, and his shining mane free-falling to his shoulder blades, revealing glimpses of the silver earring in his left ear.

He took her to a classy French restaurant where they began at last to resume the easy conversation they had been used to, although the air between them was hot and crackling. They were honest with each other about their fears and insecurities and he saw the fragile, vulnerable girl that she tried so fiercely to hide. It made him stronger. As he helped her on with her coat, he bent and kissed her softly and she turned up her face to receive him. Suddenly she felt small and he felt powerful.

Finally they were alone together in her room, the forbidden inner sanctum where no one else was permitted. He shivered, overcome by the enormity of his success. Then he was undressing her and she was offering herself to his ministrations, trembling slightly at the touch of his fingers on her skin. The dress slithered with a whisper to the ground and she stood revealed in her stockings and suspenders. He gasped and his heart pounded wildly. He had never seen anyone so beautiful or so desirable in his life. He was already erect, swollen rigid and pulsing with a terrible hungry longing, flushed and aching. She was quivering and breathing heavily.

He unpinned the suspenders in a state of rapture, his prick leaping in a hard curve towards the gap they created at the apex of her thighs, framing her curling, downy triangle.

She took his potent and rigid penis again in both hands, this time gently, cupping the balls with one hand and stroking the solid muscle beneath them with her fingertips. With one hand firmly around the base, she lowered her full, luscious lips over him and teased her tongue lightly around the exposed dome, flicking the edges of the helmet and prising into the tiny eye where a tear was forming. She ran her tongue lithely down the length of him, feeling out the seam, zigzagging up and down it and the trickles of heat that were darting through him brought a low moan from deep in his chest. No one had ever had this expertise, always in too much of a hurry and skimping the details, but she was patient and thorough, teasing out every last nerve-end and finally embracing him fully in her mouth, tightening her cheeks, lips and tongue to suck firmly until he began to push and retract against her.

At first he was careful, thinking he might choke her, but she encouraged him with tiny grunts and hard suction to release his inhibitions, and then he was pumping and thrusting with hungry abandon. He expected her to withdraw as other girls always had and was astounded into a vigorous explosion when she remained firmly around him, swallowing the warm mouthfuls of come as he shot them ecstatically down her throat.

Then she made lingering love to him with her hands, and they discovered each other searchingly. She taught him where her pleasure-spots were and how to awaken and arouse them with his hands and his tongue. They took their time now that his urgency was quelled, and when he arose again she chuckled.

'That's the big advantage of being twenty,' she mused. 'Ever ready.'

'While you, on the other hand, are just arriving at a woman's peak, so we should be well matched. Shall we see who can come the most times in one night?'

'You cheeky young devil.' She laughed. 'OK, you're on.' And he entered her slowly and tenderly, his virile young cock solid again and eager, pushing deep into her honeyed, slippery tunnel which gripped him tightly, and they ploughed the furrow until early morning, losing count of how many times who came or how.

'Oh, well,' she said dreamily, when they were both fully sated and exhausted. 'We'll just have to try again tomorrow night.'

They fell asleep in each other's arms, Luke still dazed to be sleeping in this holy of holies, united with this sumptuously mature woman of his adolescent fantasies, and Maeve amazed and full of wonder to find that her deepest needs and desires were being satisfied by a passionate and tender youth she had helped to raise.

The Locker Room Incident

*H*e placed his hand over his full crotch, squirming in discomfort. Somehow, he would have to unburden himself of this throbbing, aching hunger swelling in his groin. This experimental training with the young female cadets was driving him crazy. As an unmarried Education Officer with time to spare, he had volunteered for this new duty, but a bunch of adolescent girls in army uniform was more than he had bargained for. It was particularly unnerving when he called them to attention and twelve pairs of tits in varying shapes and sizes enthusiastically thrust themselves out in his general direction.

He didn't know whether he loved it or hated it: constantly tempted and unbearably tormented by the unrelieved arousal, especially in his capacity as swimming coach. He looked out the door at the girls running about in their swimsuits, splashing each other, and screaming playfully, and knew he would have to do something about this or they wouldn't be able to help noticing, and he couldn't risk that. Where would be safe? He'd have to be quick about it. He pressed his hand into his anguished, bulging groin and the pressure made his cock leap with anticipation, striving upwards out of his trunks, the head squeezing free and climbing up his navel. Oh, God, he groaned.

They were all in the pool now, so, with a quick glance around the locker room, he took the torturously insistent erection in his hand and furtively began to rub. He'd have to be quick or they would miss him and send someone to fetch him. He felt the urgent surge of his climax begin immediately, undeniable now, and lost all sense of his whereabouts as his pulse quickened, his blood raced and his loins blazed. Faster and faster, massaging up and down as fast as he could vibrate his fist, enjoying the sight of himself thrust up, stretched smooth and solid, like a greedy python. Then, just a second before the delicious release of his juices raced out of his cock in violent, gushing spurts, a girl stepped out from behind the lockers and stood before him. Too late to stop, he shot the pulsing creamy jets straight at her as she suddenly appeared before him.

'Oh, sir: what are you doing, sir?'

He stared at her aghast, speechless.

She looked back at him and down at the naked dick, spent now, in his hand; then, wetting her lips with her tongue, she whispered, 'Next time, sir, let me help you with that,' and vanished.

It took more courage than he thought he possessed to gather himself and go out and face the group for the lesson. The training for their life-saving certificates was something of a responsibility, especially the diving and the recovery of submerged objects. It took a monumental effort of will not to run away screaming with embarrassment. Somehow he brazened it out but he was sure they were all laughing at him, and he was careful not to catch that particular girl's eye in case she looked at him knowingly.

He couldn't bear it if they all knew, but he knew what girls were like – they shared everything – it would get around. He wasn't so worried about this getting back to his senior officers. Girls liked their little secrets and he suspected they would probably keep this among themselves, but the idea of being the laughing stock of the entire regiment brought a blush to his cheeks. Finally it was over and he sent them all to get changed. He didn't dare go near the locker room but busied himself tidying up outside until long after they had all gone.

It was a privately-owned Armed Services pool, hidden from public sight down a long pathway through ancient oak and beech woodlands. A river ran by it and the far bank was densely covered in trees and undergrowth. It was deserted and secluded. He heaved a sigh of relief as they all disappeared up the pathway, leaving him alone, then dived into the pool for a few invigorating lengths to clear his head and recover himself. The rhythmic strokes helped him to think and he tried to plan ahead for all possibilities. He could ask to be replaced. He could get reassigned elsewhere. He could pretend it had never happened and carry on as normal. He could just brave it out, ignoring the nudges and winks until it all blew over. He could . . .

No, he couldn't. That was the one thing he couldn't contemplate. He didn't want to end up in a sex scandal. No, he wouldn't: not under any circumstances. But the perfidious seed had been planted and seemed to be finding fertile soil. All right, then, say it out loud. He could take up her offer.

He trembled, gulping a mouthful of water as his stroke faltered. No! Don't even think it! That way lies disaster. She was easily seventeen and probably experienced but she was still a junior cadet in his charge and he was an officer. He loved his career and he didn't want to jeopardise it by an enquiry or, worse, a court martial. Above all, he certainly did not want to be hounded out of the army altogether by a foolhardy escapade with some lascivious nymphet that he didn't even fancy. Or hadn't fancied, until now. That all seemed to have changed and he wasn't sure whether to blame her suggestively veiled invitation or his own disgusting lack of self-discipline.

He sighed, heaved himself out of the pool, dried himself vigorously, dressed and set off up the path through the woods. Grateful for any distraction, he watched the early evening sun dappling in golden glints through the rustling midsummer leaves. It all seemed so simple suddenly. Why wasn't it ever this simple? He didn't want these sordid complications. He was good at training the youngsters, and he just wanted to enjoy this walk through the woods, the satisfaction and rewards of his career, some physical invigoration now and then, and relaxing with his fellow officers over a pint. Was that too much to ask? He strolled lazily through the trees, not in a hurry to emerge into the world of people, and was abruptly startled out of his reverie by the appearance of three girls on the pathway in front of him.

It took him a moment to register the confrontational manner of their stance. Resenting the interruption, he resorted to his official status.

'Now then, girls, what's all this? You should have left long ago.'

The tall, voluptuous, full-bodied girl in the centre was a troublemaker by reputation. She was too precocious by half and knew more than she should of the art of seductive provocation. Innocent, she was not. The one on her left was a deliciously ripe-looking, buxom wench with a soft pluckable mouth and an air of availability; jailbait for sure. The third girl was his pert little miss, blonde, winsome and flirtatious. Usually the quiet type, she readily conceded authority to the amazon in the centre. The luscious dark one was a follower. She would do as she was told for the sake of belonging and being accepted. He computed all these details in the few moments before anyone replied, and when they did, his skin prickled in alarm and he knew he was a marked man. He was wide awake and alert now.

It was the amazon who took charge. 'So, sir. We hear you need a hand. We're here to make sure you get one.' She smirked and the dark girl giggled.

He tried again to reassert his authority. 'Now, come on girls. Back to barracks. Chop, chop.'

They stood firm and the amazon tilted her head back in a long appraising gaze, a curling smile playing over her wide mobile mouth.

'Do it,' she finally muttered, so low he almost missed it.

Without warning, the three of them together lifted him off the ground and carried him swiftly into the cover of the trees and the undergrowth. Before he could gather his wits, they placed him in a clearing in the bracken, stripped off all his clothing and lay him naked on the grass. He was breathing in ragged gasps, caught totally off-guard and incapacitated by this sudden bewildering turn of events. They were expertly tying him hand and foot with some twine they had conjured up from their kitbags, completely immobilising him. Then they leaned him up against the trunk of a huge oak tree. It never occurred to him to yell for help. No one would have heard him anyway. There was no one for miles.

'Well, I don't know what all the fuss is about. Looks pretty unimpressive to me,' said the amazon, and she flicked his limply shrivelled member with her fingernail. He grimaced, still too stunned to comprehend the reality of his plight. 'What a naughty boy it was,' she said. 'What should we do with him, Sarah?'

Sarah giggled again. 'I think we should punish him,' she said in a high little girl's voice. 'What do you think, Louise?'

Louise's voice was a husky whisper. 'I think so too,' she replied.

'Well, I don't know.' The amazon sounded doubtful. 'I can't see anything to get excited about.'

And quite without warning he felt a hot surge flooding through his loins. With dismay he knew that, without his permission, his prick was playing their game. It quivered and began to uncurl in his lap, putting the lie to her derision.

'Well, well, lookie here,' she taunted him in her fruity drawl. 'Perhaps he is a bad boy, after all. Perhaps we should whip him for his audacity.' She laughed low, removed her beret, and, untied her long, glossy, luxuriantly waving hair, then bent over his lap and swished it briskly back and forth, whipping it over his rapidly swelling organ. In response to the swiftly delicate brush of the teasing hair, it jerked to attention and thrust itself insistently and proudly upright, stretching hard and full, eager for a more engulfing touch.

Then they were all at it. Black, brunette and blonde, whipping him lightly and teasingly with the unbound, copious, velvety sensuality of their youthful tresses across his lap, softly tormenting him into an agony of aching, straining, anguished desire, desperate for the firm clutch of something to enclose his naked need. He groaned aloud.

'Oh, stop, please stop. This is not right.'

'No, sir, this is not right, you naughty boy. You shouldn't have a hard-on here in the forest with three innocent young cadets. Whatever would people think? Come on, girls. Let's show him how innocent we are.'

She began to undo the waistband of Sarah's trousers and lower the zip. Sarah raised her arms for the khaki jersey to come off. Slowly, the hooks of the bra were unhinged and as it fell to the ground he stared, thunderstruck. Sarah was fully, lavishly breasted and her skin was shockingly smooth and white and firm. The nipples were large, soft, pink moons.

Down came the trousers; the boots were unlaced and

removed; and, finally, off came the white cotton, virginal knickers. Sarah stood revealed like Venus arising from the waves, the dark triangle of her mount stark against the pure white flesh. She was both a woman and not a woman, simultaneously pure and ripe, untouchable and overwhelmingly inviting.

The amazon put her mouth on one large nipple and her finger and thumb on the other. Sensually, lingeringly, she sucked on the one and tweaked on the other. His cock lurched and thrust; his bursting inability to enclose it, with his hands bound, was unbearable. He tried not to look but couldn't tear his eyes away.

The amazon had begun to unzip and reveal the fair Louise. Louise had her eyes closed in rapture and already had both hands on the amazon's still clothed breasts. She massaged in hungry caressing circles as she was being undressed; then she also stood naked, pale, lean and lissom, with perfectly formed little apples sporting pertly erect nipple-pips and a furry blonde triangle adorning the peak of her long slender legs. She turned to Sarah and they began to enjoy each other's breasts with their fingers and mouths, taking turns to suck gently on the hardened buds of each other's arousal and running their hands longingly up and down each other's flawless thighs.

He found the sight of their lovely, nubile, woodland nakedness shocking and berated himself for the importunate craving of his ravenously lustful response. He felt the pulsing heat infusing his dick and thought he must explode. The amazon stood over him while Sarah and Louise continued to enjoy the pleasure of each other and slowly began to undress herself. She arched her back seductively as she drew off her jersey and T-shirt and dropped them on the grass, uncovering a deep, luscious, womanly cleavage, the bra-straps dangling down her arms. She ran her fingers underneath her bra, revealing only the crease and a tantalising glimpse of the soft, full curve sweeping up towards the still invisible nipples, then she leaned the fulsome globes of her mature, demanding breasts down over him until they almost touched his upwardly-thrusting penis.

She reached behind herself and unhooked the bra with deliberation, dropped it over his shoulder and took a glorious breast in each hand, pushing them upwards and together. She squeezed and massaged them, closing her eyes and moaning with feigned rapture. As she knelt astride his legs, she allowed the long, hard nipples to brush lightly across the hairs on his chest and over the tip of his engorged penis. He was groaning now and squirming against his constraints.

The pulsating, throbbing fire in his groin was threatening to explode and the heat was rising to flush his chest and face with fever. He was sweating and his breath came in jagged, panting gasps. She leaned back on his legs to remove her trousers, knees bent and pelvis lifted, and the sweat was dripping freely from his face. Thrills of hunger were rippling up his cock and, when she raised her hips, slid down her trousers and panties and flashed her cunt straight in his face, he cried out in anguish.

He watched, stunned and dazed with disbelief, as she placed her hand over the darkly downy folds of her vulva and began to play there with her fingers, pushing them inside, withdrawing them covered in cunt-juice and rubbing the wet fingers against the clitoris. His prick was twitching and jerking and pulsing. She was all woman, possibly virginal but certainly not innocent. To one side of them he could still see Louise with her face between Sarah's legs. Sarah's eyes were closed, her head thrown back in ecstasy, and she was writhing and moaning. Then she was crying out in sharp, piercing cries of gratified satisfaction.

He screamed out, 'Stop this! Oh, God, please stop this!

I can't bear any more!' He struggled against his ropes, burning his wrists as the twine dug into them.

The amazon laughed mockingly and sat harder upon his legs. In pain in every direction, he stopped struggling and gave himself up to the delicious torture.

The satisfied Sarah's hand was now between Louise's legs and the amazon was rubbing herself to a climactic frenzy. He felt the corresponding response begin at the base of his root and, as the spasms of her peaking orgasm engulfed her in waves of convulsing self-gratification, he surrendered himself to the obscene release of his lust and erupted spontaneously in shudderingly forceful gushes of hot, sticky come, shooting high to land upon the smooth, white, full globes of her breasts. At the same moment, vaguely registering the shrill, surprised, birdlike cries of Louise's pleasure, he watched with a strangely superior triumph as his thick sperm oozed down the valley of the amazon's cleavage and dripped on to her flat belly.

Spent and helpless, he wanted to weep at his powerlessness and humiliation.

'Untie me girls, please. Let me go now.'

All three began to dress themselves, ignoring him and chatting gaily amongst themselves.

'What do you think, then?' asked Louise in her light whisper. 'Was I right? Isn't he just disgusting?'

'You were right,' replied the amazon. 'I've never met anyone so disgusting. He needs to be severely punished. We'll have to think of something properly suitable.'

He was dimly aware that this was not yet to be the end of his anguish.

Once dressed, berets set at a jaunty angle, they turned back to him.

'You're a very bad boy, sir.' The amazon grinned at him. 'We'll have to take care to cure you of these filthy habits. We'll see you again next week.' Chuckling smugly, she took a Swiss army knife from her bag, sliced swiftly through the twine around his hands and ankles, and the three of them raced off in high mirth back through the woods.

He remained where he was for a long time after their girlish laughter had wafted away in faint echoes on the breeze. Next week! Oh God, oh God, oh God, it wasn't over yet! They hadn't finished with him! There would be more!

A frisson which was not the chill night air overtook him and with a lurch of despair he knew he was already looking forward to it. He dared not think where it might all end. Donning his clothes, he found his way back along the now dark path which would never look the same again. Were they virgins? he wondered. Did they even like men, or was he just an easy target, a toy? The erotic thrill of the challenge, together with the dread of exposure were accompanied by a heart-thumping rush of adrenalin, the soldier's drug, and he knew he was hooked.

The following week he approached the swimming pool with a cold cramping knot in his stomach and his heart pounding wildly. He couldn't look any of them in the eye but felt sure they were all smirking. He brazened it out with bluff and breezy authority but the anticipation was unbearable. As he watched them all finally leave up the path leading through the woods, he breathed a sigh of relief, his mouth dry and his pulse racing. To gain time before facing his potential ordeal in the woods, he dived into the cool, clear, refreshing water.

The first he was aware of their presence was two shadows slipping up beside him from below and two pairs of hands grabbing his swimming trunks and stripping them off down his kicking legs. They were also stark naked and they must have slid stealthily into the water. As he continued to attempt swimming to the end of the pool, the two pairs of hands wrapped themselves around a leg each and ran glidingly up and down the thighs and calves. His body, of average size and height with no unnecessary bulk, was in superb condition, at the peak of fitness, hard and strong, the etched muscles gliding and tensing visibly under the olive skin. Dark brown hair lightly covered his chest and belly and shaded the contours of his legs and forearms.

It was not long before the swooping hands evoked a response from his willing loins and, as his released penis lifted its head and peered hungrily up at his navel, a third naked body emerged from underneath him, gliding along his underside caressingly, her breasts softly tantalising his belly and chest and her trailing hand teasingly brushing over his swelling erection. The two other pairs of hands were sliding up over his tautly curved buttocks and down his back and sides. He spluttered, gulping water and missing his stroke, and twisted over on to his back. His engorged prong was now exposed for all to see.

He must have arrived at the shallow end because one pair of hands, belonging to the willowy Louise, were grasping him by the ankles and another had pulled his arms above his head and was holding them there by the wrists. They had more twine and neatly tied his ankles and wrists, disempowering him and restricting his mobility. He had been caught napping. Had they accosted him in the woods as they had done last week, he would have been ready and more than a match for them – but they had caught him unawares, just as they had intended. It flitted across his mind that they would make good tactical soldiers. Their teamwork was superb and their forward-thinking impeccable. He felt the helpless despair of trapped prey, out of control, not knowing what lay in store, but the anticipatory rush of adrenalin cleared his brain, made his heart beat faster and his rock-hard erection slap ferociously against his navel. His lust was indescribable, hotter than he had ever known it. Whatever they might do to him, whatever danger he was in, he craved it. To hell with the risk. That only made it more exciting. His mind was whirling, trying to second-guess them, even though he was rendered passive and there was nothing he could do to regain control.

A forceful jet of water stung his protruding cock. It was the amazon, whose name he now knew was Gwen. She took another mouthful and aiming it efficiently, fired it all the way along the fully stretched, solid length. It hurt. With a third mouthful she hit him square on the glans, causing a delectable sensation of pure pain. He cried out and squirmed, trying to keel over and protect his agony under the water, but the others held his hands and feet firmly.

They were all laughing uproariously at his discomfort.

'Honestly, it's the most obscene thing I've ever seen,' shrieked the amazon. 'Just look at all those hideous veins, like worms, and it's a pukey colour. What colour would you call that, Sarah?'

'Puce,' replied Sarah, laughing hysterically, which set them all off again.

'Puce!' shrieked Louise. 'He's got a pukey, puce prick!' – which brought forth more gales of mirth.

'It looks positively strangled,' Gwen managed to splutter.

'It looks like it might explode,' giggled Louise, 'which would be utterly disgusting.'

'Men are disgusting,' stated Sarah. 'One look at that revolting obscenity puts me off for life. Give me a nice warm pussy any day.'

'Speak for yourself,' retorted Gwen. 'As far as I'm concerned, either will do.'

'As far as you're concerned, anything will do,' Louise asserted, which caused more raucous guffaws. 'Personally, I'll wait and see what it's capable of,' she continued, playing safe. 'Shall we find out?'

He felt annihilated, as if he didn't exist, being talked

about like a thing, but some libidinous corner of his brain wanted to prove his prowess. His pukey, puce prick gave a mighty lurch at the thought of it and, seeing it, the amazon clearly decided the next move.

'OK, let's put it to the test. Are you ready? One, two, three, heave.' And the three of them hoisted him by the shoulders, hips and ankles, out of the water and on to the grassy surrounds.

'Take your positions,' she ordered. They had obviously worked it all out. 'Now, sir, we know what you can do with your hands, but are you any use to anyone else? Your future might well depend on what happens next.'

She was mocking him with her lopsided, superior smile and his panic thumped loudly in his ears. He wanted to shut his eyes but didn't dare.

The amazon stood over him, majestic and magnificent, hands on hips, grinning broadly.

'Are we all ready?'

'Well, he certainly is,' quipped Louise, and they all giggled.

'Take positions,' Gwen commanded. The other two stood behind his head while Gwen lowered herself into his lap.

Before he had time to understand her intention, she took his quivering shaft, held it upright and speared herself upon it, sinking slowly and grinding hard until he slid past the tightness into the juicy depths and was fully encased. It was so sudden his brain jammed. At that moment Louise knelt over his head and he was almost suffocated by a face full of cunt. In some kind of heaven, he adjusted to breathe and extruded his tongue to lap at the musky-moist, furry swellings, parting the inner lips and seeking the entrance. He did not feel Sarah free his hands but with what was left of his brain he noticed her guide his right hand under her bush as she knelt over it. He inserted two fingers into the slippery warmth and saw her lean into Louise's hands, which were playing with her large, globular breasts.

They lifted their hips to lean forward to kiss each other, which allowed both his mouth and his fingers more access. He jiggled them both and pushed deeper. Meanwhile, the amazon was gliding wetly up and down his blazing, red-hot poker. Mentally, he clung desperately to his concentration, grateful for the military training which enabled him to accomplish several tasks at once, knowing his future career might depend upon it.

Of necessity, the rhythm became mutual to all four of them as his dipping tongue and delving fingers responded to the mounting tempo Gwen was performing upon his dick. As his fingers probed into Sarah, his tongue probed deeply into Louise. When he moved his hand to tease up Sarah's swollen button, his tongue moved to flick at Louise's nodule, and all the while Gwen rode him wildly, pleasing no one but herself and increasing her pace to suit her own rising climax.

They were all three wet and slippery and his whole body was tingling with rippling, prickling trickles of sheer pleasure and expanding desire. He wished it could last forever, and with his mind focused on his tongue and his hands, he was in no danger of achieving his own release too soon.

Louise came first, against his face, sighing with satisfaction as he flicked back and forth relentlessly with his athletic tongue. She lifted herself off him and embraced Sarah from behind, cuddling up to her closely, kissing her shoulders and playing with her breasts. She reached down to the thick, black bush and her hand joined his as she pressed the excited bud and he vibrated firmly inside the sucking depths. Sarah came like a rocket, gasping and shrieking and pushing herself against their fingers, clenching in rapid spasms against his intruding fingers. Then she turned into Louise's embrace, trembling.

He was now free to concentrate solely on the wildly bucking amazon and himself. Hearing her moans increasing in intensity and pitch, signalling her imminent arrival, he surrendered at last to the fire in his own loins. The intensity of his desire to fill her forcefully with his seed was so violent, it was almost aggressive. He raised his pelvis high off the ground for further penetration and held himself there for her to spike herself upon. This unexpected depth charge thudding against her cervix took her by surprise. Her eyes flew open, wide with consternation, shock and awe. For a split second the world stood still as their eyes locked, then with a blazing rush he erupted inside her with a terrific spurting of what felt like gallons of vigorous sperm.

'Aaaaaaaaaaaah!'

He'd never heard such a yell. It pierced the evening air and set the birds flapping out of the trees. As her cries tailed off to a whimper she slowly came to rest with his cock still inside her and her long, rich hair draped over his belly.

'Well,' he challenged them after a moment, 'do I pass?'

They just stared at him in silence, and in silence they gathered their clothes, dressed themselves, sliced the bonds around his ankles and walked away. Before she disappeared into the woods, Gwen turned to look at him. She reminded him of a frightened deer – she looked so vulnerable and uncertain. Aha! he thought to himself. Got you!

He put his hands under his head and remained for some time lying on the cool grass, gazing up at the twilit sky, listening to the breeze in the leaves and grinning to himself. He knew he was back in command. Before we're through, he promised himself, I'm going to have all three of you.

Indian Summer

Aisha had been married to Selim for six months and the marriage was still unconsummated. The marriage had been arranged and she had willingly concurred. Selim was a business friend of her father's and just a few years younger than him, but Selim was a good man: sophisticated, intelligent, kindly and attractive. His body was still hard and youthful and his full black hair greying only a little on the temples, which added to his distinction.

He was also a good husband, attentive, courteous and generous in his provision for her. They had a beautifully furnished home, several servants and they entertained frequently and lavishly. Whenever he went on a business trip she always accompanied him and his conversation was stimulating and witty. They had become companionable and were comfortable with each other, so she was very puzzled. Aisha knew she was lovely: doe-eyed and curvacious, her skin creamy smooth and mocha-coloured, her bosom, belly and hips luscious and firmly rounded, and her manner artful and flirtatious. She had been brought up to please and knew how to flatter and tempt a man. Hers had been the most sought-after hand in town, especially with her dowry added to her charms, and she had been delighted that her father had chosen the steady and reliable maturity of the elegant Selim.

On the night of their wedding, he had carried her to her luxurious bedroom, placed her gently on the bed, made sure all her needs were supplied and then, with a fatherly peck on the cheek, had retired to his own room. This had happened every night since. He came to chat with her and sometimes they read stories to each other but he always retired to his own room and displayed no sexual interest in her at all. She had tried everything. Her long ravishing black hair had been perfumed with jasmine oil. She had been anointed with various musky fragrances. She always wore brightly colourful, softly draped clothing which flattered her delicate hands and feet, and she tinkled and jingled with little bells and bangles whenever she moved. She sat at table in such a way as to reveal the curve of her long neck and the silhouette of her breasts, and looked at him seductively from under her kohl-blackened eyelids. Still nothing. She knew hungers in her body and palpitated with longings that could not be satisfied by the ministrations of her maids or the sweetmeats and delicacies always on offer. Her skin prickled and thrilled to any soft touch and her lower regions felt an aching emptiness. She was at a loss.

Only once had she seen Selim aroused and it had confused her even more. They had been in the country on a trip and he had taken her to visit an ancient temple. As they had climbed the steps to the hilltop, there had been many monkeys chittering and scampering and, right on the steps into the temple, two of them had copulated in front of their eyes, the little male taking the female from behind, pumping his tiny pelvis fast against her with apparent disinterest. When he had withdrawn, the female had examined her private parts intently, prying with her fingers among the long pale hair. Then Aisha had noticed the protrusion appearing in front of Selim, jutting out to form a peak visible even through his tunic, and his eyes had been shining. She was relieved to discover that he could become aroused but even more mystified as to why he never seemed interested in her. He had turned away quickly but she had felt a spark leap to inflame her empty belly and was determined to get to the bottom of this. She pondered on what to do next and began to watch him more closely for any clues.

Her bathroom was sumptuous, tiled in bright colours from ceiling to floor with the bubbling spa-bath recessed in the centre. On all the walls between the tiling there were mirrors here and there at various angles. Her maids washed, oiled and perfumed her, shampooing and brushing her long, shining hair, and bathing was one of her few sensual enjoyments. One day she had been ministered to and had dismissed the maids while she wallowed in the frothing bubbles when she spied the figure of Selim in a mirror. He paused in the doorway as he caught sight of her and, suddenly inspired, pretending she had not seen him, she began to pleasure herself with her fingers.

She took both her heavy breasts in her hands and massaged them, bending her head to take the nipples between her lips and sucking them to perky stiffness. Then she ran her hand between her legs, threw back her head with the hair draped around her in the water and began to rub blissfully under her pubis, all the time watching the reflection of Selim. He was wearing a long western bathrobe made of black silk and covered in dragons. To her gratification she saw him reach down and take hold of his rapidly swelling organ as it arose and extended out of the robe. Reassured that he wasn't averse to her sexuality, she watched secretly, rubbing herself to a climax and he also began to pump faster and faster until with a little cry she arched her back, the water rippling around her and gave herself up to the pervading peaks of pleasure, noticing in the mirror that Selim spurted himself frenziedly into the air as she came.

Now she was very confused. She knew that he was sexually responsive and did enjoy some sort of erotic pleasure. She knew also that he could be aroused by the sight of her but could not understand what was stopping him from coming to her as a husband should. He was apparently not homosexual, as she had suspected – she had seen no signs of any other men visiting the house who might have been sexual companions. She watched him even more closely, particularly at night, and one evening she had her best clue. She had hidden herself in his inner closet and was peeping through a crack in the door. Selim turned on the television, took a video from the cabinet and lay back on the divan to watch it.

Very soon his cock was erect and manly, hungry and solid as she most desired it. Her loins turned to jelly as she watched and her juices flowed from within her. She just managed to stifle a moan. She looked more closely at what he was watching and saw that it was a sexual video depicting a man and a woman in coitus. The full length of the man's penis was shown entering and retracting from the woman in close-up, while Selim took his own excited organ in his fist. The couple were doing as she wished Selim would do with her but all he did was watch while pumping himself to a swift ejaculation. As he erupted, shooting high in thick, white, gushing streams she felt her thighs sticky with her own fluids, waves of desire flooded her and she grew desperate. When the video ended, Selim turned off the television and left the room. Aisha went back to her own room and lay in the dark, thinking hard. Somehow she had to get him to be involved with her in such a way that they both achieved fulfilment but it seemed to her now that his only pleasure was to watch. For her, masturbation was no longer sufficient.

There appeared to her a way forward but it made her feel bold and wanton. However, if they were to have a satisfactory marriage, something must be done. She plucked up all her courage, having had the maids perfume and oil her particularly carefully, her luxuriant hair loose over her shoulders and breasts, and she presented herself in Selim's bedroom one evening as he lay reading a book. She dropped the lacy white robe on the floor and stood revealed in her full naked loveliness before him.

'Please don't say anything,' she whispered. 'Dear husband, I know that it is not I you want but I also wish to be a real wife. I ask nothing from you. I do not expect you to touch me but I have one request. Would you grant me one request?'

'What do you ask?' he replied.

'Would you watch me while I pleasure myself?' she whispered, feeling brazen and expecting to be banished from his presence.

In the ensuing silence, she saw his erection arise and give him away. The bedsheet covering him rose like a tent and swayed silkily before her eyes.

'I only wish to please you,' she said softly and began to run her hands flowingly over her own curves, luxuriating in the caress and the wickedness of being watched at her own sensuality.

Laying aside her shame, she surrendered to the erotic wantonness of her exhibitionism and closed her eyes to enjoy herself more. Lying at the foot of his bed, she spread her legs apart and pulled the outer labia aside with her ringed fingers, exposing the pink, wet folds of her cunt to his view. He groaned and reached down to his lurching, twitching prick, taking himself in hand. Now watching each other avidly, they rubbed and massaged, moaning gently and thrusting their hips against

175

their own kneading fingers until the rhythm quickened pace and the surges began, which washed over them in hotly pulsing waves, as she clutched with rapid spasms of her vaginal muscles at the hungry space within her, and he splattered himself over her fecund but empty belly. Encouraged by her success, she reached forwards with her mouth and sucked the final traces of semen from his spent and slowly deflating cock.

They sat together on the bed holding hands until he spoke first.

'You are a true wife, Aisha. I do not deserve you. I see you have learned my weakness – I will not ask how – but now we must find a way to fulfil your needs and desires. I am unable to achieve penetration. I am only able to be satisfied by watching others but you, my dear, are a full woman and have the potential for many kinds of gratification and I ask only that I be allowed to be included as an observer. This way we can be truly united.'

'What are you suggesting, Selim?' she enquired.

'I will find you lovers, Aisha, as you require. Men or women – or both – whatever you wish for your own pleasure. I will deny you nothing but I ask you to promise that you will have no secret affairs that are hidden from me. In order to be husband and wife, your sexual gratification must always include me. Can you promise me that?'

'I will do anything you ask, but I only favour you, Selim. You are my husband and it is you that I love and desire. How can I love another?'

He leaned over and kissed her lips gently and lingeringly. 'I love you with all my heart, Aisha. I will find someone to satisfy and please you. Will you trust me?'

'Yes,' she whispered, her heart beating wildly, and that night, for the first time, they lay and slept in each other's arms like lovers.

Two weeks later, their friendship deepened by their

new understanding, Selim provided a particularly delicious and lavish meal by moonlight, with fragrantly scented flowers abundant in every room and a multitude of candles burning seductively all around the courtyard. The magnolia tree in the centre was in full bloom and its sensually satiny pink and white froth filled their senses, the rich food and drink making them drowsy. They had eaten their fill, feeding each other titbits with their fingers, and were lying beside the lily pond, dreamily languid in the moonlight. Aisha's head was upon Selim's chest and her hand was beneath his tunic, idly stroking his inert sexuality, tickling beneath the hanging sack and gently threading her fingers through the dark curling bush. It was not a sexual touch, just friendly and affectionate. Although it did not arise for her, she wanted to know every detail of his physique and he hers. His hand was fondly caressing the curve of her rump.

'I have a present for you, Aisha. I hope you like it.' He clapped his hands and before her eyes, from nowhere, it seemed, there stood a creature who could only have been a god. He was unbelievably beautiful. He was draped in only a white silken cloth from his loins to his ankles, and his skin glowed golden and radiant. He was young and supple, his lean, sinewy arms muscled and strong, his smooth chest sculpted in gentle curves and his belly flat and curved into his achingly beautiful, slender hip-bones. His hair was black and waving down to his shoulders and his face was that of an angel, his black eyes almond-shaped and his smiling lips full and shapely in a curving bow.

She gasped at this apparition of virile loveliness, her eyes admiring his every line and her legs suddenly weak and trembling. She felt herself open like a lotus flower in the sun. Selim had stood up and disappeared into the shadows. The young man knelt down in front of her, took her dainty bejewelled fingers in his long, sensitive hands and kissed both palms. She melted at his touch.

177

'I am Malik, your new masseur,' he whispered in a low, mellow baritone. 'Allow me to please you.' She sat upright as he carefully removed her tunic, unwinding her scarf expertly and laying it aside. She stood while he gently lowered her trousers over her hips, unbuttoning the ankles and sweeping the garment to the ground. Then he took her feet in his hands and bent low to run his tongue up the insides of the sensitive arches and, taking each toe singly, sucked them lingeringly one by one and licked searchingly between them with the tip of his agile tongue. The rivulets of sensation trickled up her legs into her pelvis and trailed tentacles of delicious longing through her loins, loosening and dissolving her willing flesh.

She lay back upon the cushions while he filled his palms with perfumed oils and anointed her back and buttocks with a strong, firm touch that filled her corners with delicious hunger. He massaged every muscle, line and curve with careful concentration, focusing his whole attention on her pleasure, sensing which places responded the most and giving more or less pressure whenever her soft moans guided him. He placed his hands between her buttocks, parting them, and gently inserted one oiled finger into the puckered anal rose. She felt the fire blazing within and awakened to his searching touch.

He turned her over and began to enjoy the bounty of her breasts, kissing, sucking, pinching the nipples as they hardened to little stalks, running his long, slender fingers down the sides of her neck, over her breasts, down her small waist to her thighs and then between them, stroking the inner thighs with his fingertips until they ran with moisture. He placed his lips on hers as his fingers furrowed into all her openings and crevices, and when he pressed the hard little bud of her pleasure, she cried out as the shock waves streaked through her emptiness, electrifying nerve-ends she never knew she had, creating an aching deep within. She clutched at him hungrily, eager after months of waiting for the fulfilment she so craved.

He stood up and dropped the lightly draped silk from his hips. She groaned, an animal growl from deep in her throat. His long, solid cock curved hard up against his navel, the circumcised, glabrous head proudly crowning the swollen veins snaking along the dark shaft. She raised her knees and parted her thighs in welcome, open and expansive for this pleasure-god. He lowered himself slowly and deliberately and she sighed as she felt at last the lovely weight of his maleness upon her soft body, his rigidity digging hard into her yielding belly. He lifted his hips to place it against her pulsing node and, using her abundant juices, stroked it back and forth until the darting currents of electricity threatened to blow her fuses. Her mind was blank and filled with nothing but impatient sensuality as she thrust her hips towards this potent delicacy, craving and urgent. She could feel the light touch of his balls like a velvet bag against her buttocks and nearly screamed out her need of him. She completely forgot about Selim, ardently watching the candlelit seduction of his virgin wife from among the shrubbery, his own arousal feverishly in thrall to his creation.

The spongy, engorged dome was now playing inside her inner lips, pushing insistently against the virginal tightness and little by little finding a track into the undiscovered hinterlands. The veil of her virginity broke so quickly and sharply that she barely noticed it in the ravenous, craving ache of her desire. With his lips upon her breasts, moving all over them like butterflies, stoking up her searing fires even hotter, he continued his inexorably slow entry into her clinging softness until he was fully insinuated. Then he relaxed himself upon her and she felt at last his powerful weight within and without. She softened and surrendered, fully open and yielded. He placed his mouth upon hers, seeking with his tongue until she responded, twining her tongue about his and sucking him in as she sucked and clenched with her cunt against the smooth, solid prong. He began to move, sliding easily in and out of her moisture, and she knew herself filled and flooded with release and wild abandon. She thrust back and soon they were tossing and plummeting like ships on a stormy sea, plunging and rearing in unison, while Selim, forgotten and invisible, frantically rubbed himself to ecstatic release in the bushes.

The inferno rose to a crescendo slowly and steadily and when it broke over her, blazing through her loins, down her belly and over her thighs to her fingers and toes, she cried aloud and flew apart, dissolving into molten sensation. It was only after she began to return to herself that she felt his pounding increase and knew the pleasure of his seed squirting forcefully into her as he gave one final lunge hard against her womb and shuddered several times until completely void. He collapsed into a trembling weight upon her and she sighed as she clung to him, sated and satisfied.

After some moments he whispered into her ear, 'You have a gift for pleasure, little one. We will spend much time together and I will teach you to know yourself. We will discover every enjoyment that there is in each other, some you have never dreamed of.'

She stroked his smooth, dark skin and lay back in bliss. There was a barely discernible rustle in the bushes and over his lean golden shoulder she saw her husband step into the moonlight. He smiled, blew her a kiss from the fingertips of both hands, then disappeared into the house. She smiled gratefully in the shadows, her pleasure somehow intensified by knowing that they were being watched, and began to dream of the many-splendoured delights awaiting them both with this perfect young Adonis that he had so lovingly provided.

The next day Selim ordered ornately gilt-framed, two-way mirrors to be installed in every room.

Stage Fright

*I*t was a highly dangerous atmosphere. They were risking a huge public scandal, the loss of all their jobs and, if money was withdrawn, the possible closure of the theatre. But they were so far down the road now and it had all happened so slowly and gradually, that no one was fully awake to the risk.

They couldn't remember exactly when it had begun. Perhaps it was when they were on tour and had started giving points to each other for the Sunday dinners. As they were all staying in self-contained units in the same self-catering flats, they took turns to cook for each other on Sundays, their only day off. Once the competition had begun, the meals had gradually turned into lavish, epicurean affairs with the very best wine and five-course food to die for. Or perhaps it was the orgy which had accidentally occurred some weeks ago at a party and which they were still not freely acknowledging had happened at all. Or perhaps it was the boredom setting in, as they all knew each show so well and had little left to stimulate their creativity. Perhaps it was a combination of all these things, but boredom and over-familiarity certainly contributed.

The company had been rehearsing and performing together with few cast changes for over two years and they knew each other intimately. Because of their unsociable working hours they also partied, relaxed and, in some cases, lived together. Their lifestyle, working six nights a week and all day as well, left them little opportunity to mix with other people.

All four shows in the repertory season had been running now for three months and they needed something new. Once, when they had been on tour, they had actually tried swapping parts and taking each other's lines, just for fun. It had worked quite well, and kept them on their toes for a change, but the director had found out and they'd got a right bollocking. He had called them amateurs and questioned their right to work in a professional environment, which kept them docile for a while. After that, they'd invented a version of 'murders' to play onstage. The 'murderer' was drawn secretly out of a hat. Whoever it was had to catch the eye of someone else onstage and wink at them. Whoever caught the wink had to 'die' in such a way that their fellow actors knew but no one in the audience would notice.

It had been a challenge. There were points given for how many could be 'killed' per performance. It was difficult trying not to catch each other's eye to avoid being winked at and sometimes they got the giggles but eventually they had become good at it and in one performance a very clever 'murderer', taking advantage of his superior position on stage, had managed to 'kill' everyone, their heads dropping subtly to one side as they 'died'.

Being so used to each other and sharing dressing-rooms, and often showers, there was no body-consciousness among them at all. They had a favourite naturist beach where they would camp out for the last two summer holidays, with the kids and all the family, and no one would wear anything on the beach if they chose not to. During a very hot summer one night at a party, someone, no one could remember who, had stripped off in the living room and soon they had all followed suit and the party had proceeded in the nude. One night, they had all run out into the street and sat naked in the middle of the road. No one knew why – just for laughs.

Then the orgy had happened, quite spontaneously. Everyone had been there and for a week afterwards they could not look at each other. Then the giggles had started, and a few days later they began to admit what they could remember and finally, after a week or two, it all came out. Kit said that he had gone into the garden for a pee and when he came back in there was a writhing mass of limbs and bodies on the floor in flagrante delicto, and everybody seemed to be up everybody else. He'd walked around it wondering how he was going to get into it, when someone had grabbed his stiff dick and pulled him in and that was that.

Relationships had begun and ended as a result, one marriage collapsing, and Beth had lost her virginity. She said she didn't know who was first, exactly, but she was glad it was this group of wonderful people, all of whom she considered special friends. It was a one-off, being so accidental and unpremeditated, and could never happen again – but all constraints and inhibitions had been dissolved between them and there was a relaxed and easy sense of familiarity.

And that was what had led to this very dangerous atmosphere. The new onstage game was called 'spot the sex'. The idea was to have sex, which was defined as prolonged contact with the naked genitals, onstage during a performance, and not get noticed. Whoever succeeded got five points, but success had to be corroborated by one other person, presumably the partner. If someone thought they had spotted sex they would wait until everyone was backstage and then name the sex, the participants and the place it had occurred. There was one point for each correct detail and a bonus of two for getting all details correct. However, the same number of points were lost if the details were wrong. Liz already had minus five points. It turned out that no one had started yet.

The first to claim success were Bambi and Thumper. Those were not their real names of course but they were a middle-aged gay couple who bore a tenuously vague resemblance to the originals. They claimed they had mutually masturbated each other in the wardrobe during Act One of the farce. As the wardrobe was on the stage and was opened to reveal to the audience whatever or whoever was inside several times during the show, it was considered to be 'onstage'. It had an exit through the back to the offstage area and Bambi and Thumper had chosen fifteen minutes when it was not in use. No one spotted them so they got five points each.

Bambi said they'd both achieved ejaculation but Thumper said they hadn't, so no one knew for sure, but orgasm was not entirely necessary for points. There was something excitingly erotic about the thought of two naked dicks being pumped to fruition in the wardrobe during the play, and two fountains of semen spraying into the air so close to the public, with the risk of the door flying open at any moment. Everyone was fired up now and imaginations ran wild.

Tanith and Nate were the next. They planned it and rehearsed it in private. They were both fresh out of drama school before joining the company two years ago and were still almost students. The orgy had been the beginning of their relationship and, being young and successful, they were both still full of brash self-assurance. This challenge was too good to miss.

One of the plays was dressed in period costume. Tanith played a whore with a tight, low-cut bodice revealing her rouged nipples and a vast, circular skirt with petticoats beneath. It was so huge that it was held out on a bamboo frame which made it difficult to sit down and going through doors was a crablike exercise. Nate thought he could fit underneath, and with practice, he could shuffle along crouched down inside the frame as she walked. In the courtroom scene, she only came on to the stage to deliver a couple of lines, joined a group of other whores for the remainder of the scene, then eventually exited the same side she had entered.

After some rehearsal they decided to risk it, and Nate positioned himself beneath her skirts when no one was looking. She walked onstage, almost helpless with giggles, controlled herself, delivered her lines, then moved back to join the other whores. She shuffled in between them and stood with her legs apart, knees slightly bent in a t'ai chi position that she could hold for hours. She wore no knickers. Nate's hands were caressing up the inside of her thighs as he got himself into a comfortable position. Her legs tingled at the soft touch and her juices ran moist.

Then suddenly she felt two fingers thrust hard inside her cunt and she gasped. Liz looked at her sharply and she fluttered her fan in front of her face and looked steadily back. Nate's fingers were delving and dabbling and ripples of pleasure coursed around her pelvis. As he thrust inside her wet warmth with two fingers, he explored forward to her hard little nub with his thumb and rubbed it back and forth. She could barely stifle a moan. The glow was spreading around her belly and down her legs and she felt flushed and faint.

Always aware of the audience, she kept her mind on the play and concentrated on staying in control. The harder she tried, the harder it became. Her mind wanted control but her body was being manipulated from elsewhere.

Then Nate did something he had never done before.

Using her own generous lubricating moisture and his other hand, he began to insert one finger gingerly inside her tight anal ring. She was now penetrated in every orifice and her clitoris was still being aroused. Her belly and thighs melted into one another and she prayed fervently that she would not come here on stage with the whole world watching. Liz was looking hard at her again, her eyes narrowed, and Tanith felt the flush begin to rise. Sweat stood out on her upper lip and brow. Her heart was pounding and the hot tidal wave was surging inexorably. She wished Nate would stop but knew he wasn't about to. She bit down on it, willing it away but Nate's fingers were everywhere within her, digging, thrusting, vibrating, pushing and beyond her control. She was dripping wet, sucking and slippery. She fluttered her fan rapidly, praying that the scene would end and she could get off. Then, just as she heard the final speech being delivered, the orgasm broke hotly and violently throughout her and swept her mind into an numbness of sensation as waves of sheer torment blazed deliciously along her nerve-ends. Her legs wobbled, she panted slightly, and Liz looked triumphant. Tanith flapped the fan furiously and, with legs made of jelly, stumbled off the stage as the curtain came down for the interval.

When the others had all vanished, Nate appeared grinning from under her skirts, sniffing his fingers wickedly.

'What gives you the right to stick your finger up my bum?' she hissed.

He was unrepentant. 'I had you by the short and curlies, so to speak, and thought I'd make the most of it. Go on, you really enjoyed that. Your arse and your cunt clutched so strongly around my fingers in those spasms, I thought I'd get stuck in there. Admit it. It was a good one.'

She hit him. 'Go round the back of the stage and down the other side, so they don't see us together.'

She went down the stairs to the dressing room. Liz was watching for her. As Nate appeared from the opposite direction, she jumped up triumphantly.

'I spot sex!' she crowed. Everyone turned to look at her. 'Tanith had sex during the last scene with someone under her skirt and it must have been Nate.'

Everyone turned to look at Tanith.

She blushed. 'Fair cop. Five points to Liz.'

There was a roar of laughter from the others.

'Good for you! What a bloody good idea,' said Jenny admiringly. 'I'd never have thought of that. Did you come?'

'She certainly did,' said Nate shamelessly. 'I thought it was raining.'

There was another roar of laughter and the atmosphere livened considerably.

Later in the dressing room which was shared by the four whores, Jenny said, 'I think we can expand on your idea, Tanith. What say the four of us all manage to do the same thing in the same scene at the same time? I bet they won't spot that.'

Liz grinned widely. 'I'm on. You and I can get Mark and Dave under our skirts. Tanith's got Nate, who knows what he's doing now. What about you, Joan? Are you in?'

Joan was over fifty and they were not at all sure of her approval, but she had been at the orgy, though no one could remember how much of a part she had played. They all looked at her uncertainly. She was powdering her face and did not turn around.

'Oh, I'll find a way. Just let me know when.'

The others grinned conspiratorially.

It took a bit of planning. Mark and Dave were young, single, backstage crew and, although willing and capable, needed to be well rehearsed for such a huge risk. They practised shuffling under the bulky-framed skirts for ages until they felt ready.

Then the day came. It was to be a matinée. They all felt an evening performance was a bit too dangerous for this undertaking. They told Joan and she nodded and said she was ready. They didn't ask the details.

Nate, Mark and Dave positioned themselves under the skirts. The three other whores went on first and Tanith made her own entrance a little later. Then they were standing onstage in a group, the four of them with their tarty, painted faces, carmine-reddened nipples jutting and the swelling mounds of their breasts pushed up over their bodices, and men under their copious skirts. Liz giggled and that got them all going. They shook and trembled with the effort to control themselves. The onstage men were looking at them, wondering what was going on, what they were missing. The skirts were fluttering as the boys positioned themselves.

'Oooh!' squeaked Liz suddenly and pretended to cough. Jenny breathed in sharply with a hiss and her head jerked back. She flapped with her fan. Joan had a concentrated look on her face. Their nipples were tight little rosy stalks. The male characters stared at them suspiciously. Tanith could feel Nate's tongue exploring her swelling moist crevices languidly. She went a little dreamy. She had shown the others how to stand with their legs apart and their knees relaxed for stability and space. In a few moments the four of them were frozen and glassy-eyed with concentration, their bodies focused on the experience of sensuality and cresting pleasure and their faces carefully composed for the audience, revealing nothing but a glazed stare, fans fluttering madly.

Surprisingly, it was Joan who moaned first, just a tiny sound, barely audible. The other actors were all looking very puzzled. The play was proceeding as normal, the audience completely unaware of the sub-text. Then

Jenny's knees collapsed and she staggered slightly against Tanith, recovering quickly. Liz got the giggles again and covered her mouth with her fan, but her skirt was quivering and riffling violently. Tanith could feel the lithe, steady lapping of Nate's tongue as he ran it firmly up her honeyed rift, pushing it into her cunt, digging as deeply as he could, then withdrawing to flick and suck on the swollen, tender bud of her clitoris. He had a finger up her arse again, and she had to admit it increased the lovely sensations by plenty. The tide of climactic pleasure was slow and warm and lingering, coming in long flowing waves this time, just as the curtain came down for the interval.

In the wings, Liz was playfully slapping at Dave and telling him she was supposed to be the one getting sex, not him, and he was grinning and ducking and saying he didn't think it mattered which one of them it was, as long as someone was. They went down singly to the dressing room to find all the others waiting for them silently.

Robert spoke first. 'I'm pretty sure I've spotted sex. I think it was Jenny in the last scene under her skirts. I don't know who with.'

Kit spoke up. 'I spotted sex but I think it was Liz, and I think it must have been with Mark during the last scene, under her skirt, because he's the only stagehand available I can think of.'

'Is that it?' said Tanith, and the girls all roared with laughter.

'I don't know how the hell we're going to score this,' chuckled Liz, 'but you're both right and both wrong. It was all of us. Who gets the points?'

'All of you?' Robert was agog. 'At once?' The thought was clearly exciting. 'Who with?'

'Tanith and Nate again. Jenny and Mark. Me and Dave. And Joan, too, but we're not sure how.'

'I'll show you,' said Joan. She held up the skirt of her

dress. All the layers, skirt and underskirts, had been stitched together but there was a large gap opened up in the side-seam where she could insert her hand easily through the layers and gain access for masturbation beneath the concealing fullness of the material.

'Does it count if you have sex with yourself?' she enquired. They decided that it did and awarded her five points. Tanith and Nate got five each for not being spotted, Robert and Kit got two each and Dave got five for having been completely overlooked and managing an unscheduled wank into the bargain.

The air was now electrically charged. Erotic possibilities were all they could think about and the whole point of every show had become the illicit sex. It did not occur often because it needed ingenuity and careful planning but it occupied all their minds twenty-four hours a day. Those who had not so far been involved began to get a twinkle in their eye, and during performances everyone was alert and attentive to any minor alteration in the action. Several people lost precious points by spotting sex that wasn't there, for they were seeing it everywhere they looked.

Then Robert and Beth pulled off a coup. It was a masterstroke and incredibly daring, albeit unplanned. In fact it left them all a little afraid of what they were doing and things went a bit quiet for a long time afterwards. Robert and Beth had been attracted to each other for some while but had not admitted it to each other, so they had not begun a relationship. They were at that stage when the air was electrified and crackling between them and each felt the sensual magnetism of the other wherever they were. Everyone else just wished they would get on with it but Robert was married. The marriage was on the rocks and it was only a matter of time, but Beth was inexperienced and not at all sure she wanted to get involved. It actually began on stage during a performance, which gave it all the more piquancy because it was real. Having been repressed for so long, it was intense and explosive and not exactly under control.

The farce had two bedrooms on the set, each with a double bed. They were not on the stage level but up the stairs and one floor above on a sort of balcony. While the action was taking place in the living room below on the main stage, the lights were off on the bedrooms above, leaving them in darkness, but the beds were still in view of the audience.

When the lights had gone down on the scene they were playing, Robert and Beth had not left the stage. They had not planned anything to happen but had 'accidentally' bumped into each other in the dark, one going one way and one the other. The accidental nature of this occurrence was questionable for they had been playing this scene for weeks and could both accomplish the exit blindfolded without incident. But there they were, alone on the upper deck; they had fallen into a ravenously desperate first embrace. It was an all-engulfing, grinding kiss that finally exploded upon them in the dark but they were still on the stage. They collapsed together upon the bed, locked in close embrace, tongues deep, legs entwined, and something, perhaps the erotically charged atmosphere, the added stimulation of risk, the agonising restraint they had been imposing on themselves – whatever – something snapped uncontrollably and they began to undress frantically upon the bed. Totally naked, in full view of the public but still in darkness, they had pulled up the duvet cover and coupled wildly in the onstage bed: writhing, thrashing, heaving and pounding furtively but furiously like six ferrets in a sack, forgetful of the next scene shortly due to be played on that very bed.

It had been a full coitus – an explosive, violent, bestial, rampant fuck which had ended in a mutually erupting climax with both parties breathlessy heedless of their surroundings as they surrendered blindly to the hot peaking spikes of their swiftly urgent passion. It was extremely lucky that neither of them cried out, or, if they did, the cries were muffled beneath the covers.

As they subsided quivering and sobbing, they came to themselves with horror and crept hurriedly out of the bed, aware that the lights were due to go on for the next scene at any moment: they gathered what they could find of their discarded costumes and hastily beat a sheepish retreat. When the lights went up, they had only just disappeared into the wings and there were a few odd bits of clothing left on the floor which Kit and Liz managed to sweep under the bed with their feet.

It was Kit and Liz after the play who declared, 'We spotted sex but we're not sure who it was. Someone actually dared to fuck naked on the set during Act Two Scene Three on the prompt-side bed. We know because we found this –' and Liz held up a bra. 'Whose is it?'

'It's mine,' admitted Beth quietly. 'It wasn't meant to happen. We didn't plan it. It was me and Robert. Do we get any points?'

There was a moment's pause while all this information was digested, then Liz conceded, 'Yes, I suppose you do, but don't anybody do anything as risky as that again. That was too bloody close for comfort. The bed was a mess and there were bits left on the floor. We had our job cut out to make things look normal out there.'

There was an abashed silence.

But some weeks later, it started all over again. It was just too good a game to stop. Jenny gave Kit a blow-job during the banquet scene in 'the Scottish play', hiding under the table and taking advantage of his long gown. He sat close to the table and very still while she did all the work, but just as he uncontrollably shot the streams of his ejaculation down her throat they were spotted by Thumper, who had a unique, elevated vantage point that they had forgotten.

Five points to Banquo's ghost.

Open Invitation

*T*he moment I entered the room, I knew there was something going on. I felt the eyes hard upon me, the atmosphere heavy with expectancy, and knew that I had been set up. I quickly assessed how I felt about this and decided to enjoy myself. Where would be the harm, after all? I'm willing to try anything once and I was free to do as I pleased.

He was there, of course, and a fair-haired couple in their thirties, who were introduced as being married to each other, and there was a younger, intelligent-looking, dark-haired girl. They were looking at me intensely and the air was so thick and sticky I could have licked it.

Knowing I was on display, I preened. I had only known him for two months and it was not and was never meant to be a relationship. It was for fun, for play, for sex, and we both understood what we wanted from each other. He was some sort of rock musician, with his own recording studio next door, and this added to his magnetism. Very lean, wiry, tense and taut, he had a surprising amount to offer when undressed and he seemed to be able to keep the playfulness and exploration going for hours, never arriving at orgasm first, which is unique in my experience. I'm not sure whether he ever reached satisfaction completely as he always had a hungry, predatory air, but this was not my business. He didn't invite intimacy.

I knew he had plenty of others and was constantly on the lookout but this didn't bother me because he was always available when I wanted him. He was lust on legs. He had made sexuality an art form and was skilled at creating pleasure, drawing it out, responding to my needs and making me feel special and desirable. I always left physically satisfied. The room itself was designed as a pleasure-den, with large cushions on the floor and a huge blue silk parachute draped across the ceiling. In its voluptuous folds tiny red lights winked and blinked continuously.

But today he had something planned and I knew what it was. Knowing myself the centre of attention, I became flirtatious. I was wearing a light, strapless summer frock with a full skirt and, especially for him, had put on suspenders and stockings. I flopped down on to one of the cushions, allowing my skirt to flounce up and drape above my knees, baring a suspender and showing the top of one stocking. Wriggling seductively into the cushion I manoeuvred the skirt even higher and pretended not to notice that my thigh was exposed. I leaned over to the table for my glass of wine, stretching my torso sensuously and allowing the top of my dress to pull down, revealing cleavage and tightly straining against the contours of my breasts. Arching my back, I tossed my long, blonde hair, and artfully began to regale them with the day's adventures, making a joke of its vicissitudes and laughing brightly. I questioned each of them, making the usual small talk and taking an interest in them. I could feel his eyes questing and knew that he was not quite sure where this was going. Head back to display my long throat and downing my wine in one gulp, I stretched my legs to full length, revealing the suspenders as my skirt rode higher; I sank deeper into the cushion and stretched my arms luxuriously above my head, throwing back my hair.

Finally, the fair girl put down her glass of wine and got up from her seat on the settee.

'I can't stand this any longer,' she said and, kneeling beside my reclining figure on the cushion, placed her hands under my skirt and began to caress the inside of my exposed thigh.

We looked at each other directly and in this moment everyone knew that my permission was granted. They all arose from their seats and knelt on the ground on all sides of me and then there were hands all over everywhere. I relaxed and surrendered myself up to sensation. Closing my eyes, I allowed myself to be caressed from top to toe and no longer knew how many hands were upon me or whose or where.

It was clear that I was only expected to receive so I gave myself entirely to the pleasure of it. I felt the dress being lifted and pulled upwards, so I raised my hips to allow for its removal. Deftly, a hand slipped under my back and slid the zipper down; as I lifted my shoulders, the dress was up over my head and discarded on the floor. I wore no underwear. The stockings and suspenders were left to excite.

Hands stroked up and down my legs through the silkiness, hands stroked my thighs and the thick, curly down of my mound, hands stroked my belly and breasts, my arms, my face, my hair. I spread my legs to allow hands to stroke my moistly soft pubis and floated away on a sensation of touch. There were no edges, no definitions, no inhibitions, no identity. It may have been fingers or a mouth that took my nipples and teased them into erection, pulling on them until it was just deliciously short of painful. It may have been a man or woman, or both, who gently stroked the densely furry folds and swells between my legs until I no longer knew inside from outside. I forgot who and where I was and became pure sensation, pure pleasure, one with the room, one with them, one with the hands, softly, gently, exploring and caressing, delighting and delicious.

Drifting mindlessly, I floated and wafted in a timeless, formless, breathless sensuality, unaware that I was moaning. As I surrendered myself, eyes closed, bathed in touch, no longer sensing my body as separate, I felt a pleasant heaviness covering me and a solidly potent insistence pushing into me. I did not know whose. I did not open my eyes to look. It didn't matter. He entered easily, his hardness sliding smoothly into the ready, silky-smooth, wet warmth. I felt every deep, receptive corner touched and filled, ignited and on fire. Moving slowly, stroking, stroking, sliding, slipping, inside, outside, all the same, no thoughts, no mind, no edges, moving quicker, gaining speed, thrusting, throbbing, invading, deeper, higher, now, oh, now, oh, now, oh, more.

I felt the hot explosion begin from where? Inside? Outside? Everywhere? From toes to crown, from deep within, I felt invaded by the mounting molten flush, cresting slow and easy to breaking point, and abandoned myself utterly as wave after shuddering wave of ecstasy broke over me, drowning me, engulfing me, uplifting me, becoming my entirety.

Dimly, from a distance I heard two voices cry out and then he was exploding inside me: spilling, spurting, pulsing, pumping, emptying his fullness into my depths. On and on and on; it seemed to last an eternity. Then, slowly subsiding and emerging, I began to return to consciousness and felt the fluttering hands withdraw and gently leave as my skin returned and I regained my shape. Grateful, gratified, my eyes still closed, I sank into the cushion with a deep sigh.

After long, empty, satisfied moments, I opened my eyes and looked about me. The dark girl was sitting naked on the settee with her legs on either side of the fair girl, who was kneeling up in front of her, her mouth suckling one low-hanging nipple and her hand caressing the heavy fullness of the other deeply-slung breast. The dark girl's hands were on the blonde's shoulders. He was kneeling tight up behind her, his hips grinding slowly and his hands circling the handsome curves of her smooth buttocks. The husband was sitting on the arm of the settee, watching the girls and rhythmically stroking his own swelling arousal.

Unobtrusively, I got up from the cushion and padded barefoot into the kitchen, quietly closing the door so as not to disturb them. I would like to have been included but did not want to appear too greedy and wasn't quite sure of the proper form regarding group behaviour. I turned on the gas, put the kettle on and lit a cigarette, vaguely regretful that I was missing the experience of breasts. I have always been a big fan of breasts but as a heterosexual woman, have never found a suitable opportunity to enjoy them. As I stood by the bench, smoking, I could hear the muffled moans and murmurs from the next room. Suddenly, it was too much. Stubbing out the cigarette, I opened the kitchen door and looked out. I tried to figure out how I was going to get back in.

The dynamics had changed, and the dark-haired girl was now sitting astride the husband, with her head thrown back and bucking vigorously up and down. The fair girl was concentrating on the pumping she was still receiving from behind as he continued to grind hard and fast against her hips. Her hands were on the seat of the sofa and her breasts were bouncing freely to and fro beneath her.

Seeing my chance, I strode across the room, still in stockings and suspenders, climbed over the back of the sofa and slithered down, spreading my legs and sliding them on either side of the body being ravished from behind. Placing the fair girl's hands on my parted knees,

197

I took both swinging breasts in my hands and pushed them hard together and upwards, squeezing them tight so that I could sink my face into the delicious softness of the deep valley of the cleavage. Turning to one side, I took one large, soft nipple in my mouth and felt it stiffen and lengthen as I sucked. It felt miraculous. I licked all around it with the tip of my tongue, in tiny circles; then I took it between my lips and tongue and pulled on it firmly. The fair girl cried out sharply. Then I moved my mouth to the other breast and erected its nipple in the same manner, at the same time taking the other one between fingers and thumb, teasing and tweaking gently. The girl was moaning softly now.

Out of the corner of my eye, I could see the other couple still rearing and heaving violently and noticed that the girl now had her hand behind herself and underneath him and was gently cupping his bouncing balls in the palm of her hand, and stroking the solid base of the undershaft with her fingers.

Wriggling down even further below the breasts, I reached with one hand under the enthralled, thumping body to the moist fur and, with my index finger, found the hard, swollen button, and beyond that, placed my squeezing fingers around the base of his wet, slippery solidness as he thrust in and out. He groaned. Taking lubricant from around his busy member, I returned my finger to the hungry clitoris and, pressing it firmly, vibrated against it. The fair girl came to climax instantly, with a sudden rush of rapid spasms which brought forth sharp, staccato cries rising to a squealing peak. This had the effect of stimulating the others, and, in a burst of group ecstasy, the room was suddenly filled with joyful shrieks and harsh grunts as they all climaxed together and their four bodies were wracked simultaneously by an orgy of erupting gratification. The air was thick with the reek of cunt-musk and semen and even I was breathing harshly in the overpoweringly erotic atmosphere.

I remained a short while with my face in the becalmed breasts, sucking gently and rhythmically, feeling soothed and unwilling to relinquish the cushioning comfort. Men have all the fun, I thought, and then amended it – well, maybe not quite all, but breasts are a definite bonus. As we all came back to ourselves, we gradually became aware of a shrill whistling which we hadn't noticed while it was mingled with the orgasmic cries, but which now, shrilly alone, sounded rather pathetic.

'Oh, yes.' I chuckled. 'I forgot. Does anyone fancy a cup of tea?'

After the tea, it came to light that this was only the hors d'oeuvre. It had been planned that we would all go out to dinner, returning to the flat later for a resumption of the festivities. My body responded with a tremor to the idea of continuation, and I knew I had become hooked on this form of entertainment. Over dinner we discussed past sessions and teased out the ingredients most desirable for the next. Imaginations went wild, and outrageous ideas caused huge mirth for the physical impossibility of their execution.

It was not long before it was obvious that the combination of wine and erotic conversation was seductively making us all hot again and, now that the ice had been broken, inhibitions were abandoned entirely. We began to caress each other surreptitiously, both over and under the table. I could see both the men squirming and knew that they were already upright and straining. Moistly excited again, I was doubtful of the wisdom in my own case of leaving my underwear at home and, seeing the other girls flushed and bright-eyed, knew that I must also look feverish. I ran my tongue over my lips and could barely resist the temptation to place my hand on my own crotch. Which of the many possible combinations presented would we eventually choose? I wondered, as the options continued to multiply.

Finally, we left the restaurant, stimulated and ravenous for sex, and once inside the flat wasted no time in removing extraneous clothing and eagerly sharing our nakedness without hesitation. The blatancy of it increased the hot anticipation and it was not long before hands and tongues and probing members were once again hungrily reaching for everything within their grasp. The fair girl and I were in tandem sixty-nine, she kneeling above; we were sucking each other's nipples with enthusiasm and lavishly licking all over each other's breasts, while the dark girl and the husband were behind us respectively, licking our cunts and stimulating them with deeply probing tongues, encouraging up the swelling buds of our clits and the lubricant moisture. My man was hard up behind the fair girl's husband, his hands gently stroking the stiff cock and the soft dangling balls.

We all responded to a common rhythm, changing places now and then and swapping tongues for fingers or organs until it was impossible to know any longer who was doing what to whom. All inhibitions dissolved; I yielded to the liberation of total absorption in sensuality. As I was wallowing in the malleable softness of someone else's breasts, a cock presented itself before my face, so I took it willingly in my mouth. As it pumped back and forth, my vulva was being attended to by a lapping tongue, gliding along my sucking slit and stimulating searing waves of pleasure. Rough hands massaged my bouncing breasts, and someone nibbled my exposed, suntanned buttock.

Relieved of the migrating cock, I took a large handful of pliant breast and guided the tightly budding nipple into my mouth. With my face buried in deliciously suffocating breast-mounds, I felt fingers delving into my wet crevices, probing, dabbling and pulsating. I thrust back at them, my pelvis awash with rising hunger which was lingering and dallying in the certainty of eventual satisfaction.

The pleading cock was back in my face, or perhaps it was another one. I circled the dome with my tongue before engulfing it completely, tasty the salty-sweet juices of the hot-box it had just been in. The deeply digging fingers were driving into me harder and faster and the atmosphere was erotically charged with urgency. The pumping piston in my mouth grew harder and angrier.

Then, following another sudden shift of positions, there was pussy in my face. Blindly, I sought out the little node and sucked it, feeling the furry bush damp and musky against my nose. I was almost fainting with lust and carelessly dug my fingernails hard into her smooth thighs. A large, solid greedy root thumped into me, replacing the fingers and filling me, and I wrapped my legs tightly around his narrow hips and thrust back violently, meanwhile pressing my tongue hard against the rhythmically grinding cunt in my face. My senses were obliterated by the rising, expanding arousal.

My edges disappeared again in thrall to the all-encompassing sensuality and the group blended and disappeared into a single unit and a single sensation as the long, unifying, mounting heat of the climax became more and more intense, the rhythm gaining urgency, and all separate identities dissolved into the oneness. It was void, it was oblivion, it was vanishing, it was unity beyond imagination, and as the inevitable burgeoning, engulfing, exploding ecstasy of the climax swept us up and over, we all cried out as one, and darkness took hold, carrying us beyond consciousness as the whole group blacked out together. My body blew apart, but there was a brief moment of nothingness in which we harmonised and I knew them all intimately and in detail, a moment I will never be able to forget. Then, very gradually, uncomfortably, the room began to return and I came back to my separate self.

'God Almighty!' I dimly heard a man's voice say from a far distance. 'What the hell happened to us there?'

We sat for some time with our arms around each other, slowly getting our breath back and reclaiming our individual identities. We all instinctively knew that we could never repeat this, so we quietly, silently savoured the moment together before saying goodnight.

We will never see each other again. There's no point. This was somehow ultimate.

Blood Relations

*H*e drifted aimlessly about the hospital wards with no particular intent, just exercising his insatiable curiosity. He spent most of his time here now and knew the place as well as most people know their own homes, closely following the rhythms of the shift changes and familiar with the names of each member of staff and their personal idiosyncrasies. He knew the ailments and treatments of every patient in every bed and was astounded by the huge range and variety of humanity that congregated here.

His special fascination was the tiny babies in the labour ward. The creation of a new life never ceased to amaze him and fill him with envy and a hungry, aching sense of loss. Tonight he was interested in the patient who had recently been admitted to gynaecology. There was something different about her, something lighter and more ethereal. She was suffering from acute anaemia and had been put on a transfusion drip, and this he could identify with, bearing some similarity to his own situation. Also, he suspected that of all those who came and went she, along with a very few others that he carefully avoided, might be able to communicate with him.

Generally, people couldn't. He was invisible and anonymous, although always there among them. He had a name, a sort of a name, but it was not like most names and did not translate easily into English. It was more of a description and not so much a label the way names tended to be these days. It was a sound, or a collection of sounds that would perhaps seem rather like a series of musical notes to most ears, and it meant something like 'the lonely one who travels between the spheres'. Having no translation for it, he thought of himself as Skydancer.

He appeared beside the bed where she was lying, only semi-conscious after a general anaesthetic, and his breath caught in his throat. With her eyes closed and her blonde, dishevelled hair framing her serene face with its pale, translucent skin, she was quite the loveliest thing he had ever seen. Her long graceful limbs barely defined the bedclothes, appearing weightless, and she was so completely still that he wondered if she were truly human at all or whether she was in reality a misplaced angel. As if in confirmation, he felt the light touch of mind as her consciousness wafted loosely outside of her, temporarily disconnected from her bruised body by the anaesthetic and the pain, and the touch of it was like fairy gossamer.

His heart turned over. This waking state was the most dangerous time for him and he knew it would not last, but he suspected that she had the gift, even when fully conscious, and was never entirely engrossed in her earthly body. He gazed at her, entranced, for a brief moment, afraid she might notice him, then turned quickly before she could and fled back along the corridor to a private room where he could recover his composure. This racing of his heart and quickening of his senses had never happened before and he did not know how to assess it. His very peculiar circumstances did not allow for this.

* * *

enata's mind was not in her body at all, leaving it to
eal by itself from the battering it had suffered during
ne operation, her awareness blessedly released by the
naesthetic to a blissful dimension of no thoughts or
elings, and no sharp edges. She was used to this from
ears of meditation and had found that she preferred
nis state to the real world, but had disciplined herself
) operate effectively within both. Today it helped.
ided by the anaesthetic, it was a welcome relief not to
ave to experience the physical discomfort and to be
ple to drift pleasantly in this twilight world of peace
nd dreaming and otherness.

She was sure she had felt the presence of another, but
as unable to focus her attention sufficiently to ascertain
ne exact nature of it. It had felt like a male presence,
ut gentle and wistful with a strange hint of sorrow. For
brief second she had felt a tender, loving compassion
hich was quite beautiful, but then she had drifted back
to unconsciousness and when she awoke in the morn-
ng it seemed more like a dream, the details fragmented
nd meaningless. The sensation of being cared for was
ill powerful, however, and did not fade, so she made a
ental note to chase it in meditation when she was
rong enough to concentrate properly.

It was two days later before she made the effort and
e was not far away. He felt the pull as she reached out
find him and was completely unable to resist. His
uriosity had always been stronger than his will and she
with her tall, elegant, graceful beauty, so like his own
was a magnet to him. His mind had not been far from
er the whole of the two days and he was with her in
n instant. She felt him arrive and smiled softly, her eyes
osed in concentration and he paused in astonished
ve. He was nakedly visible to her and her own pres-
nce glowed with a pure radiance that felt like
nchantment.

'You can see me!' he spluttered.

'Yes, of course I can see you. Who are you? Why a
you here?'

'I shouldn't have let you see me! You shouldn't
talking to me! This is not supposed to happen! I've be
here for years and no one has ever seen me. I've ma
sure of that. I don't want to hurt anybody. This pla
was perfect but now I mustn't stay.'

'Why ever not? I don't want to upset you. Tell n
who you are and why you're here. No one else will ev
need to know. You're not a spirit, are you? You're no
ghost and you're not an angel. What are you? You'
very beautiful.'

'You won't like it. You have a nasty name for us ar
we have a horrific reputation but it is not accurate. I
based on fear and misperception. I don't want you to
afraid of me.'

'I'm not afraid of you. Your presence is delicate ar
gentle. I know you mean no harm, but what makes yo
so sad?'

'My envy.'

'Envy? What of?'

'Your life. Your feelings. Your emotions ar
sensations.'

'I don't understand.'

'I am a kind of spirit but I'm not dead and I dor
truly belong here. I belong in a different dimension qui
unlike your planet. The best I can describe it is betwe
worlds. We are called the "undead" but that is n
correct. We are the "unborn". I have never had a bo
like yours and never will, so the only way I can expe
ence emotions or feelings or sensations is to "borrov
the life from within a body like yours. That allows me
become a little more substantial, so that I can feel as yo
feel and have emotional experiences, but if I stop "bo
rowing" I return to the insubstantial, spiritual real
where there is only consciousness and mind. My appea
ance is created by my thoughts and has no substan

206

ithout the regular input of life-force. Until recently, the
ıly way we could do that was by taking blood from a
ving body, with their consent, of course, but now with
ıe technology of blood transfusion we have an alterna-
ve. Most of us stay close to a blood bank or a hospital
ıd it has been a great relief to us to be able to keep out
sight and escape that dreadful reputation that your
ar has created around us.'

'You're a vampire?'

'I hate that word. My only crime is my envy. I cannot
born but I crave your feelings. Without blood I can't
ve any.'

The wave of sorrow and grief that radiated from him
oke into her consciousness with a blast like an icy
ind and Renata shivered uncontrollably.

'I'm sorry.' Aware of her as she was of him, he was
stantly remorseful. Concern and a tender wave of
mpassion followed equally powerfully. 'I had forgot-
n that you can receive me so clearly. My feelings are
o powerful for you. I must try to control them so that
ou don't get overwhelmed.'

Renata's heart broke within her and the tears flowed
om under her closed eyelids. 'You must be so lonely.'

'Lonely? Yes, I suppose I am. I hadn't thought about
' As soon as he spoke he realised that this conversation
ıd companionship was the most stimulating and invig-
ating experience he had ever known and his gratitude
ıd joy upon realisation sent another tidal wave of
notion flooding through Renata, which filled her with
armth and pleasure. Her heart began to pound and
r breath quickened and with their acute mutual telep-
hy he received it back to himself. In loving silence they
lowed the sensation of communion to expand and
ower within them, dissolving them both into an ecstatic
ate of shared soul. The billowing clouds of colour
afted and flowed around them in a kaleidoscope of
ear blue-pink-mauve-sapphire-indigo-magenta-crystal

light and bathed them with a shimmering butterf
softness, falling and flying slowly through time ar
space beyond self to eternity.

He broke away suddenly and left her with a shar
cold, brutal separation. 'No!' he cried. 'You belong her
We can't do this!'

Disconnecting himself from her, he fled back dow
the corridor and withdrew his mind completely, leavir
her bereft. Renata came to herself with tears streamir
down her cheeks and her body on fire with unsatisfie
desire and hunger for his touch. She was both gratef
and grief-stricken. The beauty and purity of that unic
was all she had ever dreamed of, always knowing in h
heart that it was possible, and now finding it only
lose it.

He did not come to her again, no matter how desperate
she called to him, and when she finally left the hospit
it was with a deep sense of bereavement and loss. On
at home, she was forced to rest and had to rema
inactive for several weeks. She spent many hours
meditation and her heart sought him every minute.

He was hiding, trying not to listen to his own heart b
unable to stop replenishing himself from the blood bar
because even this passion and pain was better than r
feeling at all and he could no longer resist the insiste
craving to be alive, with feelings, even these. He agor
sed with his conscience for he knew there was a way f
them to be together but at great cost, and that cc
would be hers. He had made his sacrifice long ag
leaving the realms of spirit, where there was only perfe
bliss, for this crazy hotch-potch of sensations. He kne
what it would cost Renata and would not ask it of h
This was the measure of his love.

He could feel her calling him, and with the fine
tuned nature of their connection he could feel her hea

reaking as much as he could his own. Gradually his
esistance was weakened until he knew he was no longer
nable to live without satisfying this aching desire. He
ent several days filling himself from the blood bank,
ausing some consternation among the staff when
lasma bags were found mysteriously empty, but he
eeded to be fully substantial before he approached her
ith his offer.

Veeks went by, and Renata recovered her health and
itality, apart from the sorrow that deadened her heart
id drained her spirits. It was now more from habit
ian belief that she reached for him in her meditations
ut although her mind was resigned to the loss, her
eart and body were not and it was on the wavelength
f this love that he found her, flying through the open
indow and alighting beside her bed. She greeted him
ith such rapture that he wept for the joy of it.

They clung to each other, embracing into a deep kiss
lled with passion and urgency. Their tall, lithe, willowy
odies, both pale and smooth and long-limbed, twined
ngingly about each other and drew sustenance greed-
y. Their tongues explored searchingly and their hands
ught and caressed with quivering desire. The loosely
raped clothing seemed to fall away of itself and their
akedness glowed with a softly vibrating sheen, his
palescent darkness inversely mirroring her radiant fair-
ess. He traced the contours of her neatly rounded
reasts with wonder, cupping the gentle curves with his
ensitive fingers and placing his lips around the hard-
ned, tight nipple, he licked and sucked lingeringly,
arvelling and wallowing in the newly awakened sen-
uality and tingling pleasure of touch. Sensations rippled
id pulsed like rivers between them and hot hunger
azed across the melding flesh, sending flames of lust
oursing and sparking with such intensity they could
arcely breathe.

With an anguished cry, he pushed her away from him, gulping for air with a sob from deep in his belly. She clutched at him as if she were drowning.

'There is a price to pay for this!' he gasped. 'You have to know the consequences. For full union I must take a little of your life-force. I cannot make love to you without it. But I will not take your life nor make you ill, and you will not become like me, I promise you. I will never hurt you. But neither can you remain as you are. And there is more.'

'I don't care what I have to do to be with you. Never leave me again. Please. What must I do?'

'You will become a creature of two worlds. You will not belong fully in either but with each drop I take from you, you will become closer connected to my dimension. Your body will behave as a normal human body and will age and die normally but you will be unable to relate to it properly for your mind will be pulled by another sphere of being, a different kind of consciousness. It will be very painful for you.'

Renata laughed. 'Is that all? Don't you know it has always been like that for me? I don't really feel at home here anyway. Being somewhere else most of the time would be a blessing, not a curse. And I'll be with you. Just promise me I'll always be with you.'

He knelt before her, his head against her belly, and wept like a baby. She stroked his dark hair and he ardently began to kiss the creamy-smooth flesh of her navel, lingering in the curves of the hip-bones. She raised him up and guided him to the bed and together they fell upon it, entangled in close embrace. He lifted her thick blonde hair away from her face and she stretched her long, milky-white neck towards him, her eyes alight with love and desire.

He looked into them intently for some moments and reading there only willingness and surrender, sank with a long, guttural moan upon the tender valley at the base

f her throat. Two needle-points emerged from his eye-
eeth and, as he pierced her flesh, a sharp spark flashed
deep into her cunt with a hot current of undeniable lust.
As he drank from her, pulling the skin tight across her
throat and constricting her breath, his erection sprang
hard and swift between her thighs and drove fiercely
into her like a knife. Wet, tight and achingly hollow, she
drew him inside her, then drove back vigorously against
the penetrating spike. As his mouth sucked and guzzled
at her life-blood, her cunt sucked and clutched at his
thrusting phallus and locked close. They plunged and
pounded wildly, their hands seeking out the curves of
breasts, buttocks and thighs and the thudding hips
crashing hard, driving deep. The constriction across her
throat and the taste of her blood in his mouth brought
them both quickly to a climax that took them straight
through the roof. Renata did not know where they were
but it was nowhere she had ever been before. The
midnight-blue sky was shot with starlight sparkling and
twinkling like Guy Fawkes' night, and he was there with
her, flying freely through the exploding sky, laughing
and crying and blending in the expanded space, their
arching bodies thralled in the grip of the peaking
spasms. Thick streams of his seed shot deep into her as
her warm red blood trickled down his throat, sending
fiery spirals of gratification orgasming throughout them
both again and again, until they collapsed upon each
other, exhausted and utterly spent.

Mentally they remained entwined, drifting among the
clouds and the ethereal sounds and colours of another
world, in bliss and unmindful of the consequences. Their
bodies slept while they flew through the night, touching
the minds and thoughts of other lighter beings, wafted
by angel wings and permeated with the glory of a
heavenly loveliness which does not normally belong to
mortals.

Tomorrow he would care. Tomorrow he would try to

teach her to live in both worlds. It would be hard for he
not to want to remain in his all the time and even harde
to convince others that she was not going mad, but the
would think about that tomorrow. Today was for love
The happy sound of their laughter rang through th
astral spheres, sending ripples of joy straight to the hear
of God.

Turkish Delight

Phyllida, known to her friends as Philly, was twenty-seven and had never had an orgasm – at least, not with someone else, in spite of three long-term affairs, all of which were now two years in the past. In utter despair and frustration during the two-year drought, she had bought herself a sex manual for women and had discovered from that how to stimulate and satisfy herself. It had taken a long time the first time and had not amounted to much but it had been an enormously significant triumph. Up until then, she had thought there might be something anatomically or medically wrong with her and it was a great relief – without much pleasure, so far – to find that all was as it should be. And she had got better at it, but she knew there was more to it than this.

She had also discovered from the manual practices and pleasures that she had scarcely dared to dream of, with weird and preposterous names like 'fellatio' and 'cunnilingus', which terms evoked a sensuality all of their own. Now that she knew that they were normal human activities that almost the whole world except herself seemed to indulge in, she was aching for the opportunity to explore them for herself. Technically and theoretically, she was an expert. The book had explained the use of the tongue to twine and flick and suck and tease, and how to avoid the danger of teeth by the agile use of her mouth. She knew there should be a lip, a tiny slit-eye, a seam and an undershaft which responded mightily to the touch and timely pressure of fingers, but had still to venture into such mysteries in practice. She now knew that she had something called a clitoris and had found her own, although nobody else ever had, and she had explored enough with a mirror among the folds and swellings and moist crevices of her own body to know what pleased her. She had found her sex-spot with a sense of accomplishment and felt nothing but smug derision for those anatomists who said there was no such thing as a vaginal orgasm. Her experiments with the vibrator had put the lie to that. But it was not the same and she just knew she was missing something significant.

The first of her lovers, whom she had lived with for some years, she now thought of as 'the wanker'. He was a nervously anxious, guilt-ridden and neurotic man who had had to have sex compulsively every single day, becoming morose and moody if she ever declined. With a cursory suck on a nipple to arouse himself, he would then push straight into her and come almost instantly. Fairly soon, she had given up hoping and just lay there passively. That was their sex life, but she continued to endure it because she still thought then that love was more important than sex. It would be many years before she realised that she hadn't actually loved him at all.

Her second lover, with whom she never lived but saw regularly for two or three years, she had termed 'the monk'. He never allowed her to touch him at all unless he wanted sex, which was no more than once every two or three weeks. Then he would fondle her breasts with vigour, allow her to kiss him wherever she pleased

bove the waist and feel his cock with her hand until it
vas ready, when he would enter her with no further
reamble and stroke away for ages in a steady, monoto-
ious, regular rhythm with no ardour or passion
nvolved until he stopped suddenly with a little grunt.
he presumed he ejaculated, for she had to deal with the
nessy results, but neither of them seemed to notice it
nuch as there was no change of tempo or temperature.

Her third lover, who had come and gone from her life
qually rapidly, she thought of as 'the animal'. He liked
iolent, wham-bam, non-relational sex with no finesse,
o foreplay and no emotional involvement. He usually
ook her from behind very roughly or with her legs over
is shoulders, pounding hard and fast until he shot his
oad, and was then quite finished and no longer inter-
sted. He never stayed the night. At first she had been
ttracted by his lustiness and ardour, because he had
eemed so different from the others, but had soon recog-
ised the similarities. That affair had ended swiftly
vhen, on one occasion in his blind self-serving way,
nistaking one entrance for another, he had attempted to
enetrate brutally where there was too much tightness
nd no lubrication, which had caused her pain and she
ad objected. It had seemed to make no difference to
im whatsoever. One orifice was much the same as
nother. She decided on the spot that she would never
ntertain him again and had not.

She had become very wary and nervous of her
nability to choose a satisfactory lover. She wasn't even
ure that there was such a thing, although other women
eemed to find fulfilment. She blamed herself for this
ailure and for the insensitivity of her partners, suppos-
ng there was something wrong with her and never
hinking for one moment that the fault might not be
ers, or that she, quite simply, might just be in the
vrong country.

Philly had never been abroad, so when her friend Di

suggested that they spend two weeks in southern Tur
key, she became greatly overexcited. She depended on
Di to tell her what clothes to take, as she had no idea
how hot a hot country became or what sort of dress was
demanded by what occasions. In the end, she bought it
all new: bikinis, a couple of summer dresses, a wrapa
round skirt, shorts, lightweight tops and one warm
jumper in case of coolish nights, when, according to Di
they were unlikely to be in bed – at least, not their own.

On the way from the airport to the tiny coastal village
they had chosen as their base, her eyes were out on
stalks. The colours seemed so vibrant and the heat
shimmered. And how could she fail to notice the preva
lent public presence of men? There were men every
where and they all looked gorgeous. They were not tall
on average, but dark, virile-looking, neatly square with
dark eyes, dark skin and thick, wavy, coal-black hair
They had clean-lined features with full, defined mouths
clear eyes and strong jaws. They lounged, as if time was
all they had, and their direct gaze was disturbing and
arousing. They looked hungry and available. The aura
of masculinity on every street corner was enough to
dampen her knickers. Her heart began to pound and she
suddenly became excited by the possibilities; every eye
seemed to undress her and linger over her contours. She
preened, flirted and displayed herself.

She loved the heat. She loved the sun and she loved
the turquoise sea. But she could not take her eyes off the
men, nor they off her, it seemed. She was very fair and
tall, unlike the local women, and with a European air of
self-assurance. They followed her like a bitch in heat
Even Di noticed and joked about it. Di was looking a
little sparkly-eyed herself.

After they had unpacked, got settled, explored the
shops and wandered along the beach, they settled in a
charmingly open-air restaurant covered in grapevines
and surrounded with fig trees. The waiters swarmed like

bees in a hive. Nothing was too much trouble. They struck up conversation with several of the waiters and two German girls sitting at the next table, and later that evening all four were taken upstairs to a delightful mezzanine balcony room above the restaurant, with kilims on the wooden floor, pottery vases, and in the tiny arched window overlooking the stone harbour, a tall brass coffee pot. The only seating was huge, soft, tapestried cushions on the floor. The waiters kept bringing up bottles of wine and would sit and have a cigarette and a drink with them whenever they had a few minutes. The music was loud and cheerful and people were dancing on the stone-paved floor below. The atmosphere was energetic, jolly and convivial. The waiters were lovely boys, gentle and attentive, with plenty to say for themselves and a ready joke.

Much later – much, much later – several bottles later, she was lying on the cushions in a pleasantly lethargic stupor as were the others, the crowds had thinned and the boys were with them, when the lights quite suddenly went out. It was pitch dark, not a glimmer of light, save the reflection of the crescent moon on the sea shining up through the tiny window.

One of the boys said, 'Oh, shit. Hold on a moment. Don't go away.'

They all laughed. No one could see the nose in front of their own face, let alone the stairs. Then there was silence as they sat and waited. Presently, she could hear whisperings and faint rustlings, and the slither of something moving across the floor. Without warning, she felt a silky-smooth, hard rod of flesh slide up between her slightly parted thighs and a soft voice whispered, 'Would you like a present?'

Somewhat light-headed from the drink and the atmosphere, she thought that might be a nice idea, so she parted her thighs wider. A pleasantly heavy male presence with a lightly perfumed whiff of Paco Rabanne drew near and the smoothly rigid pole continued its journey up between her thighs until it met her panties. She held them aside to allow it access, her crotch already wet and liquid with desire. She felt a soft and searching mouth upon hers and a tender hand folded itself over her breast. She had absolutely no idea which of the boys this was. They were all sweet and very attractive. The bulbous nosing dome found its way past her knickers and pushed gently at her soft, swollen cunt-lips. The seeking mouth was still drawing sensation from her mouth and a probing tongue was calling up a deeper craving which connected itself to her pelvis in trickling rivulets of warm arousal. This was new. It felt like he cared whether or not she wanted this. He was not just taking for himself without her response. She softened and her legs parted wide, her hand still holding aside her knickers, feeling with her fingers the lovely, lusting, thrusting shaft with the silky skin and the furred, dangling balls tickling her buttocks.

Using the generous lubricant of her own flowing juices to slide its way up and down the greasy furrow, nosing into the hard, excited nodule that had always until now been ignored, the engorged cock sought out her response patiently. The trickling rivulets turned to fiery waves and she began to thrust her hips against him, aching for his fullness to enter her void. Her hopes were high. These molten, pulsing sensations had never occurred before. Cautiously but insistently, the anonymous gift was inserted and eased deep within her. Then they were moving together in a gathering rhythm, hips thrusting at first slowly, then quicker and quicker, synchronised. She could hear other rhythmic sounds and soft moaning in the dark, which inflamed her all the more. Her climax was growing and she knew that finally, this was going to be the fulfilment of all her longing. She sighed and yielded.

Then a voice from below called, 'I've found it. It was a fuse. Lights coming on.'

The lovely full sensation suddenly withdrew, leaving her gasping and brutally void. Her skirt was swiftly pulled down and a second later, when the lights came on, she could not tell who it was that had been inside her. But she was bitterly frustrated and her heart was still pounding fit to burst.

The next day, after self-relief and a good, long swim, she felt grateful, because she knew now for certain that a delicious satisfaction was possible and she felt hopeful that it would probably occur here in the sun with one of these sensually alive and pleasure-awakened young Turks. Apparently, Di had had a similar experience in the dark, and they giggled wickedly at what they were planning for the next two weeks.

That night, she and Di were taken to a different bar by the German girls, where there was live music. The singer was a folk-guitarist who looked like he'd been left there in the seventies. Although he was young, his hair was a wild, tousled mop bleached by the sun. His eyes were a dreamy nutmeg brown. He was tall and lean and loose, and wore only a pair of long swim-shorts with an elasticated waistband. He had fair hair curling across his chest and seemed oblivious to all save the music.

She was smitten immediately by his aura of coiled tension, and sat close to him, listening avidly to everything he sang and joining in the tunes she knew with a lyrical harmony. He bent towards her when they sang together and they spent an hour in a gentle communion of music and wine.

Eventually, he put down the guitar and taped music was turned on for the dancing. He remained languid, laying his head in her lap and smoking while she played her fingers through his unruly curls. His hand caressed the inside of her thigh up under her skirt as if it was a familiar place, undemanding and somehow natural. She mused on how nothing seemed outrageous or unacceptable in this place. The way things happened felt easy and right. Everybody was part of everybody and she relaxed to his touch, the soft, sensitive skin responding with tingles and thrills to the delicately stroking fingers.

After a while he sat up and lifted her up so that she sat in his lap, facing forwards, her back against his bare chest. She could feel the hardness of his erection beneath her and was immediately aroused, releasing moisture. Her cunt throbbed, still hungry from its rude denial of the previous night. She had decided after that experience not to wear any underwear, so when he positioned her skirt discreetly over his knees and subtly lowered his waistband beneath its cover, freeing his naked, striving erection underneath her thighs and inserted himself into her from below, jiggling his hips to achieve full penetration, she was ready for him. In the dim light, with the music playing, although they were surrounded by people, if they were careful, no one would know. She jiggled back, pushing down hard, and together they eased and wriggled and bounced in time to the music until he was fully enclosed inside her slippery and aching tunnel, invisible to anyone who might be looking. She tightened her muscles around him and her pleading moan was drowned by the music.

Careful to stay in time to the beat, and giving nothing away with their faces, they bounced up and down gently and steadily and she felt the circles of fever flush out from her core and ripple out to her fingers and toes in expanding waves of mounting hunger. There was nothing like the thick, fat length of a good solid cock to fill your emptiness and she thought she could never get enough. The position they were sitting in was hitting her clitoris square on and she rocked forwards into it to increase the gathering waves of her climax.

They could not speed up, for fear of exposure, so they jiggled and bounced and moaned gently and quietly, as if carried away by the music. Just as she was about to surrender to the swell of her first orgasm, he gave one sudden jerk, followed by a couple of smaller ones and began to subside and soften.

Oh, no, she thought in despair. Is this ever going to happen?

She lifted herself from his lap, kissed him gently on the mouth and left the bar for a midnight swim.

The following day, she and Di hired a boat with two of the waiters from the first night. They were free for the whole day. Murat was energetic and boisterously in charge and Hakan was quieter, more thoughtful and more thorough. She thought Hakan probably achieved more, although he kept it to himself. Murat was flirting with Di, trying to display his virility to effect. Hakan was silent and reserved but attentive, watchful and competent. He took the rudder while Murat helped them into the boat. It was quite a big boat, able to take about ten tourists, with a blue covering for shade over the top, and the four of them had it to themselves. Murat and Di sat in the bows in the full sunlight while she and Hakan sat at the back.

The moment she sat next to him, she caught the faint whiff of Paco Rabanne and knew that it had been he on her first night in the dark. She was glad. He was gentle and unassuming. She looked at him more closely and was pleased with what she saw. There was more than a passing resemblance to James Dean, with his luxuriantly glossy thick quiff of hair which was blue-black and his unusual clear, grey-green eyes, framed dramatically and heart-breakingly with dark black lashes. His mouth was full, firm, defined and sensual and his body, though not tall, was nicely proportioned, tidy, strong and spare. He wore only blue denim shorts cut off at the knee and frayed at the edges, with open leather sandals. His chest, legs and forearms were very lightly covered with fine black hair and she noticed that he was exceptionally efficient in his movements, gaining the most result with the least effort. This indicated an intelligent ability to weigh up the circumstances and think ahead. She was impressed. He was capable but without arrogance. Remembering that first night and its rudely interrupted promise, she felt her legs give way and her bikini bottoms dampen with a rush of moisture. Her nipples erected and jutted through the thin cloth. In the bows, Di had removed her bikini top and was sunbathing in only the bottoms. She and Murat were caressing each other mutually with their hands, in personal places, and it was clear that they were not intending to be shy of company.

Hakan took them to a nearby bay which was enclosed and secluded with a lovely deserted, white-sand beach, away from the crowds, where there was no access by road, and they anchored, bobbing gently in the lazy sea, some way out from the beach. Murat was lying on top of Di and they were writhing about oblivious of company, pleasing only themselves. The sight was arousing the already frustrated and desperate Philly and she glanced sideways to see what effect it was having on Hakan. There was a serious bulge in his denims and he did not look comfortable. As he was no longer responsible for the rudder, his hands were free and he seemed not to know what to do with himself. He was looking at the floor of the boat.

'Hakan.'

Without raising his head, he looked up shyly at her from underneath his dark lashes and the pleading puppy-doggedness in his startling grey-green eyes nearly stopped her heart. Slowly and deliberately, she removed her bikini top and stood with her proud, firm breasts and the tightly stiffened nipples thrust towards him. He continued to gaze silently with his forlornly hopeful, gentle eyes. The bulge was solidifying in his lap, stirring and straining for release. She leaned down and unzipped him.

Freed of its restraints, his cock sprang sharply alert and jerked upright, lurching eagerly towards her. She stared, fascinated. He was circumcised. Then she remembered that, of course, all the men in this culture would be circumcised, and her pussy clenched tightly with a spasm of delight. She could see the shape of the glabrously spongy, shiny helmet fully revealed and unsheathed, with all the livid veins snaking down the rock-solid spike. He seemed to be longer than average, disproportionate with his height, and his organ, curving up beyond his tanned belly button, was dark and powerful. He reminded her of the satyr Priapus.

Her legs dissolved and threatened to give way. A spasm of pure lust gripped her pelvis and her loins melted in a greedy hunger that threatened to engulf her and turn her into a wildly ravenous beast. Her cunt remembered the thwarted pleasure of the last two nights and she was reminded that he, too, had been rudely interrupted mid-coitus. She also remembered how considerately he had drawn down her skirt before withdrawing and a tenderness for him seized her. He was still hesitant, unwilling to take her for granted to satisfy his own needs alone, and waiting for her to take the initiative.

Down at the other end of the boat, Di's head had disappeared between Murat's legs and there was much moaning and groaning. They were in a separate world of their own pleasure and mindless of company. She took permission from their licentiousness and was determined at last to take all the time she needed. She knew Hakan would grant whatever she wished and would not rush her. The knowledge of time without limit relaxed her and she knew her moment had come. She knelt and took the silky-skinned, striving shaft in her mouth and ran her tongue around its infused knob, feeling out the edges of the dome and flicking lightly with the tip up and down the seam running down the front. It jumped, and she felt encouraged. With her hand clasped around the base, she pulled her lips over her teeth and ran them firmly up and down, and was gratified when he retracted his pelvis and pushed himself into her mouth. She sucked harder and he thrust himself deeper into her mouth to touch the back of her throat, forcing her to readjust or choke. She wound her tongue – in accordance with the manual – lithely and strongly around the full length and girth of him and a groan issued from deep in his chest. She held herself tightly around him with her cheeks while he pulled and pushed in and out of her virginal mouth. She drooled saliva wetly down into his pubic hair, cupping his balls with her hand to feel them swing, digging with her fingers underneath where the muscle was rooted, and hearing the slurpy sounds of herself sucking upon him.

As she felt his desire begin to increase, he gently removed himself.

'Your turn,' he whispered.

She quivered. She'd never had a turn before. He untied the strings on her bikini and it fell to the floor, revealing her blonde, curling bush, coyly concealing its bold invitation. His fingers probed beneath to locate the nodule that was swollen and pulsing.

'Oh, how ready you are,' he sighed. 'How swollen and wet and excited.'

She almost swooned. It was overwhelming to be appreciated. She was not used to even being noticed. He began to massage in tiny circles, teasing up the currents of desire that dissolved her edges and blew her inhibitions to dust. He delved with two fingers inside her wetly clutching cavity, digging and vibrating, and she yielded in a mist of melting sensuality and gave way to the unleashed beast within.

With her back against the back of the boat and her

feet planted up on the little seat to support herself, legs shamelessly wide apart, she opened herself and her cunt to him, wet, throbbing, and aching for his solid cock inside her. Standing on the seat, knees bent, he drove himself upwards into her slippery, clinging warmth with a soft cry. Bracing herself with her feet and her back, her hands gripping the rope along the sides of the boat and his hands clasped tightly about her neck, she heaved downwards to meet him as he ploughed upwards, and felt the sharp thud of his long spear against the neck of her womb. A streak of pleasure-pain shot through her and did not subside as he drove hard and deep into her again and again, hitting a spot she didn't know she had and conjuring up a furiously fiery hunger that blotted out consciousness. Utterly oblivious to all but each other, they ground and thrust with harsh, jagged, animal grunts as he plunged as forcefully up into her as he was able.

Suddenly it was there, without any effort whatsoever, rising inexorably to a violently explosive crest that blew the top off her brain, tore apart all her nerve-ends and roared through her with a shriek that must have been heard in her home town. She let rip a yell that blended with the blazing, violent, wracking thrall of her first orgasm, and cried out again, and again once more, her body wracked by an arching rictus of spasms that drew from Hakan one final ecstatic plunge and a yell of his own as he fired his gushing sperm with unexpected force in hot spurts deeply into her. They collapsed, whimpering.

Di was staring at her in astonishment. 'You don't do things by halves, do you?' she teased admiringly.

Hakan lightly caressed the curve of her breast gratefully and said softly, 'I didn't know it could be like that.'

'You and me both,' she replied with a trembling kiss.

After some contented moments of recovery, she arose and plummeted over the side of the boat, still naked, relishing the cool feel of the fresh, clean, sea water on her skin. With a splash, Hakan was in the water with her and as he came up from the dive, his naked body gently grazed against hers, his lips brushing her nipples and his soft penis rubbing against her thighs and belly. This was another first. A man who did not think that sex ended with ejaculation. What a gift he was.

They played sensuously with each other in the cleansing sea like water-babies, then lay, sated, hand in hand, on the boat seats in the burning sun. She wanted an all-over, golden-glowing tan. She knew this would not last. She knew it was not the one and only love of her life, and she suspected that Hakan was capable of this kind of focused intensity whoever he was with. He would not miss her when she left, nor she him. They had opened a door within each other and would move on without regrets. Meanwhile, she was going to make the most of every single moment that they had together in the next few weeks, to perfect her technique – and his. This was just the beginning.

Oberon and Titania

*H*e knew his body was superb. It had to be. He was an actor and a dancer and his livelihood depended upon it. He gave himself a quick last-minute once-over in the mirror before getting in the car and setting off up the motorway. He worked out every day to keep himself at peak and his tall, heavily muscled, black torso was taut and hard and chiselled solid.

He was aware that his penis was unusual in its proportions. Although he had never actually measured it, he knew it was exceptional. When it was relaxed and inert, he had to tuck it up around his waist; fully extended, it reached way past his navel towards his chest. The boys at school had teased him about giving himself a blow-job and he had tried it once. He certainly had no trouble getting his mouth around it, but it hadn't worked.

The girls it had been presented to had stared at it with a mixture of awe and terror, and some had even refused to have anything further to do with it. Those that had still been willing had asked him to be careful. He was sick of being careful. Sometimes he thought it was more of an encumbrance than an asset. It was a favourite party trick when he was on tour to sit the chorus girls on his lap and let them discover with their fingers the end of his knob away round the side of his waist. They would oooh and aaah and then come back for another feel, egging each other on to touch it through the cloth. That was the only chat-up line he needed, generally speaking.

He had little trouble getting work as there was plenty of demand for black dancers, especially if they could also act and sing as he could, and most especially if they were heterosexually butch as, again, he was. His presence glowed with a vibrantly virile energy which he channelled almost exclusively into his work. He had loved the theatre since childhood and had not known a minute of his life when he hadn't been involved, and now he was off again, on tour in a musical version of *A Midsummer Night's Dream*, playing Oberon. He whistled as he packed his case. This was a long tour, six months, and it was a good company; everyone got on and they enjoyed partying together, so the prospects for a fun time were high.

The theatre was not only his professional life but also his social life and, every now and then, his love life. He knew very few dancers who had families and mortgages. It just wasn't practical, especially when touring, being on the road for such long stretches of time. There was someone in this company that he had noticed and had hopes of, but he was still wary of her as she was not giving off any signals of availability. That didn't tend to happen anyway until after the rehearsal period was over and the show was on the road, so the jury was still out and his breath was bated.

She hadn't been at the first rehearsal. He had looked nonchalantly at the 'talent' on the first day and no one had immediately caught his attention – not that that meant anything, at this stage. People grew on you. The next time he was called to rehearsal it was 'Oberon,

Titania and fairies' and she was there, playing Titania, so they would have scenes together: wonderful scenes, provocative and fiery.

That was a very appropriate word in her case – fiery. The most eye-catching thing about her was her hair, a cascading abundance of bright copper curls frothing down to her shoulder blades, accentuating the creamy smooth, lightly dappled silken skin. She was petite, as a fairy queen should be – as petite as he was statuesque – but there was nothing frail or delicate about her. From very early in the day she had shown herself to be forthright, earthy, energetic and independent. She threw herself into rehearsals with total commitment, but she was not without a sense of fun and laughed loudly and often in her husky, throaty, whisky-sounding voice. He suspected she would be a raver on tour, once they got going, but while they were still working on the scenes and the characters she had given nothing away that was not totally focused on her work. She was as dedicated as he was and they had been very comfortable working together. Their scenes were vigorously alive and very sensual, as the relationship between Oberon and Titania demanded; their voices, both deep, were perfectly matched for the duet; and the physical contrast between them was inspired, making their dance routine riveting.

Arriving some hours later at the theatre, he located his dressing room, shared with Puck and Bottom, next door to Demetrius and Lysander. The room on the other side was shared by Helena, Hermia and Titania. The 'Mechanicals' and 'Oberon's fairies' were in two rooms on another floor with 'Titania's fairies'. One room had been left empty for the dancers to warm up in, which was an unusual concession and one for which everyone was most grateful.

Over the tannoy he could hear the four lovers rehearsing one of their scenes and, having finished his workout, feeling hot and sweaty, he wandered back along the corridor to his dressing room to have a shower. He walked in and heard a throaty female voice singing and the water running in the shower cubicle. He was rather taken aback and disoriented. What was going on? Was he in the right room? He checked the names on the door. Yes. He glanced at the cubicle and noticed that the outer door was ajar. There were two shower cabinets and neither of them had curtains. Titania was visible in one of the cabinets and quite unaware of his presence. She was naked and covered in soapy bubbles, singing softly as she lathered herself unselfconsciously in the steamy water. He could not prevent his instinctive reaction as the unsuspecting organ in his baggy rehearsal tights, surprised by this unexpected treat, began to stir and unwind. He was wearing nothing but his tights and his smoothly sculpted ebony chest gleamed with perspiration. As she soaped herself in blissfully ignorant solitude, the uncurling erection expanded and extended inside his roomy tights and solidified into a gigantic peak pushing uncomfortably against the brushed cotton.

She was utterly exquisite, with perfect, curvaceous, dance-refined legs, tapering slender ankles and long firm thighs that widened sweetly to the copper-gold apex of her mons. The two symmetrically rounded globes of her delectable rump were smooth and flawless, the valleys between her hip-bones and flat navel invited his tongue and the milky-soft, pink-nippled full moons of her breasts, which jiggled and swayed as she bent over to wash her shapely legs, cried out to be cupped and cradled in his large, sensitive, black hands. Her unbound hair was a fluffy confection of coppery red-gold candy floss framing her elfin face, and with her peaches and cream skin she was so delectable he could have eaten her.

As he watched, rooted to the spot, she began to wash under her pubis and the two pink nipples stiffened to pert little buds that cried out to his mouth. His constrained prick lurched and insisted on release. Instinctively, his hand strayed down inside his tights and clasped the huge shaft. Before his enraptured gaze, she began to rub more purposefully and his hand slid up and down in sympathy. With one hand she played with her breasts, tweaking the nipples and riffling them with her fingers, and with the other she rubbed beneath her golden bush, her lips parted as she breathed heavily, eyes closed in pleasure. As she rubbed, he began to rub; and as her fingers moved quicker and quicker, his own hand massaged his swollen, strangled member faster and faster, in unison.

Suddenly, she arched backward with a spasm and, as she cried out with a soft, mewling cry, he released his orgasm in great convulsive jets of liquid fire, ejaculating wetly into his loose-fitting leggings. He remained invisible behind the door as she draped herself in a big fluffy towel and disappeared out the other end through a door he could not see.

It seemed the two dressing rooms shared the adjacent showers. Careful to lock the door on both sides, he turned on the hot water and showered.

He looked at her differently now. He wanted her. He hungered for her and it was going to be unbearable until he had her. Later, as they rehearsed their scene, he felt sure that his lust was nakedly visible, although no one but she would notice as it was quite in character. He wasn't sure if she felt the extra heat or just thought his Oberon was in especially good form.

He could not get her out of his mind. When he was backstage alone while she was still on stage, he glanced into her dressing room and took note of her place set out with the make-up and good luck charms typical of all actors. Lying open beside her tissues was an anthology of erotic short stories. His blood pounded in his ears and he felt guilty suddenly, so he quickly left and returned to the auditorium where he tried to piece his image of her back together.

The costumes of all the fairies were completely transparent strips of indigo-blue gauze. Nothing was worn beneath and nothing was left to the imagination. Huge curling silver wigs adorned their heads and their make-up would be a mask of silver and blue with flyaway eyebrows. His own costume was simply skin-tight, silver leather trousers with a polished bare chest. He also had an enormous mane of silver hair. It would be incredibly sensual and now that his lust had arisen with such craving, he knew that she was going to drive him wild night after night and twice on matinées.

He began to plan his campaign. It was obvious that she was as hungry as he was, but was she hungry for him? He was going to make sure of it and he knew he had an edge on the other dancers. Puck was gay, for a start. The tour began to look very promising indeed.

It did not happen as planned. Later that evening, during the performance, he was winding down with the other dancers in the spare room, his scenes now over. She had also finished a scene and was due for a long break. Suddenly she appeared in the doorway, all but naked in the filmy gauze strips but without her wig, her red curls ablaze.

'I've finished my book.' (That was quick!) 'Has anybody got something I can read?' There was a desultory chorus of 'no's and a lot of head-shaking as everyone continued stretching and winding down on the floor.

'Well, then,' she continued undaunted, 'does anyone fancy a fuck?'

Incredible! It was the kind of thing actors sometimes said to each other and no one took any notice of – but not usually this early in the season.

Before he could stop himself, he heard himself say, 'Yes, I do.'

She turned to him with mischievous eyes, surprised. She clearly hadn't expected an answer. Well, you don't.

'You wouldn't dare!' she challenged him.

'Oh, wouldn't I?' he returned and got up off the floor.

Laughing merrily, she fled down the corridor and he raced out after her. No one took any notice. This kind of horseplay happened all the time but it didn't mean anything: except he was in earnest now.

With loud giggles and deliberately overacted cries of, 'You asked for this and you're going to get it,' he chased her to her dressing room.

She was returning with, 'I dare you, I dare you, I'll bet you wouldn't dare,' and laughing wildly.

They disappeared into her dressing room and he locked the door loudly, amid shrieks of hilarity and protest. Once inside, she turned to face him and her eyes were bright and wild. He stripped off his tights. There would be no denying him now.

Fully aroused, he stood naked before her, his stallion's erection thrust in a pulsing curve up against his ribs. Her eyes nearly fell out of her head.

'Oh, my God!' she gasped, and for the first time in his life he saw the awe tinged not with terror but with greed. She licked her lips breathlessly. 'Well, hullo, big boy,' huskily now. 'Where have you been all my life?'

He felt a surge of joy as his desire was fanned by an exciting new sense of unrestricted abandon. No care was going to be needed here. He was going to be able to do exactly as he pleased. His prick twitched eagerly and she gasped.

He guided her towards the divan-bed provided for resting between shows. She went willingly.

'Get on your knees!' he ordered her and she promptly obeyed, sticking her luscious, milky-white arse in the air and presenting to his view the moistly flossy pink and gold, softly swelling curves and folds of her vulva. Her ripe breasts swung beneath her, nipples alert. His bursting cock nearly exploded.

Kneeling behind her, he decided to tease her a little, tickling and tempting the tantalising curves with the head of his gigantic phallus, rubbing the moisture of his oozing dew-drop over the nub of her clitoris. She arched her hips against him, moaning softly. Using her rapidly increasing juices, he slipped and slid among the folds and the creases of her sucking pussy, teasing up her pleasure and taunting her with his restraint. He placed the bulging tip just inside her cunt-lips and played about the entrance, exploring, able to wait. He was in no hurry. There was time to dally.

When he felt her quivering on the verge of her climax, he very slowly sank his enormity into her clinging depths, and sank and sank and sank, and was overwhelmed by the blessed relief of being fully encompassed at last. He groaned out loud, an animal sound deep in his chest, with the sheer agony of his bliss, and his whole body shook with anticipation. In response, she gripped her cunt-muscles and clenched him tightly. He groaned again, as she sucked and sucked, pushing into him, hungry and impatient. With slow, steady strokes he began a langourous build-up, sliding smoothly in and out, relishing the sensation of the friction as it stimulated every gratified inch.

He was going to make this last. She was moaning into the pillows, her hips pushed back hard against his groin, arching her back to lift her arse high, grinding into him as deeply as she could, seeking ever deeper penetration. He obliged, plunging his extraordinary length full into her. He reached corners no one had and hit pleasure-spots she had only dreamed of, touching the core of her centre and creating surge after surge of searing ecstasy throughout her belly, flushing out to her extremities. She shuddered with the satisfaction of being filled at last. He never varied his rhythm, long and easy and deep, until she came in slowly cresting molten waves which broke and washed again and again with loud, muffled cries.

He did not stop. He knew he could keep this up for hours if he wanted, so he continued stroking in and out in his unrelenting, steady rhythm, on and on. She came again, this time with short, sharp piercing cries, biting into the pillows to stifle them as the sudden, jagged peaks took her by surprise. The full, rigid length of his shaft was slamming into things in her depths, arousing a gasping pleasure-pain that she had never felt before and she couldn't stop coming as he relentlessly bore down on her with his monumental self-control.

Now he wanted to wait no longer. Yielding to his own hunger, he began to buck and rear with vigour, pounding and pounding, faster and faster, gripping her by the hips, enjoying the sight of his ebony-black satin against her creamy-white silk, still draped in the frothy ribbons of midnight blue.

He barely noticed as she came the third time, breathless now, trembling, her knees too weak to hold her any longer. She collapsed on the divan with her legs still wide, drenched and slippery, and he thrust easily in and out of her tightness until he felt the surge of his own explosion begin to ignite. Slowly, inexorably, it built to a long, blazing crescendo, snaking along the immense length of him and finally, convulsively, firing his rich spunk into her in hot gushing spurts, which drained him and left him exhausted on top of her soft pale buttocks. He stayed inside her for a minute, reluctant to leave the clinging warmth, and when he withdrew he saw his seed also leave her, forming a large pool on the divan. She sighed a long tremulous sigh.

Coming to, he heard the applause for the 'Mechanicals' scene. Helena and Hermia would be on their way back to use the dressing room. Time to go; they were due back on stage in a minute. He leaped off her and ran to the door as she rearranged herself.

235

Laughing loudly, he unlocked it and returned to the corridor, exclaiming for all to hear. 'Thanks a bunch, Titania. That was lovely-jubbly!' Then he swaggered off, chuckling.

No one suspected a thing. He grinned widely as he headed for the stage and the last scene. Oh, yes, this was definitely going to be the best tour ever.

A Weekend in the Country

*T*he young man stared at the invitation in his hand
with mystified disbelief.

The Marquis and Marquise de Bacchanale request the
pleasure of the company of Mr Julian Wentworth and
friend at the Chateau Valdésir for the weekend of June
20th–22nd. The theme for the weekend will be Nymphs
and Satyrs. You are invited to stay Saturday and Sunday
night. Costume obligatory.

The gilt lettering was embossed on a satin-glossed, mar-
bled and watered card edged with gold. He did not
know any Marquis or Marquise and none of his friends
would indulge in a joke this elaborate. It had to be a
joke, of course. He couldn't possibly take it seriously,
yet the expensive invitation looked unsettlingly serious.
Still staring several minutes later, he suddenly thought
of Rupert. He would know. If there was anything in this
at all, Rupert would certainly know. He mixed regularly
with this class of person and knew all there was to know
of the local nobility. He would give Rupert a call.

'Rupe, hi! Something really peculiar has just happened. Couldn't shed any light, could you? Ever heard of a Marquis and Marquise at somewhere called the Chateau Valdésir?'

There was a long pause at the other end. 'Why do you ask?' Rupert sounded cagey.

'Well, it's just that I've received an invitation to a weekend there, but I've never heard of them.'

Another long pause, then a chuckle. 'You jammy bastard.'

'What the hell are you talking about?'

The chuckle was louder now.

'Oh, they're quite famous, or should I say infamous? In some circles, their weekends are very hot property. How the hell did you get an invite? Those are very much sought after, don't you know, and very hard to come by. I don't know if you're quite ready for this. It's, um, how shall I say, not for the faint-hearted.'

'What are you trying to say?'

The ensuing chuckle was distinctly fruity. 'We're talking saucy – and that's an understatement. You lucky devil!'

'Well, in that case, would you like to come with me?'

'What?'

'Well, it says "and friend". If what you say is true, I'd better not take a lady friend. Why don't you be the friend? Sounds like I could be needing some moral support.'

'You're going to go, then?'

'I should say so. Sounds too good to miss. What do you think?'

There was an exceedingly long silence, then a hearty guffaw. 'I don't believe this! Yes, why not? Wouldn't miss it for worlds. Bloody hell!'

It wasn't easy choosing what to wear. Rupert insisted that the weekend themes were taken as a creative challenge by the guests, and costumes would be dramatic and imaginative. They would look most out of place if they were not suitably attired. After much discussion, they both decided they felt more comfortable with 'satyr' than 'nymph', although Rupert gave it serious thought. He cherished a personal fantasy about Diana, goddess of the Hunt, but finally settled for Herne the Hunter, in his guise as a stag.

Julian took longer to decide, unable to choose between Leda's swan and Pan of the pipes. Pan won. The swan looked a bit too complicated to maintain for a whole weekend, rather likely to moult. Shopping for the materials and accessories was hilarious, never mind their clumsy attempts to assemble the costumes. In the end, they took their designs to a professional seamstress, telling her it was for a fancy dress ball, which fired her to a flurry of enthusiastic inspiration.

The leather costumes were magnificent. Rupert's horns were perhaps a little cumbersome but impressive, and Julian's bare chest caused him some concern until the seamstress pointed out that it would be a shame to hide such an asset when he had the opportunity to reveal it. He was quite proud of his rippling, muscled tan, with its light covering of curling dark brown hair, which arrowed into a line down his navel. Rupert was smooth all over, leaner and paler, with lighter, honey-warm hair worn loose and waving to his jaw, somehow suitably godlike. Their lower halves were clad in different styles of animal skin, for Rupert long, brown leather trousers and in Julian's case, furry britches revealing his naturally less furred and strongly muscled legs. He even sported a short tail and tiny budding horns. Rupert's antlers were attached to a leather headpiece which could, if inconvenient, be removed.

By now they had talked themselves into a frenzy of anticipation. Rupert had reported back all he knew of these weekends, which wasn't much, mostly gleaned from rumour, sly hints and salacious jokes overheard at the Club. They realised they had no real facts to go upon but the possibilities and assumptions grew in their heated imaginations, the more they discussed it. Both were up for anything – or, rather, hoped they were. On this point there was some anxiety, only to be expected since the exact expectations of their prowess were as yet unspecified.

Saturday the twentieth finally dawned, a beautifully hot, perfect, midsummer's day. The countryside was emerald green and sparkled in the sun as they drove through it in Rupert's racy little red Mercedes. The suspense had become so intense that neither of them felt like conversation. The driveway up the chestnut-lined avenue from the automatic gates was a mile long. The wrought-iron gates were ornately decorated with the naked, twining bodies of mythological creatures performing impossible physical feats designed to raise eyebrows, among other things. Atop the pedestals were the laughing, quaffing, grape-eating figures of Bacchus and Venus, which set them both aquiver. They began to wonder whether they were in deeper than they could manage, but it was too late to go back now.

The driveway finally opened out to reveal the house. It was a truly magnificent sight: classical, in white stone, with parapets and turrets and two wings flanking a huge central building with vast, ground-length windows fronted by pillars and colonnades. The wide expanse of steps leading up to the front door was lined with more mythical figures, this time in white stone. It was three floors in height and must have contained hundreds of rooms. They parked in a roped area filled with other cars, and carried their small cases up the acres of steps to the imposing front doors. Julian pulled the bell-rope and a deep, mellow ringing sounded within.

After what seemed an eternity, the door was opened by Neptune. At least, it was an elderly gentleman with shoulder-length, silver hair, a long, loose white frock and a trident. He gravely demanded their invitation and, upon viewing it, ushered them into the entrance hall.

Their mouths dropped open. Neither of them had ever seen anything so opulent or sumptuous: every different colour of marble from greys and beiges, through reds and browns to a glorious shiny jet-black; watered silk drapes, huge vases of richly perfumed flowers on pedestals, and crystal chandeliers, already lit and glittering. The marble-balustraded staircase was broad and central, ascending majestically to divide into two, one right and one left, on to the first landing. The walls were panelled in a variety of inlaid natural woods; oak, ash, mahogany, rosewood and others less definable. It reeked of wealth and a faint suggestion of decadence. The rich colours were overpowering and so was the scent of roses and lilies. As they stood, mouths gaping, absorbing the atmosphere, a young woman appeared at the top of the central staircase.

'Hello, you two,' she said brightly. 'We're nearly all here now. Let me show you to your rooms and you can dress, or, rather – ' she chuckled suggestively ' – undress.'

They stared at her, thunderstruck, speechless. She was wearing a softly flowing cream drapery which fell from one shoulder to the floor, tied in the classical style around her waist and revealing one completely bare white breast. Her raven-black hair was moulded up high with gold ropes threaded through it in the manner of a Greek goddess, and on her brow sat a gold band with two rearing snakes. She seemed not to notice their consternation or the cause of it. The perfect circle of the flaunted breast was superb.

'I'll have your cases taken up. Rudi!' She rang a little bell and a small man appeared from one of the doors leading off the entrance hall, grabbed both their bags and disappeared at a trot up the staircase. Already silenced by the breast, at the sight of Rudi only good breeding kept their jaws off the floor and speech was out of the question. He was no more than four feet tall with short, cropped, dark curls, his top half clad in a gold lycra body-stocking, and the brown tights clinging to the lower half of his body covered in animal fur to the knees and bulging around his hips and buttocks. His calves and feet were bare and he only had two toes on each foot. But his most distinctive feature was a gigantic, naked erection which protruded stiffly at a forty-five-degree angle from his groin in a permanent state of readiness.

'Oh, don't worry about Rudi,' she waved gaily. 'Genetic defect. You'll get used to him. Once you're dressed, join everyone in the ballroom.' She turned her back upon them, then took her magnificent breast back up the stairs and out of sight.

By now they were both feeling rather inadequate, thinking that their costumes would, after all, be somewhat tame by comparison. All the same, steady as she goes, they decided. At least they would not be out of place. Collecting themselves with an abashed glance at each other, they went up to their rooms, which conveniently shared an adjoining door. Once inside, they glanced sheepishly at each other, then burst into gales of hysterical laughter.

'Oh, Lord, what have we got ourselves into here?' Julian hooted.

'God knows, but I'm game,' replied Rupert. 'How about you?'

'Oh, I'm game all right,' retorted Julian. 'I just don't know whether or not I can rise to the occasion, if you get my meaning.'

'Well, we'll just have to find out. Better get changed and go down.'

Once costumed, they made their way back down the broad staircase, feeling very grand and only slightly foolish, and were shown by Neptune into the ballroom.

242

He flung wide the double doors and loudly announced their names. They flashed a quick glance at each other; Rupert winked, and, taking a deep breath, they entered.

In their wildest fantasies, neither of them could ever possibly have imagined what they were about to encounter. Originally a ballroom, the space had been transformed into a pleasure-parlour. The long windows were heavily curtained with plush burgundy-red velvet drapes, shutting out the daylight, and the room was lit by the candlelight from six huge crystal chandeliers. Along the full length of the draped windows and at both ends of the room had been placed sofas, loungers, cushions and divans covered in velvet or brocade in purples, ruby reds, royal blues, plums and magentas.

The opposite wall was a riot of garishly painted frescoes depicting orgiastic Dionysian frolics, and along the full length of this wall ran a table, laden – nay, burdened – with every form of tastebud-tingling, mouth-watering, epicurean delectation: whole quail and capons, suckling pig, crown racks of lamb, venison pie, succulent peppered slices of wild boar, hams studded with cloves, oysters, king prawns, lobsters, mountains of meringue swathed in whipped cream, high piles of profiteroles dripping with toffee or chocolate, mousses, pastries, jellies, cakes, desserts – a surfeit of gluttony. Wine was being served from large jugs, and multi-coloured, foamy cocktails in decorated glasses, with elaborate trimmings.

There were people sitting, standing, lounging, lying and otherwise engaged in various stages of sexual congress. No one appeared to be fully clad. Several of the men wore cod-pieces of such aroused proportions as to make your eyes water, making their own ready-access leather flaps seem inadequate. Some of the ladies, whose garments began beneath their breasts, had not only rouged their lips and cheeks but also their nipples in bright vermilion. No one was dancing although there was a waft of gentle music from invisible lutes, harps and bells.

As he looked around for the source, Julian's eye was drawn upwards to a gallery where the musicians were located, running around three sides of the room and offering bird's-eye viewing. The air was heavily perfumed with a spicy, pungent, oriental aroma and Rupert whispered that he thought he detected a faint suggestion of something more potent than spice within it.

A barefoot waitress approached them, dressed as a sylph, in a completely transparent length of diaphanous gauze with nothing underneath.

'Oysters, wine, or me?' She dimpled at them, and it would have been naive to think she was joking. Service in this household was clearly to be interpreted in the fullest sense. They settled for wine, claret-red in large, chased-silver goblets, and took stock of their surroundings.

No, no one was dancing but everyone was occupied. It was difficult to avoid looking at what they would normally prefer not to see, but also compellingly impossible to tear their eyes away. Julian was staring, transfixed. Rupert followed his gaze to a corner of the room where he was stunned by a sight that neither of them would ever have thought possible.

A woman clad in a shiny green, contour-hugging body-stocking was lying on a chaise longue, legs apart, one foot on the ground and the other with the knee bent up on the chaise. She was covered from head to foot in the lurid green lycra; the only skin visible was that of her face, hands and feet – and her openly displayed vulva, shaven smooth. Her mouth was painted green, as were her fingernails and toenails, and she sported a large pair of pointed pixie ears.

Crouched on the floor beside her, on the end of a long chain attached to a ring pierced through her fanny-lips, was a small capuchin monkey, gazing about inquisi-

244

tively, his collar emerald-studded. Every now and then she would take a chocolate finger biscuit and push it into her vagina, from where the little monkey would nibble it out, leaping up on to the chaise and squatting between her knees. Julian gulped and Rupert licked his dry lips as he tried not to stare. Strangely, the sight was not erotic, just astounding, but the message was loud and clear: anything goes.

Fascinated and bemused, they meandered over to the groaning banquet tables and began to serve themselves a selection of delicacies. It soon became evident that bodily functions were to be no impediment to enjoyment when a man alongside them beckoned a waiter with a gesture to his groin and, within seconds, a beautifully decorated porcelain container was provided and held in front of him as he fished out his penis from underneath his clothing and casually released a stream of golden liquid into it. He did not hesitate in his indulgence of the creamy, chocolate-covered profiteroles but continued stuffing himself greedily with both hands while the waiter carefully aimed the receptacle wherever it was required by the arcing stream. At the final dribble, a linen napkin was administered to the lingering droplets, then draped over the pot, which promptly vanished with the waiter.

Rupert and Julian looked at each other with their eyebrows raised. There was no reason to suppose that any other processes of evacuation would be treated any differently. Clearly no inconvenience was permitted to interfere with the ongoing festivities.

Taking their piled plates to a far corner, they plumped themselves down among the large, deep cushions, placing their food and drink on the low table between them. They ate slowly, aware of a whole weekend stretching ahead of them, savouring every rich and delectable morsel. Their goblets were kept filled by the transparently draped waitress with the dimpling smile and Julian remarked to Rupert that, in this atmosphere, it was nigh on impossible to resist feeling aroused. Stimulation was guaranteed. The tastefully muted cadences of the music continued to waft and, as they ate, reclining on the soft cushions, gazing avidly at the abandoned heavings going on all around them, they tried to acclimatise to the uninhibited hedonism. It was difficult to comprehend a social gathering with absolutely no rules and the unlimited possibilities were tantalising. They wondered aloud how they were going to get into the action.

A pair of mermaids attracted Julian's attention. One of them was facing him. Her breasts were bare and her blue-green, sinuous tail, curving over the side of the lounger, convincing. He could not see the join low on her hips where the body became scaly as her naked skin had a translucent sheen. Their shining, moonlight-blonde hair waved abundantly down to their knees and seemed to float slightly around them. As the other one turned to recover a plate of prawns from the floor, Julian realised that it was a man and he felt a slight twinge of disappointment. They must be a couple.

Was it permissible to share someone else's companion? he pondered. He presumed so, or they wouldn't be here; he felt a flutter of arousal as the one with the shimmering breasts laughed with a tinkling sound of tiny bells and lifted her blue-green tail with a sinuous tweak higher on to the recliner. He felt an urgent desire to bathe himself in that ocean of luxuriant, cascading hair and feel the powerful twining of that tail about his hips and . . . Julian knew that he was definitely rising to the occasion and felt a confident surge. Looking about, she caught his eye and smiled at him. Hers were a vivid green. He smiled back and held her look and a frisson of mutual attraction passed between them. He gulped and nearly choked. She turned away, laughing, but he had marked her and the stiffening bulge pushing against his leather cod-flap had given him away.

Rupert was remarking on the progress of the priapic Rudi, who seemed to be a firm favourite. Every so often he would be summoned. With clothing no object, access was immediate and he would pump away vigorously, thrusting his preposterous length voraciously in and out of the orifice presented until the recipient reached breathless orgasm; then he would withdraw, still erect, and leave the room, soon to return. This had already happened several times as they watched.

'Does he ever come himself, I wonder?' Rupert enquired of Julian.

'Yes and no,' he heard a light, amused voice reply from behind his cushions, and as he turned he found their hostess with the glorious breast standing behind them. She was laughing at him. Rupert was spellbound by the breast, so perfectly framed by the diagonally draped creamy folds which concealed the other.

She laughed at his confusion. 'Under certain circumstances, he does achieve orgasm but he never ejaculates and his erection is permanent. No one knows why – inbreeding, probably – but it doesn't seem to bother him. In fact he gets a great deal of pleasure from servicing others, as you see. Do enjoy yourselves in whatever manner you find most stimulating. There are no rules here, as long as everyone's having fun.' She chuckled richly and walked away.

Rupert's imagination was still in thrall to that single alabaster breast. His fingertips ached for it.

For the rest of that day and night they contented themselves with observing and stuffing themselves with food and drink. From the vantage point of the upper balcony, they watched the blatant couplings and sexual fumblings of others, no longer astounded, in a state of permanent arousal but needing to fortify their courage a little further before engaging. To Julian's chagrin, the merpersons had been borne away in a sedan chair by four chunky fauns and had not reappeared. He allowed himself to lapse into a languid stupor, his senses over-loaded but his resolve slowly stiffening. Rupert was besotted with visions of a floating breast, perfectly formed and palely glowing, inviting but always just out of reach.

Eventually, sated and stupefied, they retired to bed where they slept profoundly until late the next morning.

Before launching themselves back into the fray, they spent the afternoon wandering pleasantly around the spacious grounds and gardens, refreshing themselves among the shady trees and bushes and indulging in a brisk, invigorating swim in the clear, fresh expanse of a marble swimming pool. They lay on the manicured lawn making idle conversation in the evening sun before once again donning their costumes and rejoining the party.

The merpersons had reappeared and Julian's prick leaped to greet them. He was instantly aroused. The green goddess and her monkey were feeding themselves again, this time with fruit, the monkey delicately retracting the bananas from their usual cache, poking and peering with apparent disinterest in anything but the food. His mistress, equally disinterested, appeared not to have moved since they'd seen her the night before.

The music played on and the servicing staff were even more amenable. Their hostess and her bare breast continued to wander encouragingly among her guests and Rudi performed with unabated enthusiasm. After a lavish meal and several drinks, Rupert and Julian decided it was now or never to get some of the action. A group of nymphs were freely engaging in mutual pleasure, which activated a group of satyrs into a similar frenzy. Rupert and Julian were not tempted to join either group but the energetic gruntings and strivings were stimulating them unbearably. The merpersons had once again disappeared.

A short while later, their hostess announced to the gathering that it was a perfect midsummer's night out-

side and the grounds were available to those who preferred frolicking in the open air. Before long, the
ballroom was almost empty and, following the crowds,
Rupert and Julian soon found themselves watching the
nymphs and satyrs besporting themselves with abandon
on the smoothly lush lawn. They were both rather light-
headed and stupefied with the wine and the smoky,
hedonistic atmosphere.

'We're not frightfully good at this, are we?' Julian
complained. 'I mean, what we've been seeing is an
education and very erotic and all that, but it's not really
getting us to the point, is it?'

'Not exactly,' replied Rupert. 'What do you suggest?'

'I'm damned if I know, but this is getting me all hot
and steamy. I need to clear my head. I think I'll go for a
midnight skinny-dip; then, if all else fails, I'll see you
later back in the ballroom for more gluttony.'

'I'm going into the woods for a wander in the moonlight, then I'll join you inside and we'll see if we can't
improve our performance. I can't get that damn breast
off my mind, though.'

'No. I've got the same problem with the mermaid's
tail. Nothing else will do.'

They laughed at each other wryly, then separated and
went their separate ways.

His wits dull and befuddled, Julian almost fell into the
pool, darkly mysterious and quietly lapping in the
balmy night air, tiny glints of moonlight stippling the
surface. He removed his clothing and slipped into the
tingling coolness. As he swam lazily up and down in a
mindless haze, he became vaguely aware of another
presence. A shadow seemed to be moving in the watery
dark beneath him. He stopped and looked around him
but nothing ruffled the surface of the pool. Warily he
resumed his stroke. A soft touch lightly brushed against
his belly and chest, raising goosebumps as his flesh
prickled. He stopped and looked around again, breath

held, and after some few minutes a laughing face broke the surface of the pool, surrounded by a cloud of wafting, silvery hair.

His arousal was instant. In a swift rush of blood, his prick surged upright in greeting. She dived again and her body grazed his seductively, her trailing hand lingering over his rigid cock, testing it and teasing it. In his groggy, thick-headed state, it felt surreal. She seemed to be still wearing her tail but he couldn't get his mind around that. She glided powerfully through the water and he stopped swimming to catch his breath and gather his unravelling thoughts. She weaved all around him, her floating hair wrapping lightly about his bare flesh and her hands tickling and fluttering over him as they passed.

As he sought desperately for mental clarity, she dived. Her mouth enclosed his straining erection and she began to slide back and forth upon him. How could she hold her breath like that? His soggy brain relinquished control and abandoned him to the pleasure. Unbelievably, she wound her tail around his legs and all his fantasies were realised. Twining and untwining herself sinuously, she held him up in the water while he raised her head to kiss her and run his hands sensually through the flowing veil of her hair. As it draped itself around them both, she rubbed her body against his striving shaft and he noticed from a far distance that her skin glowed with an iridescent sheen. As he held her close, she insinuated herself hard against him, then swiftly and easily his cock slid inside the slippery aperture of her cunt and found itself enshrined within.

He couldn't feel the parting of her legs but his mind was too foggy to think with, so he simply surrendered to his fantasy. It had to be something in the food or else he was hallucinating but this was too good a dream to interrupt with logic. Dazed and entranced, he gave himself up to the all-engulfing sensations. They rode the heaving waves, apparently supported by her tail as he thrust in and out of her tight, deliciously smooth tunnel, no longer in control. He plunged and slid; his arms clasped around her; as he buried his face in the wet trails of her hair and kissed her eagerly offered, yielding mouth, Julian fell into a kind of trance and floated away on the tide.

Some magic enchantment took him to a watery dimension where he felt embalmed and enhanced, his senses sharper and more receptive than he could ever remember, every nerve electrifyingly alive and his cock monumentally huge, like a gigantic piston powering the universe, every pulse charging his veins with fire and a blazing potency that craved fusion. Her cunt clutched and sucked at him so tightly that it seared his brain. The explosion that erupted from out of him nearly tore him apart as it drained his semen from him like gushing magma. Without her muscular support he would have sunk and drowned helplessly. In the distance he heard a high-pitched keening sound which shattered his eardrums and knocked him senseless.

When he came to, he was lying on the lawn and she was sitting on the edge of the pool swinging her glistening, blue-green fishtail in the water and watching him anxiously.

'What happened?' he whispered.

'I was almost too much for you,' she replied and her voice had a weird kind of echo.

Julian found it hard to concentrate.

'You are beautiful, virile and perfectly formed. I wanted you to impregnate me and I think you have. It was extremely nice,' she continued.

'What about your husband?' Julian's head wouldn't do as he asked and he knew he must still be hallucinating.

'He's not my husband; he's my brother.'

When Julian awoke some time later, she had gone and

he was once more dressed in Pan's leather breeks. The stars looked clear and the ground was no longer moving. He supposed whatever it was he had eaten must have worn off. Swaying drunkenly, he stood up and made his way back to the house.

Meanwhile, Rupert had set off on his solitary wander through the woods. Stopping beside a knarled and ancient oak tree, he undid his cod-flap and urinated against its rough bark.

Thwack!ngngngngngng.

He looked up and just to the right of his head an arrow was embedded deep into the wood and resonating. His stream dried up immediately and he swung about in alarm.

She was silhouetted in the light of the full moon, Diana the Huntress, clad in a brief leather skirt, powerful thighs bare, leather sandals strapped all the way up to her knees and her bow aloft. Her quiver of arrows was slung over her shoulder and, although her right breast was constrained by the leather strap, there was no mistaking that other magnificently gleaming bare breast. Her black hair shone blue in the moonlight. The moment he spied her she vanished, disappearing into the dense cover of the trees.

He lingered a moment too long.

Thwack!ngngngngngng.

Another arrow quivered beside his shoulder. His heart was pounding and his mind shot into overdrive, pumping adrenalin and quickening his senses. She was hunting him, like prey. Rupert did not easily succumb to being a victim and his mental processes sought frantically for a way to regain control. As he took stock of the situation, his mind filled with the sight of that solitary breast, he registered his responding arousal. The serpent in his trousers was uncoiling and awakening, which altered the name of the game and brought a smile to his face. This was a sexual battle, his mythical fantasy enacted: Diana the Huntress and Herne, both hunter and hunted. His skin prickled with a hot flush of desire and his swelling erection jerked and twitched, arising potently from out of the open flap in his trousers and revealing him boldly upthrust and lustful. From her vantage point wherever she was, she could not miss it, clearly etched in the sharp light of the full moon.

Aware that his antlers made him an easy target, he quickly dived behind the tree and, dropping to the ground, he removed them, then crawled painfully on all fours through the brush to a fallen log and crouched behind it, thinking fast. He took a handful of sticks and stones and tossed them into the underbrush, each a little further than the last. A whizzing arrow followed the noises. Taking advantage of her diverted attention, he swiftly dashed back to the oak tree and, tugging fiercely, retrieved the two arrows lodged in its trunk. He then crawled rapidly away in the opposite direction. Peering out from behind his cover he saw her moving stealthily towards the diversion he had created. She had notched another arrow into her bow and held it ready. His blood froze and his cock stiffened. Fear heightened his ardour. He was going to have her or die. He took another handful of pebbles, heaved them into the far brush and watched her follow the sound, slowly and suspiciously, maintaining her cover. He saw her superb, marble breast silhouetted in the sharp light and his heart turned over.

As he watched her stalking him, he was filled with admiration. She was sleek and silent and powerful, moving surely and confidently through her domain, and as she moved he also moved, circling around behind her and steadily gaining upon her. She stopped behind a large, concealing tree and he saw his chance and grasped it. Rushing forwards in one fluid movement, he caught her just as she turned to face him, knocked her back and flattened her hard against the trunk, crushing her quiver of arrows and knocking the bow from her hand. He pushed one arrow against her neck and the other into her left side under the ribs. She froze, stunned, and their eyes locked. His were glittering with determination and lust and hers were wide with anger and surprise, but he thought he caught a glint of something else behind her shock – challenge.

Each time she moved, he dug the sharp metal point of the arrow into her flesh and hardened his resolve. She would not escape. She raised an arm to tear at him and bared her teeth, but he dug the other arrow into the naked flesh below her ribs, drawing blood, and she caught her breath with a hiss. He rejoiced in her feisty, courageous, fighting spirit and pressed his own raging weapon hard up between her thighs. Flesh connected with flesh and the fiery thrill that accompanied it scorched them both.

Even with one arrow pricking her throat and another piercing her side, she was still not giving in. She spat at him, at the same time raising her knee, but he was ready for her. Pushing the arrows even harder, causing trickles of blood to ooze from beneath them, he heard a small cry of pain escape unbidden. Looking into her eyes deeply, he found them sparkling and alight with passionate arousal.

He waited no longer. As she kicked at him, he twisted his leg about hers and brought her to the ground. Falling on top of her, but with the arrows still firmly in place, he parted her knees with his and, looking her straight in the eye, he plunged his virile spear hard and deep into her cunt. Now she did cry out, but her eyes betrayed her. She was on fire with lust and triumph. With the arrows still in his hands and driving vengefully and relentlessly into her, grunting with the effort, he knew it would be quick and violent. All he longed for now was her submission. He forced himself hard against her resistance, crashing into her again and again.

254

With a spasm and a loud cry, she was arching and bucking and her cunt was clenching rapidly around him. It sped him to his own conclusion and, panting and pounding, he ejaculated fiercely and furiously, pummelling viciously against her womb and firing deep, hot, stabbing jets of his semen into her as savagely as he could.

She sagged and softened beneath him and he dropped the arrows and collapsed upon her. At last he could achieve his ultimate desire. Lifting his head, he gazed in awe at the perfectly rounded, silvered globe with the assertive nipple. Gently and tenderly, he lowered his face and took it in his mouth. Placing one hand lightly on its perfect contours and, tracing the full curves with his fingertips, he sucked at the tightening nipple and felt the pliant flesh about his face. He blissfully surrendered to the sensation of its soft luxuriance and lost himself as he nourished his fantasy.

She dug her fingernails into his back. Unwilling to wilt, his cock was still couched in her warmth and, as he sucked and stroked, they remained conjoined for a long while until he began moving and solidifying within her. She succumbed with a long sigh. Still suckling, feeling her uncertain response, he allowed himself to drift as he rode upon her, hypnotised by the pulsating rhythm as his mounting desire rekindled. She began at last to writhe and grind her hips and before long, his mouth still fixed to her breast, hips undulating in unison, they once again surged upwards to a slow, steady, gradual crescendo. Fully hard again, he took her, consenting and responsive, to mutually fulfilling gratification, devouring each other and arriving together with sharp cries of pleasure, her hands gripping his hair in her ecstasy. Finally, fully satisfied, he lay with his head upon her bosom.

She spoke so softly, he almost missed it. 'You're the

first. No one before you has ever had the balls to fight back. That's why Diana was a virgin.'

It took him a minute to digest what she had revealed.

'What about all these weekends? Surely...?' He wasn't sure how you asked your hostess if she fucked all her guests.

'Oh, I don't get involved. They're for Rudi. They're his pleasure. He's my cousin and we only married to keep the family fortunes together and maintain the property. You can see he's more a child than a man. I needed a man.'

Later, back at the house, he retrieved Julian, who was still glazed and dazed and not making much sense. Diana deserted him to return to her guests, once again draped in her cream finery, breast displayed: only now Rupert watched its progress with a sense of pride. He would be back, but not on a weekend.

Julian was away with the pixies, or, as he kept muttering, the fishies. After sharing his adventure, he was withdrawn and uncommunicative, but in the light of his own experience in the woods, Rupert was not too quick to dismiss the tale as pure fantasy. Whatever it had been, it was real for Julian. The merpersons were not seen again.

They slept very late the next day, feasted heartily at lunch, then returned to the city, Julian quietly remote and Rupert sparkling with new zeal. Neither of them ever spoke of Valdésir to anyone. For Julian it remained a vivid and unforgettable dream, while for Rupert it became a recurring adventure as he and Diana battled lustily for dominance, and every sprawling detail of the house and grounds became as familiar to him as his own home – indeed, eventually became his home.

Julian never visited.

BLACK LACE NEW BOOKS

Published in March

FIRE AND ICE
Laura Hamilton
£5.99

Nina is known as the Ice Queen at work, where her frosty demeanour makes people think she's equally cold in bed. But what her colleagues don't know is that Nina spends her after-work hours locked into fiery games with her boyfriend Andrew, one in which she acts out her deepest fantasy – being a prostitute. Nina finds herself being drawn deeper and deeper into London's seedy underworld, where everything is for sale and nothing is what it seems.

ISBN 0 352 33486 X

MORE WICKED WORDS
Various. Ed by Kerri Sharp
£5.99

Black Lace anthologies have proved to be extremely popular. Following on from the success of the *Pandora's Box* and *Sugar and Spice* compilations, this second *Wicked Words* collection continues to push the erotic envelope. The accent is once again on contemporary settings with a transgressive feel – and the writing is fresh, upbeat in style and hot. This is an ideal introduction to the Black Lace series.

ISBN 0 352 33487 8

GOTHIC BLUE
Portia Da Costa
£5.99

Stranded at a remote Gothic priory, Belinda Seward is suddenly prey to sexual forces she can neither understand nor control. She is drawn into a world of decadence and debauchery by the mysterious aristocrat André von Kastel. He has plans for Belinda which will take her into the realms of obsessive love and the erotic paranormal. This is a Black Lace special reprint.

ISBN 0 352 33075 9

Published in April

SAUCE FOR THE GOOSE
Mary Rose Maxwell
£5.99

Sauce for the Goose is a riotous and sometimes humorous celebration of the rich variety of human sexuality. Imaginative and colourful, each story explores a different theme or fantasy, and the result is a fabulously bawdy mélange of cheeky sensuality and hot thrills. A lively array of characters display an uninhibited and lusty energy for boundary-breaking pleasure. This is a decidedly X-rated collection of stories designed to be enjoyed and indulged in.

ISBN 0 352 33492 4

HARD CORPS
Claire Thompson
£5.99

Remy Harris, a bright young army cadet at a prestigious military college, hopes to become an officer. She understands that she will have to endure all the usual trials of military life, including boot-camp discipline and rigorous exercise. She's ready for the challenge – that is until she meets Jacob, who recognises her true sexuality and initiates her into the Hard Corps – a secret society within the barracks.

ISBN 0 352 33491 6

To be published in May

INTENSE BLUE
Lyn Wood
£5.99

When Nan and Megan attend a residential art course as a 40th birthday present to themselves, they are plunged into a claustrophobic world of bizarre events and eccentric characters. There is a strong sexual undercurrent to the place, and it seems that many of the tutors are having affairs with their students – and each other. Nan gets caught up in a mystery she has to solve, but playing amateur detective only leads her into increasingly strange and sexual situations in this sometimes hilarious story of two women on a mission to discover what they really want in their lives.

ISBN 0 352 33496 7

THE NAKED TRUTH
Natasha Rostova
£5.99

Callie feels trapped living among the 'old money' socialites of the Savannah district. Her husband Logan is remote, cold and repressed – even if he does have an endless supply of money. One day she leaves him. Determined to change her life she hides out at her sister's place. Meanwhile Logan has hired a detective and is determined to get his wife back. But she is now treading a path of self-expression, and even getting into the ancient art of Voodoo. Will he want her back when he finds her? And what will she do when she learns the naked truth about Logan's shady past?

ISBN 0 352 33497 5

If you would like a complete list of plot summaries of Black Lace titles, or would like to receive information on other publications available, please send a stamped addressed envelope to:

Black Lace, Thames Wharf Studios,
Rainville Road, London W6 9HA

BLACK LACE BOOKLIST

All books are priced £5.99 unless another price is given.

Black Lace books with a contemporary setting

RIVER OF SECRETS £4.99	Saskia Hope & Georgia Angelis ISBN 0 352 32925 4	☐
THE NAME OF AN ANGEL £6.99	Laura Thornton ISBN 0 352 33205 0	☐
BONDED £4.99	Fleur Reynolds ISBN 0 352 33192 5	☐
CONTEST OF WILLS	Louisa Francis ISBN 0 352 33223 9	☐
FEMININE WILES £7.99	Karina Moore ISBN 0 352 33235 2	☐
DARK OBSESSION £7.99	Fredrica Alleyn ISBN 0 352 33281 6	☐
COOKING UP A STORM £7.99	Emma Holly ISBN 0 352 33258 1	☐
THE TOP OF HER GAME	Emma Holly ISBN 0 352 33337 5	☐
VILLAGE OF SECRETS	Mercedes Kelly ISBN 0 352 33344 8	☐
PACKING HEAT	Karina Moore ISBN 0 352 33356 1	☐
TAKING LIBERTIES	Susie Raymond ISBN 0 352 33357 X	☐
LIKE MOTHER, LIKE DAUGHTER	Georgina Brown ISBN 0 352 33422 3	☐
ASKING FOR TROUBLE	Kristina Lloyd ISBN 0 352 33362 6	☐
A DANGEROUS GAME	Lucinda Carrington ISBN 0 352 33432 0	☐
THE TIES THAT BIND	Tesni Morgan ISBN 0 352 33438 X	☐
IN THE DARK	Zoe le Verdier ISBN 0 352 33439 8	☐
BOUND BY CONTRACT	Helena Ravenscroft ISBN 0 352 33447 9	☐

VELVET GLOVE	Emma Holly ISBN 0 352 33448 7	☐
STRIPPED TO THE BONE	Jasmine Stone ISBN 0 352 33463 0	☐
DOCTOR'S ORDERS	Deanna Ashford ISBN 0 352 33453 3	☐
SHAMELESS	Stella Black ISBN 0 352 33485 1	☐
TONGUE IN CHEEK	Tabitha Flyte ISBN 0 352 33484 3	☐
FIRE AND ICE	Laura Hamilton ISBN 0 352 33486 X	☐
SAUCE FOR THE GOOSE	Mary Rose Maxwell ISBN 0 352 33492 4	☐
HARD CORPS	Claire Thompson ISBN 0 352 33491 6	☐

Black Lace books with an historical setting

THE INTIMATE EYE £4.99	Georgia Angelis ISBN 0 352 33004 X	☐
GOLD FEVER £4.99	Louisa Francis ISBN 0 352 33043 0	☐
FORBIDDEN CRUSADE £4.99	Juliet Hastings ISBN 0 352 33079 1	☐
A VOLCANIC AFFAIR £4.99	Xanthia Rhodes ISBN 0 352 33184 4	☐
SAVAGE SURRENDER	Deanna Ashford ISBN 0 352 33253 0	☐
INVITATION TO SIN £6.99	Charlotte Royal ISBN 0 352 33217 4	☐
A FEAST FOR THE SENSES	Martine Marquand ISBN 0 352 33310 3	☐

Black Lace anthologies

PANDORA'S BOX	ISBN 0 352 33074 0	☐
PANDORA'S BOX 3	ISBN 0 352 33274 3	☐
WICKED WORDS	Various ISBN 0 352 33363 4	☐
SUGAR AND SPICE £7.99	Various ISBN 0 352 33227 1	☐
THE BEST OF BLACK LACE	Various ISBN 0 352 33452 5	☐
CRUEL ENCHANTMENT Erotic Fairy Stories	Janine Ashbless ISBN 0 352 33483 5	☐
WICKED WORDS 2	Various ISBN 0 352 33487 8	☐

Black Lace non-fiction

| THE BLACK LACE BOOK OF WOMEN'S SEXUAL FANTASIES | Ed. Kerri Sharp ISBN 0 352 33346 4 | ☐ |

------ ✂ --------------------------

Please send me the books I have ticked above.

Name ....

Address ....

....

....

.... Post Code ....

Send to: **Cash Sales, Black Lace Books, Thames Wharf Studios, Rainville Road, London W6 9HA.**

US customers: for prices and details of how to order books for delivery by mail, call 1-800-805-1083.

Please enclose a cheque or postal order, made payable to **Virgin Publishing Ltd**, to the value of the books you have ordered plus postage and packing costs as follows:

UK and BFPO – £1.00 for the first book, 50p for each subsequent book.

Overseas (including Republic of Ireland) – £2.00 for the first book, £1.00 for each subsequent book.

If you would prefer to pay by VISA, ACCESS/MASTER-CARD, DINERS CLUB, AMEX or SWITCH, please write your card number and expiry date here:

....

Please allow up to 28 days for delivery.

Signature ....

------ ✂ --------------------------